Unbroken

NATALIE DEBRABANDERE

Copyright © 2015 Natalie Debrabandere
All rights reserved.

The moral rights of the author have been asserted.

This book is sold subject to the condition that it shall not, by way of trade or otherwise, be lent, resold, hired out, or otherwise circulated without the author's prior consent in any form of binding or cover other than that in which it is published or without a similar condition, including this condition, being imposed on the subsequent purchaser.

ISBN: 1503368815
ISBN-13: 978-1503368811

To the Different...

Chapter One

Whānau Anō Holiday Park
Hoka Tiri, West Coast of New Zealand.

Kristan Holt stormed out of her office, followed closely by her friend and business partner Mike Anderson. She walked quickly along the veranda and down the three wooden steps leading to the driveway. She glanced behind her only once, assuring herself that they were alone, before she turned around to face him.

"What the hell, Mike?" she said sharply. "I can't hire him now."

"Yeah, I know. Look, maybe we can…"

"Not a chance," she fumed. "I mean what's wrong with him? Does he really think showing up drunk at his interview is going to impress me?"

"Kristan, listen to me…"

"I can't even give him a test flight now! I don't want to do it. I won't."

The tall dark-haired man beside her nodded a little and raised his hand in an attempt to claim his turn.

"Please let me talk for a second, okay?"

"Go ahead, talk," Kristan snapped.

Mike put his arm around her shoulders and led her farther away from the office, toward the forest and the trees and completely out of earshot.

"Look, mate, I'm really sorry," he apologised. "I had no idea he was still hooked on drink. Of course we won't hire him now."

Kristan finally took a second to breathe, and she started to calm down a little. She glanced at her partner. She saw that he was a little bit pale, and clearly very upset, and she sighed in frustration.

"Mike, I am so sorry this happened. Are you okay?"

He gave her a weak shrug and attempted a smile.

"Yeah. Sure."

"You don't look it."

His face was grim and he remained silent, simply standing there with both hands resting on his hips, looking back toward the office. More than anything he looked puzzled. Clearly he had not expected such a dismal performance from their potential new pilot.

Kristan followed his gaze toward the familiar building as well, wondering whether she should go back in and attempt to talk to the guy again.

She cared about her partner deeply. He was more than a friend to her, like a brother, and so when he had told her that his own brother was in trouble and needed a job, she had been more than willing to bring him on board. They needed an extra helicopter pilot after all, and James was ex-Army, and he had all the required skills and qualifications.

Everything had sounded so perfect.

And Kristan would have loved to be able to bring him into the small team of trusted and committed people who together had been making her company successful for the past three years. But now she simply could not. Would not.

It was not Mike's fault of course.

He had been honest with her from the start, as always. He had explained to her in detail how his brother had struggled with alcoholism after he was discharged from the Army, and Kristan understood that better than most. To her, James's past made no difference, and probably just the opposite, simply because of her own personal struggle with addiction, and also because Mike had assured her that James was sober now and back in control of his life. Then James had turned up at the interview, drunk, arrogant, looking for trouble and trying to start a fight with his older brother.

Definitely not the sort of guy Kristan wanted in charge of one of her helicopters. She did not want him taking tourists up Mount Fox in one of her precious machines. She did not want him working as a kayak instructor on the lake. She did not want him working at the Holiday Park either. Despite her best intentions, she did not want him around, period. Looking at Mike's face now, seeing the disappointment in his big brown eyes, she disliked James even more.

"I'm sorry," she said in a quiet voice. "The job was his, you know that."

"Yeah, I know."

"But we're talking about people's lives. I can't risk him being drunk on the job."

"Not your fault, Kristan," Mike said with conviction. "I agree with you. Over the phone, on emails, he sounded all good. I'm sorry I wasted your time. And you know damn well I would never bring anyone into our business who might end up a liability; whether that's my brother or someone else makes no difference."

"Maybe not; but I think it should," Kristan observed, and she sounded a little sad.

Already she was thinking of ways that she could help.

She turned to her partner again, feeling calmer this time.

"Look, Mike. I know what it's like with the drinking, okay? Maybe we can talk to him again in a few months. I could try…"

But Mike shook his head.

"Don't worry about it, Kris," he said firmly.

He stepped forward to give her a quick hug, and when he stepped back he glanced in the direction of the office again. This time he looked like his mind was made up.

"You leave it with me," he said. "I'll sort it out."

Kristan hesitated.

"I should talk to him."

"No. Thank you for offering, but really, you sorted yourself out a long time ago, and this is not your problem. I should be the one to have that discussion."

Kristan relented.

"Fine. But I'm here if you need me, okay? Don't feel you can't talk to me about it."

"Absolutely. No worries. And Kris?"

"Yes, buddy."

He smiled at her.

"Thank you so much. I know you're as disappointed as I am."

"You can say that again."

Mike nodded, squeezed her shoulder one last time, and Kristan watched him walk away. She knew better than to follow. She knew her partner. He was angry. Whatever happened next should remain between him and his brother, and she wanted to respect that.

Once he had disappeared back inside she turned around and started on the short walk that would lead her back to the Holiday Park. As soon as she penetrated deeper into the sub-tropical rainforest she started to feel better.

Kristan loved spending time in the woods. It had always been a refuge for her, a place to unwind, a place to be alone. Lush vegetation and vibrant colours made for the perfect thinking hideaway, the ideal environment for active meditation. Bellbirds and tuis, fantails and bush robins tweeted and chirped in the early morning light. As she made her way along a path flanked by majestic trees, covered in ferns and beautiful orchids, Kristan unconsciously started to smile.

She had made her home in one of the existing Park cottages, a sturdy wooden building that stood on a secluded corner away from everyone else, on the edge of the forest with great views of the nearby lake and Mount Fox in the background. As she shed her clothes and stepped into the spacious shower, she did her best to forget about James and concentrate on the day ahead instead.

She was due to take a group of American tourists kayaking on the lake first thing, and she would be out most of the day doing that. Then in the evening a local rock band were coming to perform at the Park, and several of the instructors had offered to organise a barbecue.

It was going to be another amazing day.

Kristan had worked hard to craft the life for herself that she really wanted, down there in New Zealand. Three years previously she had left everything she owned in California, and walked out on her old life. She had driven to the airport, abandoned her Porsche in the lot, and thrown the keys to the guy busking on the corner. She had phoned her office to tell them she was not coming back from a pay phone in Singapore, and she had gotten outrageously drunk before getting back on the plane.

Then she had landed in New Zealand, and simply become someone else.

She rarely thought about her days in Silicon Valley now, and she did not miss her old life there either. The money, the cars, the alcohol, and the fleeting girlfriends whose names she could never remember… Life in a vacuum. She had been clean now for three years. Distance running had replaced the drugs, and although Kristan was aware that she was addicted to that in pretty much the same way that she had been to all the rest, at least this one was not likely to kill her.

She thought of James again and her stomach tightened.

She would speak to him, she decided. Of course she would. They would figure something out, and give him another chance. But she was not so far out of the woods herself that she could allow him to worm his way inside her brain.

Wary of unwanted thoughts, and eager to get back out into the sunshine and the life she loved, she dressed quickly in a pair of shorts and a red Nike sports bra and headed for the door. On her way to the lake she popped into the Park café, and helped herself to a bottle of water. She was used to it being deserted at this time of the morning, so when the door flew open just as she was about to walk out again it took her entirely by surprise. The door was solid wood, and really heavy. The sharp edge of it connected nicely with the side of her eye, hard, and she doubled over as an explosion of white heat filled her vision.

It felt like several seconds later when she became aware of a woman's voice close to her.

"Are you okay?"

Kristan looked up, dazed. She blinked in an effort to clear her head, and immediately her surroundings came back into focus. She was sitting on the floor by the door, where she had landed after it hit her square in the face. She looked up into the eyes of the woman responsible for sending her flying.

Intelligent, charcoal black eyes gazed back at her, filled with concern.

"I'm really sorry," the woman apologised. "I just opened the door, and you..."

Kristan took a deep breath.

"That's okay," she said. "My fault, I wasn't looking."

She got to her feet. A glance in the mirror above the counter confirmed her eye was swelling up already.

"Damn, that hurt," she murmured under her breath.

Liz Jackson winced a little at the comment. She regarded the woman in front of her, all of a sudden finding it quite difficult not to stare. She was absolutely stunning. And Liz had seen abs like that before in magazines, but never on a real woman. She shook her head a little, annoyed at herself for letting her thoughts run away with her so easily.

The woman in the red sports top turned to her and their eyes met. Hers were arrestingly blue and clear, framed with long, thick black lashes. Her features were angular and strong, sharply defined, and at the same time there was a softness there that was unmistakably and so interestingly female.

Once more Liz struggled not to stare.

"I'm Kristan," the woman said, holding out her hand.

Liz shook it and introduced herself.

"Not many women manage to get me on my back so quickly, you know Liz," Kristan stated with a quick smile.

"Sorry... But you did not offer much resistance."

Amused by the challenging come-back, Kristan burst out laughing.

Liz laughed with her, relieved that she was taking it so well. Only briefly, she wondered what on earth she was doing, flirting with this complete stranger... albeit an extremely good-looking one. She ran a hand through her hair and worked to regain her composure before Kristan could become aware that something was going on.

"Why don't you sit down over there," she suggested, guiding her toward a bench with a soft hand in the middle of her back.

"What for?" Kristan asked, puzzled.

She sat down anyway, and she watched as the newcomer gathered a handful of thick blond hair in her hand, and tied it in a bun at the back of her head. She was sexy in such a natural and effortless manner, and Kristan was sure that she had not seen her around before. She would have remembered those incredible eyes, for sure.

"Have you been at the Park long?" she asked.

"Not that long," the woman replied evasively.

"Where are you from?"

"London."

Liz rested her fingers against the side of Kristan's face, gently feeling around for broken bones.

"Does this hurt?"

"No... What are you doing?"

"Making sure you're okay. Making sure you don't have an orbital fracture."

Kristan held her breath as the woman's fingers carefully went up into her hair. She had no other option but to stare at her chest, inches from her nose, and the tantalizing glimpse of softly tanned skin leading down to her breasts.

Kristan cleared her throat and looked up carefully.

"Are you a doctor or something?" she asked.

She exhaled slowly as the woman's hands came to rest on her naked shoulders.

"I'm an A&E specialist," Liz said. "On holiday at the moment. Look at me please?"

Kristan looked up into those same captivating dark eyes. She suspected if Liz had not been so beautiful she would not still be sitting there getting prodded.

"Didn't look like you lost consciousness," Liz murmured as if talking to herself, more as a statement than a question.

"No, I didn't," Kristan replied quickly, frowning a little.

"Just a bit dizzy, yes?"

"Sure. Don't go all ER on me, doc."

Liz gave a quick smile, nodding absently.

"Follow my finger," she said.

Kristan sighed a little, and Liz raised an eyebrow.

"Problem?" she said.

"No. But I'm fine, really."

"I'm sure you are. Please bear with me while I make sure."

Kristan tracked her finger with her eyes, the only difficult thing about that her growing desire to simply stare at Liz's attractive face.

Then Liz dropped her hand, and she pulled back.

"Okay. You're good to go," she said simply.

"Right."

Kristan stood up quickly, intent on proving that she was one hundred percent fine, and almost instantly regretted her decision. Her head started to buzz, and she swayed. She reached for the edge of the table to steady herself, but her fingers only just brushed it, and she stumbled backward.

"Hey, not so fast."

Liz quickly caught her around the waist to steady her.

"Take it easy," she said.

Kristan shook her head in an attempt to regain her balance, only managing to make herself feel worse in the process.

"No, I'm..." she protested.

"I know you're okay," Liz interrupted firmly. "Just relax, will you?"

Kristan could only remain silent as a fresh wave of dizziness threatened to completely overwhelm her. She struggled to take a deep breath, and as she leaned a little more against Liz the woman slowly ran her hand up and down her arm in a soothing motion. Kristan's jet black hair, which softly brushed the base of her neck, only accentuated how pale her face had become.

Liz kept a soft hold on her, feeling herself tense a little when she caught a whiff of Kristan's shampoo. She resisted the urge to brush a strand of hair from her cheek. This was not a new or unwelcome feeling, this attraction to women. And she appreciated a beautiful body when she saw one, of course. Whether it was male or female had never made a difference in the past.

But she was holding this woman in her arms now, and as her hand moved gently over Kristan's warm and soft skin, Liz felt herself grow uncomfortable. Struggling a little with the sudden realization that her body was reacting to this woman in ways that she had not allowed herself to feel for so long, she reminded herself that she was a doctor, and should be acting like one.

She blew air out impatiently and winced at the sight of Kristan's eye, which was getting darker by the second.

"Where is your camper?" she said. "I'll walk you there and you can lie down for a bit."

Kristan straightened up.

She suddenly remembered her clients, and realised that she was going to be late if she did not get going soon.

"Can't, I've got work to do," she said. "But thanks."

Liz looked surprised.

"Work?" she repeated.

She had assumed, wrongly obviously, that everyone who stayed at the Park must be on holiday.

"Yeah, I have a group of clients today."

Kristan rolled her neck and blinked a few times, glad to realise that her head had cleared. She grabbed her bottle of water, and took another deep breath.

"I run the Activity Centre," she added, reading the question in Liz's eyes.

Reluctantly, Liz took a step away from her. She knew the Activity Centre offered kayaking sessions on the lake, and also scenic helicopter flights over Mount Fox Glacier.

"Are you one of the pilots?" she probed.

"Yes."

"You will not be flying today."

Even though it was a question, it was phrased and sounded like an order, and Kristan hesitated for a second before she replied. She was not used to receiving orders, not from Mike, not from anyone on her staff, and certainly not from women she had only known a few minutes, no matter how beautiful they may be.

"You will not be flying, right?" the woman insisted, and this time Kristan recognised her tone for what it was.

Genuine concern.

She relaxed immediately.

"Not today," she confirmed. "I'm just going out on the lake with a bunch of guys."

Liz nodded, only partly reassured.

"Okay. My humble opinion is you should take the rest of the day off," she said thoughtfully. "But something tells me you might disagree with that."

She was pleased when Kristan smiled.

"Yep," she said.

The colour had started to return to her face. When she smiled her entire face lit up, and again Liz felt that unusual but not totally unpleasant little stab of attraction in the pit of her stomach.

"You know me so well already," Kristan joked, "and we've only just met."

Liz easily laughed along with her.

"Will you be out all day?" she enquired.

Kristan nodded.

"Most of it."

"In this case, make sure you wear a hat and drink plenty of water."

"I will. Thanks."

There was no reason for her to stay put any longer, and yet she was finding it difficult to leave. There was something really oddly attractive about the way this woman seemed to be so comfortable issuing directives, and telling her what to do.

"So how come I haven't bumped into you around the Park?" she insisted.

"Because I just did, remember?" Liz replied with a chuckle.

She started toward the coffee machine in the back, and Kristan stared after her thoughtfully, admiring her figure, biting her lower lip as she did. She jumped a little when Liz suddenly turned around, and those amazing black eyes locked onto her face again with the intensity of a laser beam.

Kristan felt her cheeks grow hot as she blushed. Busted, she thought briefly, but Liz apparently had not noticed her looking, or if she had she chose to ignore it.

"I predict a killer headache later," she said. "If you need me, just come and get me. I'm the last camper before the pool."

"Okay. Thanks doc."

"No need to thank me. I'll see you later."

Kristan burst out laughing.

"Pretty confident, aren't you?" she called as Liz walked away.

Chapter 2

Five long hours later, and Kristan sighed as her kayaking group stopped paddling again to snap photos of one another. She glanced at her watch, then back in the general direction of the beach, disappointed to see that they were still quite far out. The day had gone very well, her clients were delighted, and it was not often that Kristan wanted to end a session early. But she was getting pretty desperate.

Mike caught up with her, smiling at her from behind his sunglasses.

"Hey mate. Got somewhere you need to be?" he asked.

"Not really," Kristan muttered as she reached for her water. "A cool dark room would be nice though," she added as she took a sip, and winced.

"How come?"

"Well…"

When Mike glided closer to her and leaned against the side of her boat, Kristan lifted her sunglasses and gave him her eyes.

"Shit, Kris, what happened to you?" he exclaimed.

She felt guilty when she caught the worried look on his face.

"Don't fret, it's nothing."

"Doesn't look like nothing. Come on, what's up?"

"A woman slammed the cafe door in my face this morning."

The concern in his eyes disappeared instantly, replaced by curiosity and a huge grin. Kristan knew she had just volunteered the wrong kind of information.

"Don't you start," she muttered.

He laughed.

"Hey, I'm not starting anything," he protested. "Just concerned for you is all. So, what did you do to that lady to deserve such harsh treatment Kris? Uh?"

Kristan threw him a dark look.

She put her sunglasses back on and grabbed her paddle.

"It was an accident, not domestic violence."

Mike snorted, looking amused.

"If you say so. Whatever happened, it looks like you're in a whole lot of pain, mate."

"Yeah," Kristan admitted. "My head is kind of killing me right now."

"Then go back if you like," he offered immediately. "We're nearly there, I can finish without you."

Kristan looked out toward the group, busy swapping cameras and yelling instructions at each other. Making wonderful screensavers for the work PCs back home, she thought.

Good for them.

"It will be fine if you don't finish with us," Mike offered again, catching her hesitation.

"Really? You sure?"

"What am I, a rookie?" he said roughly.

The pounding between her eyes finally won the battle.

"Okay, thank you," she said gratefully. "You've got your radio just in case, yeah?"

He rolled his eyes, pretending to be offended.

"Yep. Got it, Boss. Stop talking, and go find yourself some shade."

"Mike, I need to talk to you about James."

He turned her kayak around and gave her a firm push.

"Later. Call me if you need."

Kristan nodded, and she finally got going.

If she carried on a little farther beyond the beach she knew she could come to shore pretty much right in front of her cottage. So she concentrated on her paddling and tried to ignore the fierce hammering in her head, which was only getting worse as she got closer to shore. By the time she got there she was in serious pain, and seeing stars. She dragged her boat out of the water and collapsed on the grass by the side of it, struggling to get out of her spray deck.

"Damn it!" she muttered.

"Hi there. Need any help?"

Startled, Kristan squinted up at the sound of the now familiar voice. Liz's British accent was another thing that she was finding attractive... But not attractive enough that she would immediately accept the help.

"I can manage," she mumbled, pulling on her spray deck as if she were trying to rip it open.

"Are you always this stubborn?"

Kristan opened her mouth to speak, but before she could say anything Liz was kneeling down in front of her. Kristan went still as the woman lifted her sunglasses carefully, and leaned closer to scrutinise her face. She clearly made her own private assessment of Kristan's condition, and then she reached for her and as if by magic the wet skirt came off.

Talented hands, Kristan reflected thoughtfully, and she almost laughed out loud, feeling a little drunk now. It was not a completely unwelcome feeling.

"I was on the beach painting when I saw you come out of the water," Liz explained. "You looked a bit unsteady on your feet so I thought I'd better come over to check on you. How is your head now?"

Kristan considered fibbing, but she did not have the energy for it.

"Not too good."

"No?"

"No. Turns out you were right," Kristan said slowly.

Liz smiled in sympathy.

"Killer headache, uh?"

"You got it."

"Well, I am sorry that I told you so. Are you allergic to anything?"

"No."

"Good. Take these. They'll help with the pain."

Kristan stared at the tablets Liz offered, and she shook her head carefully.

"Thanks," she said. "But I can't… I don't do pills."

Liz narrowed her eyes at her. She thought of a question, but when she noticed again the shadows under Kristan's eyes, shadows which had not been there in the morning, she decided to keep it for another time.

"That's fine," she said gently. "We just need to get you lying down."

"I'm finding it a bit… difficult to talk."

"I'm not surprised. Come on, let's get you inside."

Kristan dropped her keys three times as she struggled to fit them into the lock, before Liz quietly took them from her and stepped forward.

"May I?" she said with a brief glance at her.

Kristan let her go first, wondering what it was about that woman that made her want to agree to everything she said or suggested. She was attractive, and of course that was a factor, even in Kristan's weakened state. But it was more than that, and if anything, trying to figure it out only made Kristan's headache worse. Thankfully the cottage was cool inside, and it felt wonderful to escape the glare of the afternoon sun.

Liz followed Kristan across the generous space, her eyes

growing wide at the view of the mountains and the lake that seemed to fill the entire lounge. She stared out the open bay window for a moment before gazing around the rest of the room.

There were thick and heavy rugs covering the gleaming wooden floors, green plants in dark pottery scattered at each corner of the room, and a big wood burner tucked against the stone wall, which reminded Liz that even though this might be a rainforest they were still in the middle of New Zealand's Alpine country, and it would get cold in the winter.

"Wow," she murmured, smiling. "This is a beautiful space."

Kristan squinted toward the window.

"Glad you like it," she said tiredly.

She caught sight of her face in the mirror and attempted a joke.

"I look like the lead in a horror movie."

She glanced at Liz, who had come to stand very close to her, and tried to smile.

"I'd say that's definitely a huge exaggeration," the woman observed quietly. "More like an extra," she added, when she realised that she had probably come across as way too intense.

Kristan just stared at her, and Liz held her gaze. There was no doubt in her mind what the doctor had meant by her comment. The way she was looking at her right now would have been enough to set the cottage on fire. And before Kristan could figure out what to say, Liz pointed behind her and hit her with yet another unexpected question.

"Where's your bedroom?" she asked. "This way?"

Kristan blinked.

"Excuse me?"

Liz gave her a blank stare.

"I want you to lie down. Right now."

"Yeah, uh... Sure. Couch is fine. Thanks."

Kristan turned around but immediately came to a sudden halt. She gritted her teeth as her stomach lurched and suddenly tried to turn itself inside out. She stopped moving, and she leaned against the wall for support.

"It's okay," Liz murmured, standing right behind her. "Just keep breathing. That's it, deep and slow."

Kristan felt her fingers wrap around her wrist, and her other hand coming to rest on her forehead, and she closed her eyes in spite of herself.

"You feel a little hot. Are you going to be sick?"

Kristan would have laughed if she had not been feeling so terrible. What a wonderful impression she must be making on that woman.

"No," she said firmly, hoping this was true.

"Good. Let's get you lying down then. You'll feel better once you're flat on your back, I promise."

Liz pulled the blind down on the bay window, plunging the room into soothing darkness.

Kristan stretched out on the sofa, looking white as a sheet.

"How's that?" Liz asked gently.

"Yeah… Good."

"Okay. Hold on one sec, I'll be right back."

Liz disappeared off toward the kitchen, and Kristan settled herself lower down against the pillows. She reflected she would have been in real trouble if this had happened when she was out on the lake on her own. She wondered how she was going to manage the concert later on. Perhaps Mike could take over for the night? It was becoming increasingly hard to think, and she drifted a little.

When she opened her eyes again Liz was sitting next to her, looking serious, and armed with a fresh towel and an ice pack.

"You've got a few of these in your freezer," the attractive doctor remarked. "Ice packs," she added when Kristan looked at her blankly.

"Yes... Sometimes need to ice my knee after a long run."

Liz nodded as she wrapped the ice pack into the towel.

"I like running," she offered. "How far is long for you?"

"Twelve, fifteen miles."

"That's impressive. Close your eyes, please..."

She carefully applied the towel against the side of Kristan's face, brushing her hand away with a smile when Kristan tried to get a hold of it.

"Let me do this," she said softly. "It's the least I can do for you, really."

Kristan sighed a little.

"Thank you... If only every woman was as nice as you..."

Liz threw her a little questioning look.

"Am I to conclude from this that I am not the first woman who ever slammed a door in your face?"

Kristan did not notice the quick tightening of her mouth.

"No... Women are normally nice to me," she said, and she was in pain, and really, absolutely, categorically did not mean anything funny by it.

But Liz did manage to read something into the careless comment.

"Oh yeah, I can imagine," she murmured, as if to herself.

"Imagine what?" Kristan asked, surprised at the unexpected sliver of bitterness she heard in her voice.

Liz shifted the towel to the other side of her face, not making eye contact.

"Nothing," she said. "I can imagine women wanting to be nice to you, that's all."

Once again she rested her hand on Kristan's forehead, the gentleness of her touch in sharp contrast with the harshness of her comment. Kristan stared at her for a few seconds, trying to figure out what the woman was really thinking.

"So... was that a compliment then, doc?" she tried eventually.

Looking into Kristan's limpid blue eyes, catching the pain in them, and just a little hint of vulnerability, Liz suddenly felt herself on the edge of tears.

She had been on the go for a few weeks now, always keeping on the alert, not stopping anywhere for long, not trusting anyone she met along the way. She was feeling tired and stressed out, and this kayak instructor, with her incredible looks and friendly manner, was getting under her skin.

"Sorry," she said softly. "Yes, I definitely meant that as a compliment. You look... Well. Beautiful. And I am really sorry that you're hurting now because of me."

Kristan watched her as sadness drifted into her eyes. Suddenly, the beautiful doctor looked as if she was the one who needed comforting. It surprised her, because up until this very moment Liz had been nothing but take charge and efficiency.

"So what were you painting out on the beach?" she asked, keen to bring a smile back onto the woman's lips.

Liz appeared grateful for the question.

"The lake, and the forest in the background," she said.

"Yeah? Can I see it?"

"Nice try, but you're not getting up just yet."

"I mean when the headache's gone."

"Sure."

Once again Liz sounded evasive.

"Just concentrate on your breathing," she repeated.

Kristan grew quiet, doing just that, almost drifting off to sleep. She probably would have done so if there had not been a loud bang on the door, and if Liz had not practically jumped out of her skin in reaction, startling her awake.

"Yo, Kristan," a booming male voice called out.

Kristan reached for Liz's hand as she stood up, and missed.

"That's okay," she said quickly. "It's just my friend Mike."

Liz nodded, her eyes darting toward the door, her face suddenly pale.

"Don't get up," she ordered as Kristan started to move. "I'll get it."

There was no doubt in her mind when she saw the expression on the man's face that he thought he had interrupted something juicy. Or was she just imagining things?

"Hey, is Kris in?" he asked. "She decent?"

So yes, not imagining anything, Liz concluded.

"She's resting," she informed him coolly. "Come in and be quiet."

He snorted, and he walked past her without another word. He seemed at ease as he did so, looking at home in the cottage, and comfortable with the surroundings.

"Hey," Kristan greeted him weakly when he walked into the lounge.

Her eyes drifted to Liz, and she felt very disappointed when she realised that the woman was not going to stay any longer. It felt like too soon, too harsh, her leaving now. But the woman was all business once more, and when she met Kristan's gaze this time she was clearly back into doctor mode.

"Get some sleep, if you can," she said with a pointed glance toward Mike. "Call me if you need anything. Bye."

She turned around, and she left so quickly that Kristan did not even have time to say a word. She fell back onto the pillows and sighed.

"Wow," Mike commented.

He sat on the low table facing the couch, and grinned.

"What?" Kristan asked.

"She's hot. And bossy. And hot."

"Shut up," Kristan said flatly.

"Is she new?"

"Think so."

"You know her?"

"No. Only met her this morning."

He chuckled and his eyes lit up.

"Oh, I see. She's the one who slammed the door in your face in the cafe, am I right?"

"Yeah."

"And you like her. I can tell."

Kristan closed her eyes, and she pressed the icy towel against her eyes. She winced. Mike seemed to realise that she was not in any mood for banter because he lowered his voice immediately.

"Sorry, Kris. How're you feeling, mate?" he asked her gently.

"Pretty rough just now."

"You think you'll be okay for tonight? 'Cos it's not a problem if you're not, you know? I can take care of it."

Kristan opened her eyes and squinted at him.

"I'm not sure," she admitted. "Right now I feel like I'm going to throw up every time I move. Or pass out, or something delightful like that."

"How about I set up then? You get some sleep, see how you feel later."

"You sure you don't mind?"

He shook his head emphatically.

"Of course I don't mind, Kris. We're partners, you don't always have to do all the work yourself, you know? And the guys will help anyway. You should get some sleep, get better."

"Okay then. I think I will take you up on that. Thank you."

He leaned forward to kiss her on the cheek.

"No problem."

Kristan held him back with a finger.

"How was James when you talked to him?" she asked.

Mike stood up, and a muscle in his jaw clenched.

"Don't worry about James."

Kristan noticed the annoyance in his eyes.

"What's going on?" she insisted. "What happened between you

two?"

"He's gone, Kristan, okay? Forget about the guy."

"But what..."

"I mean it, Kristan."

Mike's face had grown serious, and his brown eyes had hardened.

"Just leave it," he said. "Get some sleep. I'll handle tonight."

He closed the door quietly as he left, and Kristan sighed and buried her face into the ice pack.

Liz practically ran back to her camper and slammed the door shut after her. That guy had scared her half to death, banging on the cottage door like that. She had to remind herself that she had been careful, and there had not been any sign of Robert behind her, at any point along the way.

She had got rid of her old credit cards and of anything else that might lead him to her. The staff at her old hospital in London thought she had gone to live in France. She was not on Facebook, Twitter or any other social media site. She was in a different country, on the other side of the world, moving a lot, and there was no way he would be able to find her.

She was being jumpy for no reason at all. Damn it!

Liz rubbed her face with both hands and untied her hair. Going to the fridge, she grabbed a beer and collapsed on the couch in front of the window. She realised with a start that she could just make out the edge of Kristan's cottage from her pitch. Watching, she took a deep breath and a sip of beer.

She relaxed.

It had been a surprise, her incredible physical reaction to the sexy kayak instructor. Liz had never been much into sex before, and of course she knew it was because she had spent eight long years pretending to be somebody else, denying her own feelings, and trying to ignore her inner voice. The one that told her that she liked women. Prior to Robert there had been a few girls, of course, especially Eva, back in college. But she had been young then, and it had all been hesitant and rather clumsy. In her mind, Liz had always imagined that making love to another woman would someday be the most incredible experience of her life… and she was still waiting.

She smiled a little as she remembered the look Kristan had given her in the cafe. Liz knew what she had been looking at, and she knew she liked what she had seen. Sighing, she settled more comfortably onto the couch as the sun started to disappear over the mountain tops.

She closed her eyes, breathing deep and slow.

She stood a little way back from the stage, leaning against a tree, smiling as she watched the band. It was late now and still warm, and Liz felt pleasantly drunk. She grew still as she spotted Kristan walking toward her. The woman looked unlawfully sexy in a pair of low slung blue jeans and a loose flannel shirt. She was barefoot. She slipped behind Liz and rested her hands on her waist.

"Hi."

"Aren't you supposed to be in bed?"

"Sorry doc. I felt lonely."

Liz smiled as she felt Kristan's warm breath against her hair. When Kristan kissed the side of her neck, she stiffened.

"Stay still," Kristan whispered.

Liz nodded, but she was trembling. Kristan's hands sneaked under her t-shirt. She moved around to face Liz and hide her from view. She pushed her back into the shadows.

"You feel hot," Kristan murmured.

Her eyes were sparkling and burning with desire. Liz put her hands on the back of her neck, and she pulled her in for a searing kiss.

She opened her eyes again with a start, surprised to realise that she had drifted off. It was a lot darker now, and a lot cooler as well. Liz let her right hand drift slowly between her thighs, astounded to realise that she was trembling. She glanced toward the forest, but she could not see Kristan's cottage at all now, only darkness. She hoped that she was okay.

Music drifted softly through the night, and as Liz checked her watch she realised that it was only eight-thirty. Early. She needed to eat, and she knew there was a concert on tonight. No point staying in on her own and missing out, thinking about some woman she should not be thinking about.

She grabbed her wallet, her keys and a warm jacket, and she stepped resolutely out into the night.

Chapter 3

When Kristan showed up at the Activity Centre's office just after six o'clock the next morning Mike was already there, sat at his favourite desk with a steaming mug of coffee, and an open laptop in front of him.

"Good morning, Frankenstein," he greeted her with a wink. "Hey, you're late."

She flashed him a brilliant smile, and bent over to kiss him on the cheek.

"Morning buddy."

"What's that for?" he grunted.

"To say thank you for the plate of spinach lasagna you left in my kitchen," she said, amused at his reaction. "At least I assumed it was from you."

He grinned.

"Ha. Don't mention it. I came to check up on you after the concert last night, and you were out like a light. Snoring. Mouth open. Wasn't a pretty sight..."

Kristan rolled her eyes, and she laughed.

"Yeah, yeah, whatever."

She sat on a corner of his desk and started flipping through some mail.

"So how're you feeling?" he asked, watching her. "Your eye doesn't look so swollen today."

"Yep."

"That's good. Don't want to scare any of our clients off."

"I feel a whole lot better. Headache's gone too, which is the main thing," Kristan commented, picking up a bunch of reservation forms off the desk. "Had your lasagna for breakfast which helped also."

"Did you? Was it okay?"

"Amazing. As usual."

She nodded enthusiastically, looking at him, smiling at the serious look on his face.

Mike was 6'2 and 195 pounds. Full of muscle, and an absolute gem in the kitchen. It always surprised people when the big bearded helicopter pilot launched into animated conversations about organic vegetables, and the best way to steam carrots. Kristan was a frequent recipient of his vegan culinary creations, and always a very grateful customer.

"Thanks for taking care of things at the concert last night by the way," she said. "Everything go okay?"

"100%. Everyone had a good time, and the band were excellent. It was packed. Shame you missed it."

"I'll be there next time."

Mike gave an approving nod.

"Hope so. Your attacker was there, by the way. She seemed to enjoy her evening."

Kristan immediately lost interest in the booking forms.

"Liz? She was there?"

"Yeah."

"On her own?"

He chuckled.

"Ha! See? You do like her. I knew it."

Kristan shook her head a little, smiling.

"I don't, I'm just curious."

"Of course you are," Mike said with a quick laugh. "And I guess it doesn't hurt that she's really good-looking too, uh?"

Kristan threw him a warning look, and busied herself with more paperwork. She had no idea exactly what it was that she felt toward

Liz, although she was intrigued by her, and eager to find out more about her. But she knew if she left it to Mike to figure out he would have them married and growing old together in just under a minute.

Safer to focus on work for now.

"Looks like we're fully booked today," she observed.

"We are indeed. Will you be flying?"

"Absolutely."

"Can you see okay?"

"Of course I can," Kristan exclaimed, laughing.

Mike had a quick check of his laptop, grinning.

"Just making sure. Weather should be great. Hot and dry down here, cool and clear up there."

It was perfect flying weather, and the mountains would look gorgeous in the sunshine. Kristan was feeling great, and she was looking forward to a full day in the pilot's seat.

"Hey, guys. Morning. How is everyone today?"

She looked up and smiled at the two young women who walked in, dressed for kayaking and carrying bags of food.

"Morning Pam. Hi Mel," she said.

"Morning ladies," Mike greeted them loudly. "What's your schedule looking like today? Out paddling on the lake for the duration?"

"Yes sir!" one of them confirmed in an exaggerated booming voice.

She had ultra short blond hair and a brilliant smile, and she winked at Kristan as she sent a quick salute in Mike's direction.

He rolled his eyes.

"Don't call me sir, Mel," he complained. "Makes me feel old."

The two women laughed, and the other one, who was tall and lean and looked like the climber that she was, patted him on the shoulder.

"You are old, mate," she pointed out, smiling.

"Not helpful, Pam," Mike muttered. "Not helpful."

Pam and Melissa were two of the kayak instructors who worked for Kristan full time. Pam also doubled as a mountain guide, and she worked as a ski instructor during the winter months. They were a small team, and at the height of the season regularly put in ten to fifteen hours of work each day. Yet nobody complained, and everybody always worked hard.

It was worth it.

Situated in between the mountains and the ocean on the edge of a blue-green lake, the Holiday Park was in a prize location, and attracted tourists year round. Living at the Park and working for Kristan was a very attractive proposition for many students on a gap year who possessed the necessary outdoors skills. It was also a dream job for seasoned instructors the likes of Pam and Melissa.

After a quick chat, and after they collected some equipment from the office and left to go meet their clients, Mike turned to Kristan and handed her flying helmet to her.

"Ready to roll?" he asked, looking happy.

"All set; let's go," she replied.

She followed him out onto the tarmac at the back of the building, and she took her time checking the big AS355 Twin Squirrel helicopter she would be flying.

With a cruise speed of 120 mph, and a seating capacity of 5 passengers, the aircraft was ideal for passenger charter flights, and also shorts hops up and down Fox glacier. People came from all over the world to enjoy the adventure, and Kristan enjoyed giving novices who had never flown before the experience of a lifetime. Once on the glacier they were allowed a short walk around, plenty of time for photos, and on the way back Kristan always flew low and slow over the lake, giving everyone an extra thrill.

Learning to fly was one of the things that her old life in the States had made possible for her to do. In spite of the bad memories she was grateful for it, and appreciative of the money those crazy years had allowed her to earn. Without it her dream life in New

Zealand would have taken a lot longer to achieve.

Sometimes when she went flying on her own, high over the peaks or following the jagged line of the ocean, she could not quite believe how incredibly lucky she was.

Mike often said that luck had nothing to do with it.

It was hard work, he believed, and he was right. The money had bought the buildings and the Park, and all of the foundations of the business all right. But the main reason it was so successful was Kristan's unrelenting desire to make it so.

She worked hard for it and so did her partner.

Once all the safety checks were done, Kristan settled into the right seat, put her helmet on, and reached for her sunglasses. From out on the tarmac Mike gave her a smile and a thumbs up, and she returned the gesture.

Good to go.

An excited group of people were already queuing up to board, and as Kristan watched them take photos of her and the big bird waiting to take off she felt excited too. She started the engine, laughing a little when the guys outside gave her a round of applause.

"Okay, let's do this thing," she murmured with a smile.

It turned out to be another perfect day. Lots of good flying, and lots of satisfied customers. Kristan was feeling on top of her game, and she enjoyed herself throughout.

Right before her last flight of the day she stood outside the office catching a quick break and a snack, whilst Mike was out on the tarmac refueling. As always when she had been up in the air in one her machines, she felt relaxed, happy and content. One more trip up Mount Fox and she would be done. No tourists this time, just a local mountain guide and her client requiring a lift up, ahead of a night on the glacier followed by a day's hike.

Easy.

Kristan watched as her partner greeted the climbers and helped them load their equipment in the back, and out of the corner of her eye she caught sight of Liz slowly approaching. Immediately she pushed up off the wall, and stood a little straighter.

The doctor had not seen her yet. She was dressed in a pair of walking trousers, boots and a red tank top. She was carrying a rucksack and a pair of sunglasses, and she looked like she had been out in the sun all day. Her skin was glowing, she had a little smile on her lips as she walked, and Kristan's stomach did a nice double flip as she watched her approach.

"Hey doc," she called out from the doorway.

Liz shielded her eyes from the sun, blinking.

She smiled when she spotted Kristan standing in the shade, and immediately looked pleased to see her.

"Hey," she said softly. "Didn't see you there. How are you?"

Kristan threw the rest of her apple in the bin, and she stepped forward, drawn to Liz as if by a powerful magnet.

"I'm fine, thanks. Just taking a quick break before I go up again," she explained, gesturing toward the helicopter. "How're you doing, Liz?"

Her voice was low, a little bit husky, just that little bit intimate. Her eyes locked on to Liz, so blue they looked unreal. Unable to take her gaze off her, Liz's smile widened, and everything else around her kind of just disappeared.

"Are you all right?" Kristan asked, smiling as well when Liz just stood there, watching her with a happy look on her face.

"Yeah. Great," Liz replied, suddenly remembering that Kristan had asked her a question. "I had a wonderful time hiking around the lake today."

"Well, it's a fantastic day for it. Which trail were you on?"

"Oh, uh, a mix of purple and green I think."

"You must have been out a while then," Kristan stated, interested to notice that Liz had probably walked an average of ten to twelve miles.

Liz nodded, and she glanced toward the helicopter with an enquiring look on her face.

"Was that you going over the lake?" she asked. "I caught sight of a helicopter a few times."

"Yes, it was me. Sorry about the noise."

Liz chuckled, and she was interested in the helicopter but she could not keep her eyes off Kristan for very long. She stepped a little closer to her and lifted her hand.

"May I?" she asked.

Kristan did not understand what she meant at first, and for a wild second she wondered if Liz were asking for permission to kiss her. Then she remembered, and felt like a total idiot.

"Oh… Yeah, sure," she said. "It's much better today."

Liz gently brushed her fingers over her temple, pleased that the swelling had gone down completely.

"It is looking better," she agreed. "But that is one hell of a bruise."

"Just cosmetics," Kristan joked.

"I'm assuming you wouldn't be flying if you were not feeling okay," Liz remarked, and once again the comment sounded a little bit sharp, but Kristan was beginning to understand that Liz tended to sound that way when she was concerned.

If the beautiful doctor was concerned about her, hopefully it meant that she liked her, and Kristan had no problem with that whatsoever.

"I feel brand new, doc," she assured her. "It's amazing what twelve hours in bed can do for you."

Liz smiled at that. She nodded, and quickly averted her eyes. She did not really want Kristan to know what imagining her in bed did to her.

"I'm glad you're okay," she said simply.

"Hey Kris," Mike yelled toward them. "Ready when you are,

mate!"

"You're working. I'd better let you go," Liz stated, and she started to walk away but Kristan caught her wrist lightly.

"Would you like to come up with me?" she asked, her eyes sparkling with sudden expectation.

"What, in the helicopter?"

"Yes."

"Right now?"

"Right now."

Liz hesitated, but Kristan noticed the way she glanced toward the machine.

"Have you flown in one of these before?" she asked.

"No, never," Liz replied quietly.

"Would you like to?"

Liz met Kristan's eyes, and gave her an almost shy look.

"Yeah…" she said with a smile. "I've always wanted to."

Once again her eyes drifted toward the helicopter, and Kristan smiled at the excitement in her voice.

"I'd love to take you up, doc," she offered. "Come on; what do you say? Keep me company?"

When Liz turned back to her she was beaming.

"Okay. Great!" she exclaimed.

Her smile was contagious, and for a couple of seconds the two women just stared into each other's eyes. It took Mike's booming voice in her ear to bring Kristan back to reality.

"Clients are A-waiting, matey," he said loudly, pretending to be annoyed. "Are you going up or are you waiting for the glacier to melt?"

He glanced at Liz as he said that, curiosity getting the better of him.

"I do apologise on behalf of my friend here, she's very rude. I'm Mike. Mike Anderson, nice to meet you."

Kristan shook her head at him, and she was laughing.

"Sorry, big man. Liz, this very annoying guy is my very good friend and business partner, Mike Anderson."

"Like I just said," Mike pointed out, grinning.

"Mike, this is Liz..."

"Liz Jackson," Liz finished for her.

She shook Mike's hand, and she was friendly with him, but she could not help herself and her eyes were quickly back on Kristan.

"I don't even know your last name," she laughed.

"Sorry. It's Holt. Kristan Holt."

"Right. Hello, Kris."

Kristan nodded happily, her eyes on Liz, and once more the two women got lost in each other.

Mike rolled his eyes, amused at the mushy smile on Kristan's lips. It was nice to see really, and when he glanced toward Liz again and saw the very same expression on her face he was really glad.

"Okay ladies, let's roll," he declared.

When Kristan walked past him he grabbed her arm and squeezed gently. He gave her a silent thumbs up and a warm smile, and this time Kristan knew he was serious and not joking. His reaction made her feel ten feet tall.

"The first thing you need to know about helicopters is to always approach them from the front," Kristan told Liz as they walked closer to it. "The tail rotor is invisible when it's on. You won't be able to see it, and it's easy to forget. And it will slice your head off nice and clean if you're not careful."

Liz nodded, frowning a little.

Kristan noticed the serious look on her face, and she backtracked a little.

"Sorry," she apologised with a smile. "Bit of a stern warning, but if you're going to be around helicopters you should know."

"Yes, definitely," Liz replied, "you're right, I do want to know."

She was glad that Kristan was not treating her like any other client, and when Kristan glanced at her briefly she realised that if anything, Liz looked even more interested than she had been before. She took her own seat, and Liz sat on her left, and Kristan buckled her seat belt for her and adjusted her headphones.

Liz watched her do all this with a little smile.

"Thanks for taking such good care of me," she said softly.

"No problem. I want you to enjoy your first time," Kristan explained, and then she looked away quickly when she realised what she had said.

She was immensely glad that her partner had not been there to hear it because she suspected he would not have let her get away with it.

"Ready?" she asked.

Liz smiled.

"Yes, I'm ready," she said expectantly.

Kristan nodded, glancing behind her to make sure their passengers were all in and ready to go.

"Everybody okay back there?" she asked.

"Yep. Let's go, Kris."

Kristan glanced at Liz, noting the excited look in her eyes. She was so beautiful it was hard for her to concentrate, and so it was lucky she could have flown to the glacier and back with her eyes closed.

"And we're off..." she said.

Liz gave her a thumbs up and a grin, and Kristan pulled the heavy machine off the ground, smiling when she heard the delighted giggle coming from her left.

The first time she took off with new clients on board she was always careful, and slow. But she wanted Liz to experience the real thing, so she took off hard, and when she glanced at her again the woman looked so happy and enthralled it was all Kristan could do not to lean over and kiss her.

She climbed up quickly, leaving the lake and the forest behind, headed fast toward the mountains. Liz's mouth dropped open when they approached the glacier. She stared in amazement at the huge expanse of ice in front of them, encased in between two walls of rock. The glacier was not at all smooth as she had expected it to be, but rough and jagged. On its surface the ice was dirty and grey, and yet just underneath it Liz could see the second layer, this one a very clear, pure shade of blue. Kristan's eyes, she thought immediately. She glanced at her briefly, and nodded. Yes. Glacier blue; that was it. Grabbing her camera, she leaned forward to take a couple of shots.

"Okay, doc?" Kristan enquired over the headphones.

Liz glanced at her, catching those amazing blue eyes on her again.

"Yes. This is wonderful," she exclaimed.

Kristan pointed ahead of them with a smile, and Liz held her breath as the helicopter approached the top of a ledge, covered in snow and lost in clouds and mist. She held her breath as Kristan flew them fast and low over the edge, laughing as the ground seemed to fall off below them as soon as they cleared the snowy peak.

Then Kristan banked sharply to the right, and a few seconds later they landed smoothly on top of an icy open field surrounded by mountain tops.

Liz was silent for a moment. She took a deep breath, caught in the beauty of everything in front of her.

Kristan killed the engine and pulled her helmet off.

"Did you enjoy that, Liz?" she asked softly.

She already knew the answer to that of course. She had caught Liz's every smile on the way up, noticed the way she held on to her seat a couple of times, and enjoyed her laughter as she flew them delicately over dangerous crevasses and hidden rocky peaks.

"I loved it," Liz replied, gripping Kristan's wrist as she talked. "This is just amazing. It is so..."

She waved her hand toward the vast expanse of snow and ice

bathed in late afternoon sunshine.

"Beautiful?" Kristan finished for her, not really talking about the mountains.

Liz simply smiled at her and nodded.

"Beautiful, indeed," she murmured, and she also was not talking about the scenery anymore.

Kristan tore her gaze from her because she had a job to do.

"Let's unload these guys, and then we can take a little walk around," she said.

The mountain guide and her client quickly got their kit together, shook hands with their pilot, and were on their way. Liz gazed after them with interest.

"Where are they going?" she asked, and she sounded fascinated.

"They're going to spend the night a little further up the glacier. Tomorrow they'll do some ice climbing, before we pick them up and bring them back later in the day."

"It must be amazing up here at night," Liz reflected.

"It is, yes."

"Have you've slept on the glacier before?"

Kristan nodded as she grabbed a heavy fleece off the back seat and gave it to Liz. She put one on too, and they both walked out a little bit farther onto the snow-covered ice. It was chiseled softly, and looked just like underwater sand sculpted by waves.

"I've been up a few times," Kristan explained. "On New Year's Eve last year one of the mountain guides I work with wanted to come up. Her name's Pam, you'll probably meet her at some point. We flew up with her and a couple of the other guys. We parked the helo in the corner, had some food, and spent the night."

"Wow."

"Yes, it was just that kind of night," Kristan agreed as she remembered.

Then she made a face and chuckled a little. "

Only I had to share a tent with Mike, so, you know... Kind of killed the romance."

She smiled at Liz.

"I thought perhaps Mike was your partner… as in not just your business partner," the woman blurted out, looking a little bit intense.

Kristan shook her head, looking alarmed at the very thought of it.

"No," she said immediately. "No, no way. I love Mike, but definitely not like that."

Liz burst out laughing. She was strangely relieved, and she hoped it did not show too much. She wanted to ask more personal questions, but Kristan did not volunteer anything else, so she decided not to push. She surveyed the sea of ice and snow in front of them, and she sighed happily.

"Thank you very much for bringing me up here this evening," she said quietly. "It's incredibly beautiful. And I loved every second of the flight over."

"Good," Kristan said softly. "I was hoping that you would."

The sun was disappearing fast over the peaks, and the temperature was dropping. Liz shivered imperceptibly. It was getting late. Mike's voice on the radio wanted to know if they were planning on coming back any time soon, or was Kristan waiting for the glacier to melt.

"We should go," she said reluctantly.

Chapter 4

A couple of days passed, and life at the Park was busy as ever. Kristan did not have a single second to herself, except for when she was out running, and those were precious moments for her.

On that particular day she left the Park at five-thirty, when it was still dark, and she took the road out toward town. She wanted to do a bit of distance, and the road would be good for that. It was a perfect six miler to the edge of town, and if she went home a slightly different way she would be able to complete the equivalent of a half marathon before breakfast.

She settled into a comfortable pace and let her mind wander.

Inevitably her thoughts drifted back to the attractive doctor. They did not often get lone travellers at the Park, but Liz was on her own, and happy to be apparently. She had told Kristan she was taking some time out to travel and indulge in her passion for painting, and Kristan had not been able to find out much more. After their flight together the other day her office manager had been waiting to discuss an urgent issue with their booking system, and Kristan once again had been swallowed up by her work.

Liz had been on her mind though, pretty much constantly. So she was pleasantly surprised later on that afternoon when there was a knock on the office door, and she looked up to see Liz standing there, dressed in jeans and a blue t-shirt, smiling and looking absolutely stunning.

"Hey!" Kristan exclaimed.

"Hi, Kris. Can I interrupt you for a minute?"

Kristan stood up quickly from behind her laptops.

"Of course," she said warmly. "Come on in. How are you?"

"Good. I just wanted to stop by and thank you again for taking me up the other day."

"It was my pleasure, Liz," Kristan said, and she meant it. "What's this?" she asked when her visitor handed her a little parcel.

"Just a little thank you."

Kristan unwrapped the unexpected gift, and she smiled when she realised it was a painting. One of Liz's. She had captured perfectly the shimmering waters of the lake, the white beach, and the gorgeous dark-green trees in the background. And Kristan raised an interested eyebrow as she narrowed her eyes at the lonely paddler in a red kayak that Liz had added into the scene.

"Is that me?" she asked.

"It is."

"Wow. Thank you," Kristan exclaimed, and she was blushing a little.

She sounded genuinely delighted with the gift, and that is when Liz realised how much she had wanted to give her something meaningful, something of herself that she could keep.

"Liz, this is beautiful. You are very talented."

"Thank you. I try, although I don't always succeed."

Liz's gaze drifted around the office, and Kristan was glad when she noticed that she seemed to be wanting to hang around a little. The woman seemed very curious about everything connected with her business, she asked a few questions, and Kristan thought that was very cool.

She sat down again and watched as the good-looking doctor explored her space. A couple of pictures pinned to the back wall amongst many others obviously caught Liz's eye.

In one of them Kristan was standing with Mike in front of a big black and red helicopter, both holding a glass of champagne in their hand, grinning from ear to ear. The photo had obviously been taken on the glacier. Kristan was looking back toward the camera. She had the happiest look on her face, and she was laughing. In the other photo she was sitting in her kayak in what appeared to be a major storm, spray flying all around her, a wave threatening to engulf her. Again that brilliant smile of hers was nearly burning a hole through the picture.

Liz looked up as Kristan came to stand next to her.

"This one was taken three years ago," Kristan explained, pointing at the helicopter shot. "It was the first helicopter I ever bought, and I flew us up to the glacier for the first time to celebrate."

Liz gave her an appraising look.

"So hang on a minute; you don't just run the Activity Centre then, do you?" she pointed out. "You own it?"

"Yes. I do."

Liz nodded, smiling a little.

She said nothing but she looked impressed.

"What about this one?" she asked, indicating the other photo she had been looking at.

Kristan grinned.

"This was last year. Middle of winter. We had a pretty bad storm one day, and we took the kayaks out to the beach for a surfing session."

"Sounds dangerous," Liz pointed out, frowning.

"Not really. Just fun. One of my instructors took this one just before the wave in the back caught me. It flipped me over, and I think I swallowed half the ocean in one gulp. Took me by surprise," Kristan added, glancing at Liz and smiling.

"Easily done it seems," Liz teased.

She wanted to stay but it was getting late, and Kristan had two laptops open, and paperwork spread all over her desk. She had obviously been in the middle of something, and Liz did not want to take up too much of her time.

"Well, I guess I'd better leave you to it," she said. "I'm glad you like the painting."

"I love it."

"All right. I'll see you when I do, then…"

Liz started to go but Kristan stood in front of her, and it was as if she had been reading her mind.

"I was just about to call it a day myself," she said. "Have you eaten yet?"

Liz shook her head no, her eyes locked onto Kristan's, fascinated by the way the evening light made her eyes sparkle and dance. She bit her lip, all of a sudden quite unable to take her eyes off her.

Kristan was slightly taller than her but not by much, and they were almost eye to eye, standing close. The white shirt that Kristan was wearing was open to reveal a flash of black bra and muscled shoulder underneath. All of a sudden Liz started to wonder what it would feel like to touch her, to run her fingers over her skin, underneath the shirt, until she could make those blue eyes darken, until she could make her tremble. And it frightened her a little to realise how much she wanted to do it now.

"Doc?"

Kristan was waiting, a soft smile dancing on her lips.

"I'm a vegetarian," Liz blurted out, immensely grateful that Kristan could not read the crazy thoughts running through her head right now.

"Really? Cool. That's good."

"You too?" Liz asked, looking hopeful.

"I'm a vegan," Kristan said with a soft chuckle. "So anyway. How about I order us a VG Supreme and some cranberry juice. Would that be okay?"

"It would be perfect."

Kristan smiled, thrilled that she would get to spend a little bit longer with this woman, who she found so beautiful and so captivating. And she was even happier that the feeling seemed to be mutual.

When they reached Kristan's cottage, and Liz spotted the table and chairs on the beach a little way away, she burst out laughing.

"Oh, I see," she said, touching Kristan's arm briefly. "Very slick. I like your style."

"Well, I have a beach," Kristan replied innocently. "Why not make the most of it?"

Liz's eyes widened.

"You own the beach?" she exclaimed.

Kristan gave a soft laugh.

"Yeah. Came with the Park."

"You own the Park too?"

"I do."

Liz shot her a piercing look.

"Well," she murmured. "You don't look old enough to be so accomplished. A helicopter pilot, a successful business woman, a kayak instructor..."

She glanced toward Kristan, and noticed that she was blushing again. Once more this had a definite effect on Liz. She was finding it difficult to keep her hands off Kristan, and she touched her hand lightly again.

"Anything else I should know about you?" she teased.

Kristan chuckled a little.

"Yeah. I'm a really lousy cook. You've been warned."

Liz nodded, smiling.

"No problem, I'll keep that in mind."

She sat down and leaned her elbows on the table, glancing at the lake and then turning back to look at the cottage, just visible on the edge of the rainforest.

She shook her head a little in wonder.

"This whole setting is simply amazing," she remarked. "I don't think I have ever seen a more beautiful place in all my life."

Kristan sat down next to her, feeling happy. For some insane reason she could not really figure out, Liz's heartfelt comment made her feel incredibly good.

"You should let me take you out on the lake sometime," she offered.

"I'd really like that," Liz said softly, meeting her eyes.

"Cool." Kristan smiled. "We'll do it soon. Will you be staying with us this autumn, Liz?"

It was a very innocent question, but the woman looked startled by it. Her smile faded, her eyes lost their focus. She opened her mouth to speak but nothing came out. Taken aback by her reaction, Kristan immediately rested a hand on her arm.

"Sorry," she said quickly. "I didn't mean to, uh... Did I say something wrong?"

Tears welled up in Liz's eyes, and she blinked them away quickly, but not quickly enough.

"Liz, what's wrong?" Kristan asked, and she leaned forward, worried now.

"Nothing. It's okay. You didn't say anything wrong."

Liz smiled through her tears, and she did her best to pretend that she was fine.

"I'm sorry. I just... I don't know how long I'll be staying," she blurted out, and fresh tears came to her eyes.

She brushed them off angrily.

"Sorry," she apologised again.

"Okay. Don't worry about it."

Kristan was about to pull back, but Liz covered her hand with hers and held her in place, and Kristan twitched involuntarily. Every time Liz touched her, and she was doing that a lot, she felt like a jolt of electricity shooting straight through her. She waited, watching as a cascade of emotions flashed through the most expressive black eyes she had ever seen.

"Bloody hell," Liz murmured, feeling embarrassed now when

she caught the concern in Kristan's eyes. "I'm sorry. I don't know where that came from, I guess I'm just tired. Sorry."

She jumped at the sound of a motorbike approaching, looking as if she might run off any second.

"It's okay, that's our meal," Kristan said quickly. "I'll go get it. Okay?"

"Yes."

"Sure?"

"Of course. I'm fine, don't worry."

Kristan nodded, looking far from convinced.

She stood up and walked briskly toward the bike, keen to give Liz a minute on her own to gather herself. She did not really understand what had just happened. Looking back toward her she noticed the woman run her hands through her hair, breathe deeply, and roll her shoulders a couple of times.

"Cheers Denny," she said as she accepted the pizza from the delivery guy.

"Hey Kris. Nice shiner."

Kristan threw him a wry smile along with a twenty. She could not wait to get back to her guest. Something was obviously wrong, and she kicked herself for suggesting an outing on the lake and asking questions that were none of her business.

She was glad to see that her tears were gone when she got back to Liz, and that she was smiling again. Most of all she was glad the woman had not simply decided to run away.

"I hope you're hungry," she deadpanned as she rejoined her. "This is an extra-large."

"I'm starving," Liz replied, grabbing a slice before Kristan could even sit back down.

Kristan gazed at her with an amused look on her face.

"That's very sexy," she remarked.

Liz nearly choked on her food.

"What is?" she coughed.

Kristan flashed her a brilliant smile.

"The way you eat that pizza."

She passed her some juice as Liz swallowed hard and blushed.

"Shut up," she muttered.

Kristan laughed, happy that she had them back on to safer territory. She picked up a slice of pizza for herself, and leaned back against her seat. She was hungry but she ate slowly, her attention entirely taken up by the woman who sat next to her.

Kristan did not scare easily when it came to emotions. She was curious about Liz, and deep conversations never put her off. If and when the woman wanted to open up to her she would be happy to listen, and offer whatever support she could.

"I needed that," she said after a few silent bites of her food.

Liz narrowed her eyes at her.

"How come? Did you skip lunch?"

"Yes…"

"You shouldn't skip lunch. Especially when you're flying, Kristan."

"I know, doc. But then again, I had coconut pancakes and spicy lentil stew for breakfast."

Liz raised a perplexed eyebrow.

"Is that a traditional kiwi thing?" she enquired.

Kristan chuckled.

"It is when your business partner is such an innovator in the kitchen," she said. "When Mike wants me to test one of his creations I normally end up eating the whole thing."

Liz gazed across the lake in front of them, smiling, feeling herself relax inside once more.

Kristan was amazing company.

Soon she had Liz laughing at some of her kayaking adventures, and she kept the conversation light and flowing, keeping safely away from any dangerous subjects. She talked about life at the Park, the here and now. She did not ask Liz any more questions, and she did not talk about the past.

When all the pizza was gone, and it was getting dark, Liz looked across at her companion, her expression pensive.

She smiled.

Kristan leaned forward a little, and Liz did the same.

"What?" she smiled, thinking it was so difficult not to get drawn in by this woman. "You look like you want to ask me something."

"I was just wondering what was on your mind," Kristan admitted.

Liz bit her lower lip a little, trying to figure out what it was about Kristan that made her feel so happy and comfortable.

"I feel like I have known you for a long time," she remarked after a short while. "That's weird, don't you think?"

"Not necessarily. Time is all relative."

"Yeah, I guess."

"Some people say it is just an illusion, albeit a persistent one."

Liz smiled a little.

"Quoting Einstein?"

Kristan grinned, and her blue eyes sparkled.

"They print this stuff on the side of cereal packets."

"You're just being too modest."

Liz reflected on the four weeks she had spent on the road. She felt so detached from her previous life now it was hard to believe it had only been that long. She rested her hand on the table, and as she did Kristan spotted the little whiter patch of skin on her ring finger.

She did not know how she could not have noticed it before, but her smile disappeared, and she stared at it for a second. When she looked up she saw that Liz was watching her intensely, and that her expression matched her own. The smile was gone, and her eyes was hard.

Kristan could have kicked herself for being so stupid.

"Sorry," she murmured. "None of my business."

Liz leaned back against her chair, and she crossed her arms.

"I was with somebody," she said. "But not anymore."

Kristan shook her head when she heard the small tremor in her voice.

"It's okay, Liz," she said quietly. "You don't have to tell me."

Liz breathed deeply, and she looked into her eyes once more. She saw nothing in them but genuine sympathy, interest and a hint of concern. An opportunity for friendship. Maybe, hopefully, a lot more than that. She took a deep breath, and dragged her chair a little closer to Kristan's.

"I was married," she said. "For eight years."

"Right."

"To a guy."

"Well. It happens," Kristan simply said, and she was careful to keep her expression neutral, but her heart sank a little, and she could not quite keep the emotion out of her eyes.

"Yes. I guess it does," Liz said gently.

Kristan forced herself to ask.

"I take it you're not married anymore?"

"Officially I am still married to him. But only because I haven't been able to divorce him. Yet."

Kristan nodded. She remained silent.

"What?" Liz asked her when she noticed her hesitation.

"I just assumed that you were gay," Kristan said honestly.

She simply had to say it. She was incredibly attracted to Liz, and if the woman was out of bounds she wanted to know, sooner rather than later. There was absolutely nothing in the way that Liz had acted with her so far that had made her think the feeling was not mutual, but if she had read her wrong and it was not, then she would back off immediately.

"I am! Even though I have ignored it for so long, to try to fit in and please people," Liz immediately said in response. "People I don't even care about! But I've always been attracted to women. When I bumped into you the other day... Gosh, Kristan, I was reminded of that in a big way."

So she can be direct too, Kristan reflected, and again she felt that little jolt, and it was a little bit easier to ask the next question.

"What happened, Liz?"

Liz breathed deeply.

"When I met Robert I was single and curious. I wanted to know what it would be like to be with a guy. We became best friends. And he wanted me. It was also at a time in my life when I was feeling vulnerable and lonely, and it was good to be wanted. He was fourteen years older than me."

"So what made you decide to leave him eventually?" Kristan asked gently.

"I realised it was not true love for me, and that it never would be. It came to a point when I had to be true to myself at last, and go back to what would be right for me. But he did love me. Or so he said. He would not accept the separation, and he became abusive. Violent."

Liz saw Kristan's eyes harden, and her expression change.

She reached for her hand, needing reassurance.

"It's okay. It's over now, and..."

"Did he hurt you?" Kristan interrupted.

Liz looked out toward the lake. She nodded a little, and she was biting on her lip again.

"Why?"

"I don't know why. But he was drinking."

Kristan exhaled sharply.

"But it's okay now," Liz said quickly.

She turned toward Kristan again, and brushed impatiently at the tears shining in her eyes.

"It's okay now," she repeated.

Kristan was silent. She gazed deep into the woman's eyes, and she did not like what she saw in them. Sadness, as expected, but fear as well. Definitely not okay.

She leaned closer to her.

"Are you on the run from him or something?" she asked.

"Why would you think that?"

"You looked scared when Mike banged on my door the other day. And even now, every once in a while you look around as if you're checking that no one is coming."

Liz gave a faint smile.

"I did not realise I was. You are very observant."

She tightened her hold on Kristan's hand, and held it in both of hers. Kristan felt her trembling. She shifted even closer, her eyes not letting go. She knew there was more.

"Tell me," she whispered.

Her gentleness was too much for Liz, and she gave in to the tears she had been holding back for so long. She leaned forward, and sort of folded in on herself.

"Liz. Hey, come on..."

Kristan put both arms around her shoulders, and she held her safely against her.

"Let it go," she murmured.

"He said if I ever left him that he would find me," Liz sobbed, her voice raw and full of emotion. "He said... He promised he would hurt me."

She allowed herself to rest against Kristan as more tears rolled down her cheeks.

Kristan started to feel angry.

"Nobody is going to hurt you, Liz," she said firmly. "Not as long as you're here. Not as long as you are with me," she dared to add.

Liz clung to her, and for a while she did not speak.

Then she took a deep breath.

"He's an ex-Marine, you know," she whispered.

"And?" Kristan snapped. "So what?"

"And... What he said... He really scared me."

Kristan paused for a second.

"What are you saying, Liz?" she asked eventually.

"Just that I know him well enough to want to be careful." Kristan's eyes burned in the gathering darkness.

"Son of a bitch," she muttered.

Liz glanced at her, and she made a massive effort to regain control. She knew if she was not careful she would really go too far with this. Kristan was too easy to talk to, and Liz was way too in need of support. Especially this woman's support, she realised. Kristan looked so beautiful, and she seemed so pure of mind and spirit. It was hard not to want to seek shelter in her strength. But Liz would not let herself do it. She had learned her lessons, and so she pulled back a little.

"Sorry," she murmured.

"Don't be sorry," Kristan said immediately. "It's okay."

Liz gave a light shrug.

"I am not running away, you know. I'm fine. I'm just being careful."

It was important to her that Kristan know she was not running. She did not stop to analyse why.

"I had always wanted to come to New Zealand," she explained, rationalising. "So when I got the chance I took it. I'm spending the summer here, and I have a job waiting for me in Wellington starting in July. It's all planned. I am not running away."

Whether or not Kristan believed that statement was not the point right now. And what it did to her hearing that Liz had plans in Wellington, in the North Island, was not something she wanted to acknowledge just yet either.

So she let it go.

Instead she brushed her fingers softly across Liz's cheek, pushing her tears away. Her touch was gentle, her gaze warm and understanding.

"Thank you for telling me," she murmured. "I can see it was very hard for you."

Liz simply clasped her hand in hers, finding warmth and safety in the simple contact.

"You're shivering," Kristan remarked after a few seconds. "Would you like to go inside now?"

A strong breeze had started to blow in from the lake, and Liz realised that she was freezing. She nodded. All of a sudden she felt completely exhausted.

"What about the table?" she asked.

"Don't worry about that."

Kristan stuffed the empty bottles and pizza box in a plastic bag, and she stood up.

She took Liz's hand.

"The rest can wait until later."

They walked quickly back toward the cottage, and there was no doubt in Kristan's mind that Liz was coming in with her. The woman looked shaken, a little bit spaced out even. Kristan doubted she would be able to sleep now anyway, and maybe a nice cup of tea would help to make her feel better. She walked straight to the front door, unlocked it, stepped aside to let Liz go in first, and walked in after her. She made sure that the door was locked properly before she turned around.

"Kristan."

Liz was standing right behind her, her eyes huge in the semi-darkness, and when Kristan turned to her she just stepped into her arms. Kristan wondered only briefly about the easiness of it all before she wrapped her arms around her waist.

"Everybody I know think I'm in France," Liz murmured against the side of her neck. "He won't come here."

Kristan's skin smelt of cocoa butter and sun. She felt solid and warm, and her embrace was strong. Liz felt safe, for the first time in months. She closed her eyes when Kristan pulled her a little tighter against her, and she sighed.

"Sorry," she mumbled.

"What for?" Kristan said gently.

"I should be taking care of you, not the other way around."

"How'd you figure that?"

"You're hurt."

"No, I'm not. And I don't need looking after."

Liz pulled back until she could look her in the eye.

"There is no need to play big and butch with me you know. I'm a doctor."

Kristan looked serious when she replied.

"I'm not playing. I'm just used to doing things for myself."

Both women jumped when there was a loud knock on the door.

"Yo, Kristan," Mike's voice called.

Kristan grinned as Liz collapsed against her, shaking with laughter.

"Big and butch, yeah right," she giggled.

Kristan let her go reluctantly, and she was smiling.

"Here goes my reputation."

Chapter 5

It took a while, but eventually Kristan did manage to corner her partner, and talk to him about his brother. She was dismayed but not too surprised to hear that when Mike had caught up with him in town they had had an argument. James had been drunk again, and it had been impossible to get through to him.

Kristan was definitely upset when she found out that they had come to blows.

"You didn't hurt him, did you?" she asked.

Mike was the bigger guy, fitter, more powerful.

Fortunately he was also the sober one.

"What do you think?" he said darkly.

"I think you didn't."

"That's right. Just avoided a few drunken punches, that's all."

"Okay. Good. So where is he now?"

It was just after four in the afternoon, and for the first time in about eight weeks now it had suddenly become quiet at the Park. Summer was truly over, and things at last were beginning to slow down. It had been a wonderful season, and everybody was looking forward to some well-earned rest. Everybody normally enjoyed a bit of time off, apart from Kristan, who thrived on being busy.

She was always up at five, to fit in a training run before the day's work started. On top of her normal duties, which included flying the helicopters, running the Park, and taking people kayaking out on the lake, she also liked to speak to every member of her staff at least once a day. She liked to check in with them, make sure everything was okay, make sure everybody was happy and getting on with their job.

People enjoyed chatting to her, and always had a million little things they wanted her to do. She was run off her feet most of the time, and whilst normally she was happy with the frantic pace of her life, over the past few days she had grown quite a bit annoyed that she had not been able to catch up with Liz.

Not that the woman had asked her to, and Kristan had a feeling she would not. They had bumped into each other a few times, said hello, lingered, stared at each other and smiled a lot, but that was it.

And Kristan was frustrated.

Liz had shared an awful lot with her that first night, and Kristan did not want her to think that she was not interested, or that she was taking her trust for granted.

"Where is James now?" she repeated, as Mike stared at a pile of paperwork, and pretended he could not hear her. "Mike?"

He sighed, and stood up to shake his legs and look out the window.

"I don't know," he said, and he sounded discouraged and a little sad.

Kristan noticed the set of his jaw, and the frown on his face.

It was not often that her partner appeared worried about anything.

"I've tried his number, but he's not answering."

"Do you know if he's still in town?"

He turned to her, frustration evident in his eyes.

"If he is, he's hiding well. It's not that big a town."

Kristan nodded. She always knew what he was thinking.

"Are you worried something's happened to him?" she asked.

Mike ran both hands through his short dark hair.

He sighed and gave a little shrug.

"I have no idea, Kris," he admitted. "Maybe…"

"Well then we need to find out, right?"

He seemed to mull over this for a second or two, but then he shook his head, and his eyes cleared.

"Take that back, matey. Won't be the first time he's done a runner on me. Hey, don't worry. I'm sure he'll turn up soon. So, how is it going with you and the doc?"

Kristan was lost in thoughts as she walked back to her cottage that night, feeling tired and dispirited. Mike always wanted to change the subject when it came to James, yet she knew how much he loved his brother, and she understood what this constant fighting between them was doing to her partner. She had suggested dinner in town but Mike had declined, saying he was behind on some paperwork, and really could do with getting it completed. Reluctantly Kristan had left him to it, knowing he needed time on his own to think.

She hated not being able to help.

It was a huge boost for her when she found a note from Liz stuck to her door, inviting her to dinner. Finally. It had been almost a week since that evening on the beach, and Kristan had worried about her, and genuinely missed her. At last, she thought, a chance to catch up.

She grabbed a quick shower, and threw on a white flannel shirt, ankle boots and a pair of jeans.

As she left her cottage, and headed toward the Park, she had no idea her life was about to change so dramatically.

When Kristan was a no-show, Liz tried not to take it too personally. After their impromptu pizza on the beach the other night she had wanted to invite her over, and cook for her. Yet every single time she had bumped into her at the Park Kristan had been in a rush, usually not alone, looking incredibly busy. And even though she always looked happy to see her, Liz had been unsure what to do.

She was used to dinner parties and she was not shy about making friends, so surely she should have been able to just walk up to Kristan, and ask. Yet she felt a little too attracted to the woman to consider an invite to dinner as just that. Who was she kidding? It would have been a date, a serious one at that, and she was feeling nervous. So eventually she settled on sticking a note to her door, and cooking a vegan chili for two in the hopes that Kristan would join her.

All in vain it seemed.

Liz told herself that she had probably been delayed, probably had not even been home yet. She tried to stick with that thought for a little while, but eventually she could not resist taking the short walk over to Kristan's place, and when she got there she realised that her note was gone.

So Kristan had found it after all.

Disappointed, Liz turned around.

She was just walking past the cafe on her way back to her pitch, wondering about Kristan, when her new friend came flying around the corner.

Liz's heart jumped in her chest at the sight of her.

"Hey Kris," she called out, smiling, "wait up!"

Kristan glanced sharply in her direction, slowing down as soon as she recognised Liz. She headed fast toward her, and as she watched her approach Liz's smile literally died on her lips.

"Oh my God," she exclaimed. "Are you all right?"

Kristan came to a sudden stop in front of her, looking dazed.

Liz grabbed her and steadied her.

"What happened?" she asked fervently. "Are you hurt?"

Her eyes jumped over several bright patches of blood on Kristan's face, and on her chest. She had blood all over her, on her jeans, on her hands, and on the side of her neck. She was breathing hard, and Liz could not really tell whether it was anger flashing in her eyes, or pain.

It might have been fear.

Whatever it was, Liz knew for sure it was nothing good.

"Kristan," she called again. "Hey!"

She reached for her and rested a hand on her cheek, gently turning her head toward her.

"Look at me, Kris," she said firmly.

Kristan finally rested her eyes on her.

She seemed to come back to her senses all of a sudden.

"It's okay," she mumbled. "I'm okay, Liz."

She became aware that Liz was touching her. Her hands were all over her, urgent, searching. Kristan eventually noticed the way the doctor was looking at her, and she glanced at her shirt and understood why.

"It's not me. Not my blood," she said, and her voice broke.

She started to cry.

Liz pulled her hard against her.

"What happened?" she asked again, more firmly this time, more calmly.

"I got your note."

"Okay. Then what?"

"I was on my way to you when I remembered I'd left my wallet in the office..."

Kristan took a deep breath, finding it hard to talk all of a sudden.

Liz felt her heart tighten in response.

"Okay. Come on over here," she said, and she led Kristan to a picnic table and bench, and sat down by her side. "You're in shock. Just take a few deep breaths, try to relax."

She rested a hand on her back, kept the other one wrapped tightly around her wrist.

"Better?" she asked after a while, and Kristan nodded. "Okay then, Kris. Tell me what's going on."

"It's Mike," Kristan said through clenched teeth.

Liz tightened her hold on her as a sliver of apprehension snaked its way down her back.

"Mike? Is he hurt? Where?" she asked.

Kristan took a sharp intake of breath. She stared into space, her eyes intense, apparently lost in thoughts.

Liz had to shake her again.

"Talk to me, Kris. Where is Mike now?"

"I found him in the middle of the office lying down. He was bleeding. The back of his head was... He was cut... He was cut really bad."

Kristan glanced at her shirt and jeans again, and she shook her head a little.

"There was a lot of blood... Such a lot of blood... I called for an ambulance."

She seemed to get lost in the memory again.

Liz ran her fingers through her hair softly, and pulled her closer.

"So Mike is on his way to the hospital right now, is that right Kris?" she asked.

She needed to make sure, so she had to keep her talking.

Kristan blinked a couple of times.

"Yeah," she mumbled. "Yeah. He's on his way to the hospital."

She turned suddenly, and the look of despair in her eyes was overwhelming.

"There was so much blood, Liz," she murmured. "What if he's really hurt..."

"Hey, listen," Liz interrupted. "Head wounds always bleed a lot. Okay?"

But Kristan continued as if she had not heard her.

"He was so still in there, I thought he was dead. What if they can't bring him back, Liz?"

Liz leaned forward, and she kissed her; because she simply had to. She needed that connection, and she knew that Kristan did too. It was the only way that she knew to express exactly how much she cared. The kiss was almost unconscious. It was a reflex action, pure heart, no thinking involved.

She felt Kristan's reaction. It was shock at first, surprise, hesitation, and then Kristan leaned into the kiss and poured her entire soul into it.

"I'm here for you," Liz whispered against her lips. "Mike is going to be okay, and so are you."

Kristan was trembling.

Liz wrapped her arms around her, and she held her tightly.

"It's okay, honey," she whispered. "It's okay."

Several hours later she pushed open the door to Mike's private hospital room, and peered inside. It was dimly lit, quiet apart from the soft hum of the machines surrounding him.

Kristan was sitting on a chair close to her partner's bed, holding on to his hand. Her eyes were fixed on him, and her gaze was intense, as if he were on the verge of opening his eyes.

Liz slipped inside, and she closed the door quietly behind her.

"Hey Kris," she said softly. "Can I come in?"

Kristan glanced toward her, looking a little as if she were coming out of a trance.

"Sure," she murmured. "I was wondering where you'd gone."

She let go of Mike's hand and stood up. She smiled weakly.

Despite everything that had just happened, the sight of Liz standing there affected her in a powerful way. She could not really remember the drive over to the hospital. Or the sequence of events after she had found Mike unconscious in a pool of his own blood. Things were a little foggy.

But Liz was real. She was an anchor.

When it had become obvious earlier that Kristan was in no state to drive Liz had quietly taken her car keys, and held the passenger door open for her. She had driven hard and fast, the way Kristan would have done. At the same time she had explained, patiently and in great detail, what the ambulance crew would be doing now, what the doctors in the ER would be doing to prepare for Mike's arrival, and exactly how skilled and dedicated these people were.

She had kept a careful eye on Kristan as she drove, making sure that she was breathing okay, making sure that she remained present, hating the sight of so much blood on her, and wishing she could make that haunted look in her eyes disappear.

Now when she opened her arms Kristan stepped into her embrace without a single word. For several long minutes Liz was silent as well. She held Kristan until she felt her relax against her, until she felt her start to breathe deeper and slower.

Then and only then did she speak.

"Are you okay?" she asked softly.

"Yeah. I'm fine."

Liz nodded. She pulled back a little until she could look Kristan in the eye. Her gaze was searching, questioning.

"I'm okay," Kristan repeated.

She shivered a little, and Liz squeezed her hand.

"I found this in your car," she said, "do you want to put it on?"

Silently, Kristan pulled the heavy black hoodie over her head, and it made her want to cry again when she realised it was one of Mike's.

"Why don't you sit down, Kris, and I can fill you in."

"Have you spoken to the doctors?"

Liz nodded and she squatted down in front of Kristan, looking up into her face, one hand resting safely on her knee. Kristan's eyes were red from crying, and a little hazy, and every other second she would glance toward Mike. She was pale, and dark circles stood out under her eyes like she had been punched. Liz steeled herself for what she was going to have to explain to her.

"Mike has suffered an extremely serious injury," she said quietly, her eyes on her. "The blood flow to his brain was interrupted, and as a result..."

"That's why he's not breathing for himself right now?" Kristan interrupted.

"Yes," Liz answered, and this was not what she had been about to say.

Once again Kristan glanced over toward her partner. She purposely avoided making eye contact with Liz, as she refused to acknowledge the truth that was staring her in the face. Slowing things down, delaying the inevitable.

"There's nothing wrong with his heart," she stated. "So he's going to be okay. Right?"

Liz knew what she was doing, and she could not allow it.

"The heart can function independently of the brain for a while," she said patiently, "so long as it has oxygen."

"Yes."

"Kris, the ventilator is what is keeping it working right now."

Kristan gave a sharp nod.

"Yeah, I know. So if his heart is okay, then as soon as he wakes up we can..."

"Kristan," Liz interrupted.

She knew she had to put an end to this, and do it quickly.

"He is not going to wake up, darling, I'm sorry."

"Of course he is," Kristan argued.

She stood up suddenly, and walked over to the bed.

"He's just in a coma right now. People recover from that all the time!"

Liz went to stand close to her, and simply took her hand in hers.

"Sometimes when someone has a catastrophic brain injury," she said slowly, "it is irreversible. Mike's brain has stopped working, Kris. There was a blood clot. He's not in a coma. The machine isn't keeping him alive; it is only a way to keep oxygen going to his organs until they can be recovered."

Liz felt Kristan start to shake as she finally demolished the last of her illusions. She hated doing it to her. She was a surgeon, and it was not the first time she had told someone that their loved one had died. But it was the first time that she had had to explain it to someone she cared so much about. Up until that very second she had not even understood how much she cared about Kristan. Now she knew. She would have done anything right now to be able to take her pain away. But she could not bring Mike back.

"I'm sorry, darling," she murmured. "I am so, so sorry."

Kristan stood there looking down at her partner's body, tears rolling down her face.

Liz took a couple of steps back. It was so hard.

"I'll give you some time, Kris. Okay? Take as long as you need. I'll be right outside when you're ready."

Kristan came to find her in the waiting room thirty minutes later.

Liz was standing up at the back, staring out the window with a tired look on her face. But as soon as Kristan walked in she looked in her direction, and the smile she gave her would have been enough to power the entire city.

"Kris," she said softly. "Come here."

Kristan walked up to her, and Liz immediately pulled her against her in a tight hug.

"Hey there," she murmured.

"Hello, doc," Kristan said tiredly. "Thank you for staying."

She knew that the doctors wanted to speak to her about Mike; the police wanted to speak to her; she had to get back to the Holiday Park, cancel today's helicopter flights, and possibly all of them for the week ahead. She had to speak to her staff. She had to get back to the office where she had found her partner unconscious, and take care of things there as soon as the police said she could. This would be a manslaughter investigation now. Kristan's head was spinning, and it was a huge relief to find that Liz had waited for her.

"As if I would simply go without telling you," the woman replied, looking deep into her eyes. "How are you doing?"

Kristan shrugged a little, and stared at a spot on the wall behind Liz's head, trying her best not to cry again.

"Mike just looks asleep," she reflected. "He's warm. He looks like any second he might wake up and smile…"

"I know. I wish that were true."

Kristan met Liz's eyes.

"I felt it," she said slowly. "I'm sure I felt it. He was still there when I walked into the office, and found him unconscious, and then it was like something shifted…"

Liz rested her hands on her shoulders gently.

"You probably did. When you are this close to someone, it is not unusual to be able to feel these things," she explained softly.

When Kristan said she was ready to get going she simply nodded. She had not expected her to do anything about Mike straight away, so for now she was happy to leave.

"I can drive now," Kristan told her.

"Sure, no problem," Liz nodded, and she handed her the keys to the big Ford Ranger truck.

It was early morning, unusually cold and raining a little, and she shivered as they walked quickly across the car park. In the truck Kristan switched the heating on to high, and she was mainly silent as they drove back toward home. As they neared the end of town, just before turning right onto the main road, she leaned forward in her seat and slowed down a little. Liz had been about to ask her if she could help with all the things she had to do at work later when Kristan suddenly hit the brakes, and pulled hard over onto the gravel side. Liz turned to look at her, and she was surprised and alarmed when she saw the angry look in her eyes.

"Kris, what is it?"

Kristan jumped out of the car without a word, and she took off in the general direction of the town, walking fast, almost jogging.

Liz stared after her.

She spotted the man walking toward them on the other side; tall, lean, dressed in jeans and a t-shirt and carrying a rucksack.

He looked a little familiar.

"Did you hit him?" Kristan screamed at him.

The man frowned.

"What?" he asked.

Kristan stopped in front of him with fury in her eyes.

"Because he wouldn't give you a job? Right?"

She rested her palms against his chest, and shoved him back.

"What the fuck are you on about?" he snarled.

Kristan pushed him again, and he stumbled and dropped his rucksack.

"Don't you fucking start," he threatened.

Liz had caught up with them by then. She took Kristan's arm and pulled her back, just as the woman was about to lean into James again.

"Don't," she ordered. "Kristan. Kris!"

She stepped in front of her, right in between them, as the man started to laugh a little.

"You want a fight, uh?" he goaded her. "Want to hit me? Come on then!"

Liz kept her hands firmly on Kristan's shoulders, frightened at the intensity on her face.

"Who's that?" she asked.

"Mike's brother," Kristan said. "They had a fight a couple of days ago because Mike would not give him a job. And now he's dead," she yelled at him over Liz's shoulder. "Did you do it James? Did you have an argument again, and you lost it, is that what happened?"

His expression did not really change when she said that, but he did go a little still.

"You what?" he said.

"Mike is dead, James," Kristan repeated. "Want to tell me about it?"

"You fucking junkie bitch," he exclaimed, and he took a threatening step toward her.

"That's enough," Liz snapped, as he stopped only inches from her, breathing hard. "Both of you, stop it! Kristan, call the police."

She glanced back toward her, and grabbed her arm to get her attention. Slowly, Kristan met her eyes. She looked lost, as if Liz had just pulled her back from a different reality.

"Kris, do it now," Liz ordered.

"You little cunt. You won't pin that on me," James spat.

He was so close now Liz could smell the alcohol on his breath. He looked dirty, as if he had been sleeping rough. Kristan got on the phone and started talking to the police, and he was still yelling at her.

Liz grabbed her by the wrist and dragged her back with her toward the car.

"Come on," she urged.

"What, you think I would kill my own brother?" he shouted. "Coke fried your brains or fucking what!?"

"We're just outside of town," Kristan was saying into her phone.

At the same time she was walking backward, her eyes on James, ready to react if he tried anything.

"Yes. Quick as you can," she said.

He lunged toward Liz, but Kristan stepped quickly in front of him and tripped him up.

"Liz, get in the car."

James stood up, and he launched himself at Kristan, but she easily deflected the blow, and this time she sent him to the ground hard. The man picked himself up off the floor and screamed.

"Kris, get in," Liz yelled at her from inside the truck.

She hit the locks as James smashed his fist on the bonnet, and started banging on the door.

"You fucking bitch!" he shouted.

"Let's go," Liz said tightly. "We need to move, now."

Kristan nodded, and she hit the gas. James was still yelling obscenities at them as they drove off quickly toward the Park. Liz did not say anything as Kristan shed silent tears all the way back home.

Chapter 6

Kristan spent the rest of the day talking to the police, and to her staff, working to put things in place and organise shifts, in order to free her from work for the next week or so.

James got picked up by the cops, and spent most of his day in custody being questioned about his whereabouts. He was released eventually when his alibi checked out, and it was established that he could not have been fighting with his brother at the time that it happened.

"If you see him hanging around, or if he tries to contact you," the officer in charge of the investigation told Kristan later on that evening, "let me know immediately."

"What if he goes to the hospital?"

"I don't think he will."

"But what if he does?" Kristan insisted.

The man simply shrugged.

"Nothing I can do to stop that," he said. "You just let me know if he does, and we'll put things in place to stop it if he is causing trouble."

In Kristan's office the police had found one of the big heavy spanners her partner regularly used to work on the helicopters. The tool was bloody, abandoned right outside the door, and more than likely it would turn out to be the murder weapon. Reports of several thefts of equipment at campsites around the areas had started to trickle in, and the general theory was that Mike had walked in on a thief, and been hit on the head when the person found themselves cornered.

"He wouldn't just let someone creep up on him like that," Kristan had protested.

"He probably didn't even know there was someone there," the officer had told her.

Detective Chief Inspector Omaru had been polite with her, but dismissive. Clearly his mind was already made up. The police were concentrating on looking for a thief who may have become a murderer. They interviewed everyone at the Park, every instructor, every client, and they started to go through footage of the CCTV cameras Kristan had in place. Whoever was responsible for what had happened to Mike, they were confident that they would find him quickly.

Now as it was getting dark Kristan shuffled back to her cottage, and stepped inside. She slammed the door shut behind her, looking for an outlet for her anger. The note from Liz inviting her to dinner was still on the table. Everything looked just as she had left it, and yet her world had been turned upside down, and she did not want to be there. Without thinking, she threw on a pair of shorts and a t-shirt, laced up her running shoes, and started off toward the forest.

Liz waited. She had decided to take a step back earlier on in the day, aware that Kristan needed to have meetings, and make decisions that she could not help her with. She wanted to give her some space too, but she had been hoping that when things started to calm down a little, that Kristan would come to find her. So she was relieved, and very pleased when she heard the soft knock on her door, and spotted her standing outside.

She hurried to get the door.

"Kris. How are you?"

Kristan stood there with her hands on her hips, her hair wet with sweat, her bare legs and trainers muddy.

"I went for a run in the forest," she said.

"And how are you feeling?" Liz enquired gently.

Not surprisingly, Kristan struggled a little to answer that question.

"I'm all right," she replied without enthusiasm.

"Have you eaten today?"

"No."

"Kris…"

"Would you like to have dinner with me at my place?"

Kristan had assumed, wrongly, that she would not want to see anybody after the events of the previous day. She had discovered pretty quickly that she could not stop thinking about Mike, and that Liz was also constantly on her mind. Spending time on her own was not that great. It was lonely, and sad, and no amount of running would be able to help with that.

"I would love to have dinner with you," Liz replied immediately.

Kristan gave her a brilliant smile, and for a second she looked relieved.

"Great," she said. "I… Thank you."

She had been worried about rejection. After all the stuff that Liz had told her about her ex-husband, losing her temper with James and almost ending up in a fight with him right in front of Liz was probably the most stupid thing that she could have done. But the woman seemed to be okay with her, and Kristan was so relieved she could have cried.

"Are you cooking?" Liz enquired, feigning concern.

Kristan smiled. She reflected that it was incredibly sweet of Liz to try to make her laugh, and she loved her for it.

"Don't worry, I'm not," she said. "But you won't have to, and it's not takeaway. I'll be back to pick you up in twenty minutes."

"It's okay, I can walk on my own…"

"No, no. Please," Kristan said softly. "It will be safer that way."

For once Liz did not argue. Mainly she did not want to give

Kristan another reason to worry. She simply got changed quickly, and twenty minutes later Kristan was back at her door as promised, dressed in faded jeans and a simple black shirt, clean Nikes on her feet, and her hair still wet from the shower.

She looked sexy and dark, and just a little dangerous, and Liz felt her heart skip a beat. She locked her door, and turned around, leaning close to give Kristan a quick hug.

"You smell lovely," she commented.

Kristan smiled, and she took her hand.

"Thanks. You look beautiful."

Liz was gorgeous in simple black trousers and a dark green silk top. Her hair was pulled back in a ponytail, and a few errand strands just kissed the side of her face. Her black eyes sparkled as Kristan tightened her grip on her hand, and Kristan reflected Liz was quite simply the most beautiful woman she had ever seen in her life.

"It's good to see you again, doc," she murmured.

Liz smiled at her, and noticed that even though Kristan was smiling too the smiles did not quite touch her eyes. She squeezed her hand and threw her arm around her waist, pulling her close. Thunder was in the air, and the wind was picking up, and so they walked quickly over to Kristan's cottage.

When Liz stepped inside she broke into a huge smile.

"Oh, Kris, this is gorgeous," she exclaimed. "When did you have time to do all this?"

Kristan gave a simple shrug, looking a little lost still, almost shy.

"It's no big deal. Didn't take long."

She had set the table in front of the bay window, with the lake and the mountains in the background, and she had lit candles all around the room. Music was playing softly in the background, and Liz relaxed as soft guitars and women voices filled the space all around them. It was peaceful. Quiet. It made her feel safe.

Kristan stood behind her, so close that Liz could feel the heat of her body through their clothes.

"I wanted to make it a bit special," she said. "You were great at the hospital. And... With everything. So thank you."

"I'm glad I could be there for you Kris, there is no need to thank me."

"Would you like some wine?"

Liz nodded, smiling.

"Red okay?"

"Perfect."

Kristan filled a glass and handed it to her.

"Cheers," she said.

"Cheers. Are you not having any?"

Kristan shook her head, and her eyes lingered on Liz.

"Maybe later," she said.

She had that look on her face again.

Liz touched her hand briefly.

"What's on your mind?" she asked.

"Just about a million things," Kristan replied, and sadness flickered in her eyes for just a moment. "But when you asked just now, I was thinking about last night when you kissed me."

"Yes," Liz said a little hesitantly. "About that..."

Kristan was looking at her attentively.

"I just felt... that's what I needed to do at the time. I didn't think, I just..."

She looked at Kristan, and gave a small shrug.

"I just acted. I hope that's okay."

"It's more than okay," Kristan said softly. "I was wondering if... maybe... you'd like to kiss me again..."

She leaned closer to Liz. She gave her plenty of time to pull away, and when Liz did not she softly brushed her lips against hers. She smiled. When she started to move back Liz held her in with a hand on the back of her neck, and once more Kristan hesitated.

"What is it?" Liz murmured.

She felt Kristan's breath, like a caress against her face.

"I just want to make sure this is what you want, Liz."

"What do you mean? You?"

"Me. A woman."

Liz pulled back a little, just enough to be able to gaze deep into Kristan's sparkling blue eyes.

"You," she said, "are more woman than anyone on this planet."

She leaned into Kristan, and let her fingers travel up into her hair.

"And I want you," she said. "Precisely because you're a woman."

As soon as she said that, Kristan took her glass from her and dumped it on the table. She wrapped her arms around her, pulling her a lot closer, and a lot harder against her than she would have dared before. This time when she kissed her it was urgent, intense, hungry. Her mouth travelled to her naked shoulder, and she bit the fleshy part at the base of her neck. Liz clung to her. Heat filled her body. She struggled to keep her eyes open.

"Kris..." she murmured.

Kristan found her mouth again. She kissed her hard, deep, and slow. When Liz's hands snaked under her shirt and found her naked flesh she moaned softly.

"I won't be able to stop if you touch me," she gasped.

"Did I say I wanted you to stop?"

Liz let her fingers travel over the hard muscles etched on her stomach. When the shirt got in the way she struggled with the buttons impatiently, eliciting a soft laugh from Kristan.

"Take it off," Liz exclaimed. "Please, Kristan, I need to..."

See you. Touch you. Hold you.

That is what she wanted to say but then she never got to finish her sentence, because Kristan pulled her shirt over her head and threw it across the room, and the sight of her simply took Liz's breath away.

"Gosh, you're so beautiful," she whispered.

She stepped forward, and Kristan remained still, looking at her and breathing a little hard.

"So beautiful..." Liz said again.

She was a doctor, a surgeon, and of course she had seen hundreds of women naked before. But right now was a gift, Kristan standing in front of her, trembling and open and just everything Liz had ever dreamed a woman would be.

Kristan's eyes were on her too, tracking her every move. They darkened when Liz rested a hand of the small of her back, and let her fingers drift over her breasts. She gasped when Liz pinched her nipple, and when her mouth closed over it and started to suck she felt lightheaded, and she had to stop her.

"You're sure you've never done this before?" she asked, holding on to her wrist.

"No."

Kristan shook her head, out of breath and laughing.

"Are you kidding me?" she said. "I'm about to explode."

Liz looked into her eyes, and she knew that it was true.

"Then take me to bed, Kristan," she said quietly. "I need you now."

The sheets were tangled and twisted, and Kristan's skin felt nicely bruised and tender when she woke up several hours later, into the next day, with Liz wrapped tightly around her. It was no longer raining outside. The cottage was cool, and Liz's skin against hers felt like a volcano still. Kristan rested her cheek against the top of her head, and she allowed herself to drift for a while.

The previous night's dinner had turned into much more than that very quickly, and at first Kristan had tried to slow things down. Then she had tried to be very careful with Liz, aware that it was her first serious time with a woman, and in fact Liz was the one who had turned their encounter into raw, organic sex.

Kristan could not remember ever being with a woman who

could read her like Liz could. They had talked very little, laughed a lot. Touched, explored, pushed the boundaries all night long until both of them had collapsed exhausted in each other's arms.

It was five in the morning now.

Kristan was lying on her back, and as she started to think about what she had to do that day she progressively grew more and more rigid.

"What is it?" Liz murmured against her ear.

She opened her eyes, and smiled.

"Good morning," Kristan said, smiling back at her.

She was wondering what exactly she had ever done to deserve waking up next to such an exceptional woman. Kristan's smile widened as the woman stretched like a cat, pulled the quilt tighter around them both, and snuggled back against her. She rested her head against Kristan's shoulder, and sighed with content.

"Hi," she said softly.

"Did I wake you?"

"No... I just felt you in my sleep. What are you thinking about?"

Kristan exhaled softly.

"About Mike," she replied. "About what I need to do today. I have to go to the hospital and..."

"Yes. You do," Liz said gently when she did not finish her sentence.

There would be no romantic breakfast by the lake or leisurely walk through the forest for them this morning, and if Kristan started to change her mind about her partner, Liz would have to keep her on track. She had to see to her friend, and do what he would have wanted her to do. There was no sense in waiting.

Liz knew for sure that her presence last night had helped to keep Kristan grounded. It had been a timeout, a break, a way to hide outside reality for a few hours. She knew Kristan had needed that, and she knew she had satisfied her in ways neither of them would be able to express. As for herself, Liz knew that she had found a little part of herself that had been missing for a lot of years. Thanks to Kristan she felt whole again.

"Thank you," she murmured.

Kristan just smiled, a question in her eyes. Liz rested her fingers against the side of her neck. With her thumb she gently caressed her lips, loving the way that Kristan's eyes immediately lost their focus.

She kissed her softly.

"Thank you for last night. For being you. For loving me the way you did."

"I hope you don't think it was just because of what happened to Mike. That I needed to unwind or something. That it was a one-off."

Liz considered her response carefully.

"I think you did need to unwind," she said softly. "And that's okay. I also know something happened between us last night that was a lot more important than either of us can understand right now."

Kristan relaxed a little.

"I'm glad you feel that way," she murmured. "Because I do. And I don't just sleep around, just so you know."

"I didn't get that impression. Neither do I."

It seemed this was all they needed to say, and something was sealed between them in that moment. They showered together, both comfortable with each other, and both aware that the day had to be got through, even though it would have been tempting to just go back to bed and pretend it was all a bad dream.

Kristan in particular was finding it difficult to concentrate, and she was slow to get dressed, and slow to find her car keys. Then she got distracted checking her emails.

"Do you want me to come with you to the hospital?" Liz asked when she realised what was going on.

When Kristan did not reply she went to stand in front of her.

"How are you doing, gorgeous?" she asked softly.

Kristan just shrugged and looked away, blinking back tears she did not want her lover to see.

Liz wrapped her arms around her neck.

"Talk to me, baby."

"I don't want to go to the hospital."

Liz could hear the reluctance in her voice, and the emotion.

"You are doing the right thing, you know."

"Yeah."

Kristan was finding it difficult to think about it.

Impossible, actually.

"I'm sorry," she said softly, as she tucked a strand of silky blond hair behind her lover's ear. "You look beautiful. And I am not normally this weird in the mornings."

She looked so sad it made Liz want to cry.

So she simply tightened her grip on her.

"Do you want me to come with you?" she asked again.

"I do... But I think I need to do this alone," Kristan said after a slight hesitation.

"I understand."

Kristan wrapped her arms around Liz's waist and pulled her closer.

"I'm sorry I can't spend the day with you. Last night was so incredible for me, and there's a million things I'd like to do with you today."

"Me too. But Mike needs you honey, and I know how hard this is going to be, but you need to do it. That's what he would have wanted. We can wait, Kris."

"Will you be here when I get back?"

"If that's what you want then nothing would make me happier."

Kristan smiled.

"That's what I want. And me too."

After one last kiss she grabbed her keys, put on her sunglasses, and walked to the door.

"How long will it take, Liz? After I switch off the ventilator?" she asked, and Liz could not see her eyes anymore, but she heard the tremor in her voice.

"Not long, darling. Seconds."

Kristan nodded sharply.

"Okay," she said, and then she stepped outside, and ran toward her car.

Chapter 7

Liz decided to make herself useful. There was not a lot she could do in terms of kayaking, or flying people up to the glacier, but she could definitely help in the cafe, unpack deliveries, check invoices and all that sort of thing. Kelly, who ran the shop and also managed reception most days, was grateful for the help, and even more so for the company. The sixty-year old, who was a head shorter than Liz, and almost as wide as she was tall, spent the morning remembering Mike, and telling Liz stories of his and Kristan's adventures.

Liz did not have to say much, just listen, and she was happy to be distracted and kept busy. Her mind kept wandering, and she was thinking of Kristan, and what she would be doing right now at the hospital. Flicking that switch, turning the ventilator off, saying goodbye to her best friend. Liz was careful not to think about it for too long.

She realised that Kelly had stopped talking suddenly, and was looking at her curiously, and she shook herself.

"I'm sorry, what?" she asked.

"I was saying, did you happen to know what time Kris was coming back?"

Liz shook her head no.

"I need her to sign off on some invoices."

"Okay. Well, as soon as I hear from her I'll tell her to pop round."

Kelly gave a triumphant smile.

"So you think you'll be seeing her first, eh?" she exclaimed. "I knew you two had something going on."

She burst out laughing when Liz blushed, and she got up to give her a hug.

"If you ask me, it's about time she found somebody like you," she added. "I knew nothing was ever going to happen with Mike, but you..."

And she stopped to appraise Liz slowly.

"You look lovely, and I appreciate your taking the time to spend the morning helping out. That's very kind of you."

"Well, I want to help," Liz said simply.

"I can see that," the older woman said with an approving nod. "But before we do, I would like to have lunch with you, and find out all about you. How about it, darling?"

Laughing, and more than a little nervous, Liz agreed.

It was dark again by the time Kristan arrived back at the Park. Liz had been keeping an eye out for her. She watched her climb out of her truck, and for a few seconds Kristan just stood there staring into space. Unaware that anyone was watching her, she leaned with her back against the car, and lowered her head, and when her shoulders started to shake Liz understood that she was crying.

Her first impulse was to run to her, but then she stopped. Would Kristan want her there? Would she want someone talking to her right now, or would she want to be left alone to grieve in peace?

As she hesitated, Liz remembered the look in Kristan's eyes the previous night when she had kissed her, and the careful, intimate way she had made love to her all night. And Liz did not need anything else to know exactly what she should do.

The sound of footsteps on gravel alerted Kristan that someone was coming, and her first impulse was to hide. Then she recognised her lover, and a huge sense of relief washed over her.

"Hi baby," Liz greeted her softly.

She pulled her into her arms, and Kristan leaned into the embrace, and buried her face against the side of her neck.

"Hi, doc."

"I like it when you call me doc," Liz murmured, smiling.

Kristan breathed deeply.

"I'm so glad you're here," she murmured. "You have no idea."

Liz hugged her hard.

"I think I do. How are you? How did it go today?"

"It's the hardest thing I've ever had to do," Kristan said tightly.

Liz looked at her, and nodded a little.

"But you did it," she said. "You are so incredibly brave, and I am so proud of you..."

Kristan rested against her for a minute longer. She was feeling so disconnected from everything, and once more Liz felt like pure oxygen to her.

"How are you doing?" she asked after a while.

Liz smiled at her, touched that Kristan would ask.

"I'm fine. I needed something to do today so I spent the day with Kelly in the cafe. Helping out, and chatting. Kelly's lovely."

Kristan looked surprised, and pleased all at the same time.

"That's great, Liz. I'm glad you two got on," she said. "Thank you for helping out also. Even though you don't have to work."

"Like I said, I wanted to," Liz said softly. "It's no problem. Now, tell me about you. How are you feeling?"

Kristan just shrugged.

"Oh, you know. I'm all right."

Liz was beginning to understand that this was Kristan's default setting. Being 'all right', being 'okay', obviously would always be her first answer, regardless of what was happening to her, or how hard it was affecting her.

Liz simply nodded, not wanting to push, and she held her close as Kristan started to walk them back toward the cottage. Just letting her know she cared by being present. Letting her know it would be okay if ever she wanted to talk.

"You know what?" Kristan said then.

"What?" Liz said in the same tone.

Kristan smiled a little.

"If Mike could have seen me, he would have yelled at me for being such a softie."

"He probably did see you," Liz remarked.

She was glad when she got a weak chuckle out of Kristan.

"Probably," she agreed. "Probably made him roll his eyes a few times."

She was trying to act normal, act easy, and yet she was pale, and she looked exhausted, and when they came into view of the lake and the cottage she slowed a little, and then stopped completely.

"I think I need a minute," she murmured.

"Of course. I'll be inside, okay?"

"Yeah. Thanks. I won't be long."

"You take as long as you need, honey."

"Liz, I..."

Liz simply raised her hand.

"It's okay, Kris. You go do what you need to do. Then you come back to me."

Kristan nodded, and she immediately walked off toward the forest. As soon as she was out of sight of Liz and the cottage she started to run.

She sprinted through the trees, going hard, as fast as she could, uphill for as long as she could. She slipped on a patch of mud, fell, got up and went at it again, harder, until she fell again, and the tears caught up with her and it became too hard to breathe.

Panting, she found the nearest tree and stood in front of it. She breathed deeply, made her right hand into a fist, and hit the tree three times in rapid succession, as hard as she could. The third time brought fresh tears to her eyes, and she cried out when she connected with it. It hurt but that did not stop her, and she delivered another few hard punches. Pain flashed through her fingers and up into her arm, hot and intense and incredibly good. She welcomed it, focused on it, let it take away the feelings. It was not the first time she had resorted to self-harm. It worked. She was fine with it, now more than ever.

After a few seconds she flexed her fingers slowly. She had not hit hard enough to break her hand, but it was swollen and cut, and already starting to bruise. Kristan exhaled sharply, feeling oddly relieved. There would be no panic attack now, she knew. Just pain, and she was used to that. She leaned against the tree, and simply cried for a while.

Meanwhile Liz had turned her back, walked to the cottage, pushed the door open and then closed it quietly behind her.

She went through Kristan's CD collection, smiling when she realised they had the same taste in music. She put Lady Antebellum on the player, lit fresh candles, and started a fire.

She opened the freezer and looked for one of Mike's specials, selecting mushroom shepherd's pie which would be warming and filling, and just the right kind of food for Kristan, who she suspected had not eaten a thing since the day before.

She very consciously thought about Mike as she handled his food, silently blessing him, and thanking him for being a best friend to the woman she knew she had begun to fall madly in love with.

She poured wine and set the table, and when Kristan walked in she simply smiled at her, and took her jacket from her. She ignored the mud on her jeans, and pretended she could not see the blood on her hand.

"You're all good, stud?" she asked simply.

"Yeah," Kristan replied, and her voice was raw and broken.

"Are you hungry?"

Kristan blinked. She hesitated.

"Yes; I am," she said eventually.

Liz beamed at her, and leaned in for a gentle kiss.

"That's great news," she said.

Suddenly, Kristan became aware of the wonderful smell coming from the kitchen. She became aware of the music playing softly in the background, and as she walked closer to the fireplace it was as if something shifted inside her. She suddenly noticed the candles, felt the warmth of the fire, and she did not want to feel pain anymore.

Or be alone.

"Here you go, honey."

Kristan accepted the glass of wine from Liz, staring at it for just a second, and then she really focused on her face, and noticed the look in her eyes. It was sadness and uncertainty, and mixed in with that, strength, and a promise for the future.

Kristan set her glass on the table, and she wrapped her arms around Liz's waist. She kissed her. She took her time, and the kiss was soft, warm, and reassuring. When she pulled back Liz was smiling, and Kristan smiled back at her.

"I love you," she said with feeling. "I know I haven't known you long, and a lot has happened since, but it doesn't matter."

"Well. At last you're talking sense, woman," Liz said softly.

She was smiling still, and her eyes were full of tears. Tears of joy.

She grabbed a fistful of Kristan's shirt and looked deep into her eyes.

"It was really hard for me to let you go just now, you know."

Kristan nodded a little.

"Yes. I'm sorry. I just had to be alone for a moment."

"I don't like it that you hurt yourself when I wasn't looking. I don't like it at all."

Kristan glanced at her hand.

"I just..." She hesitated. "Sometimes it helps."

"And it's scary for me to think about you doing it."

Kristan bit her lower lip, looking down at her hand with a little frown on her face.

"Yeah. I can see that," she murmured.

"Next time you need some release, perhaps you can do it differently," Liz said gently. "You know? Like maybe you can get it with me. Talk, or whatever else you need. Just don't hurt yourself like that again, Kristan. I won't have it. Okay?"

Kristan leaned over for another soft kiss.

"You're talking a lot of sense too," she murmured.

"I always do; you just got to listen," Liz exclaimed, laughing now. "So, why don't you grab a shower and a change of clothes? Then we can eat."

And just like that, she moved them on again.

Kristan hugged her briefly. All of a sudden it felt like another layer of sadness and hurt had just been lifted off her shoulders, and she owed it to Liz. She showered quickly, put on an old pair of jeans, a jumper that was too big for her, thick socks, and she padded back into the kitchen.

"Is that Mike's food smelling fantastic in the oven?" she asked, smiling.

"Yes. I hope you don't mind."

"I don't mind at all, and Mike would be happy that we are enjoying his food," Kristan interrupted, her eyes sparkling with emotion. "I reckon he owes us a good meal after all he's put us through."

"So do I," Liz smiled.

"You know what, I really ought to learn how to cook."

"I could teach you."

"Cool."

"You could teach me to fly in exchange."

Kristan smiled brightly.

"That's a great idea, doc."

She glanced around the room and nodded thoughtfully.

"Thank you so much for all this," she said simply. "It's perfect."

The night was theirs, and so they took it. They ate slowly, kissed slowly, and talked for hours. When they went to bed Kristan lay on her stomach, and buried her face into the pillow. She was exhausted, but she looked back when Liz straddled her back.

"Relax," Liz ordered.

"What are you doing?"

"Giving you a massage."

"Really? Wow; you really are one of a kind..."

Liz gave a little laugh.

"You'll owe me one back," she joked. "Gosh, you're so tight I can't believe you can still move," she added, and she started to work on the painful knots in Kristan's shoulders.

As she worked she narrowed her eyes at the thick scar that started just behind her shoulder, and snaked its way down her right arm. She traced it with her finger, and poked Kristan in the back of the neck.

"Hey you. What's this? How come I didn't notice it last night?" she asked.

"Too busy driving me crazy, probably," Kristan smiled, her voice muffled by the pillow.

She chuckled.

"I'm serious. What happened?" Liz insisted.

Kristan just closed her eyes, and gave a light shrug.

"It's nothing," she said. "Just ligament damage."

Liz rolled her eyes.

"Oh really? Must have been one hell of a bad surgeon."

She stretched out next to Kristan, and raised herself up on an elbow.

She gazed at her, smiling faintly.

"You are such a bad liar," she observed.

"Yeah? What's my tell?"

Liz pulled back when Kristan tried to kiss her.

"No. Not until you tell me your story," she said. "I want to know."

"About the scar?"

"All of it. And also about the things that Mike's brother said on the road yesterday."

Kristan's glacier blue eyes instantly grew a little darker.

"I want to know you," Liz insisted. "I don't want any secrets between us."

"I don't want any secrets between us either," Kristan said quickly.

She smiled a little when she caught Liz's serious look.

"Okay," she murmured. "Okay, I'll tell you."

She turned over and stuck another pillow behind her back, laughing when Liz draped her leg over hers, and wrapped her arm around her waist.

"I won't run off, you know," she said softly.

"I know, I just like holding you," Liz replied. "So come on," she added with a quick smile. "Tell me about you. I don't scare easily, I promise."

Kristan snuggled closer against her, and Liz rested her right hand on her heart. Kristan covered it with her own, and she took a deep breath.

"So you know I'm American, right?" she started.

"Your accent kind of gives that away. I like it."

"I like yours too."

"Don't change the subject," Liz said gently.

Kristan nodded.

"When I was twenty-one I got a job with a computer programming firm in Silicon Valley. I was good. I wrote a program we sold to the Pentagon, and I made a lot of money, very quickly."

"You were a nerd?" Liz blurted out.

Kristan burst out laughing.

"Yeah," she chuckled. "I guess I was. Still am when it comes to helicopters."

Liz raised an eyebrow.

"How much money?" she asked.

"A lot. I had a few cars, a big house, a swimming pool; lots of invites to parties, and open access to any amount of alcohol and drugs I wanted."

Liz's expression grew troubled.

Kristan glanced at her and saw it, and her voice got a little bit huskier.

"I was young. It was hard not to take advantage of everything on offer. I got hooked on alcohol pretty quickly, and then it was only a matter of weeks until I was on cocaine."

"Oh, Kris," Liz murmured.

Kristan gave a light shrug.

"Mike must have told James about it, maybe as an incentive to get sober. From the way he was shouting at me the other day, it looks like it didn't work."

"If only it were that easy."

"It's easy to get on it, hell to stop. Of course I didn't care then. I was on my own, I could do what I wanted. It was exciting, and I didn't really have an off switch."

Liz shook her head a little.

"That's a very dangerous way to be."

"Tell me about it."

"Have you found that off switch now?"

"I have."

Liz nodded.

"So what happened?"

"Well, it's a bit fuzzy. For two years it seemed like this huge party that would never end. I had job offers coming out of my ears, I was high all the time, and rich. I was also working pretty much twenty-four seven. Until one day I went out to a party, and woke up in hospital a week later. I can't remember a single thing that happened. But I was high, drunk, and driving."

Kristan felt Liz stiffen against her.

"I crashed my car. Fortunately it was the middle of the night, and no one else got hurt."

"So that's how you got that scar."

"Yeah. I nearly lost my arm. Almost tore it off my shoulder. They had to repair some ligaments and stuff."

Liz closed her eyes for a second. She rested her hand on the side of Kristan's face, and turned her head toward her so she could look her in the eye.

"Any other injuries I should know about?" she asked wryly.

Kristan smiled at little at the way she said that.

"Nothing else, doc," she said.

Liz exhaled slowly.

"Good. So you moved to New Zealand after the accident?"

"Yes. When I got out of hospital I sold my house, the cars, and everything I owned. Then I flew down here, and used all of my money to buy the Park and set up the Activity Centre. I haven't touched drugs, or alcohol, since the day I left the US."

Liz nodded slowly.

"So that's why you didn't drink tonight either," she reflected.

"Right."

"You bought the wine just for me?"

"Yes. It's not a problem for me if you want to have a drink. I just can't."

"Why didn't you tell me?"

"Because you would have asked me why," Kristan sighed. "You know, I named the Park Whānau Anō. It means 'Born Again' in Maori. A new start. I don't like talking about the past."

Liz nodded thoughtfully, and she made a mental note to never drink again in front of Kristan from now on. Actually, it would be a good idea to be like her, and give up alcohol entirely.

"What about your family? Your friends?" she asked.

Kristan shook her head.

"I grew up in care. I have no family. And the friends I had at the time were so busy making millions they probably never realised I was gone."

"So Mike was..." Liz hesitated.

"My family?" Kristan finished for her. "Yeah."

She glanced at Liz, and softly caressed her hair.

"So now you know. Does it change anything about us?"

"Of course not," Liz exclaimed. "Why would it?"

"Well, you know, I was a little bit afraid to tell you about it."

"How come?"

Kristan hesitated.

"Because I don't want you to think that I'm like him," she said eventually.

Liz frowned, not sure she understood.

"Who, James?" she asked.

"No. I was really thinking about your husband," Kristan replied slowly. "I was an alcoholic, and a drug addict, but I would never hurt you."

Liz heard the torment in her voice, and her heart tightened in response.

"Kristan," she said fiercely.

She kissed her, because it was the only way that she could really convey her true feelings. When she pulled back Kristan was a little out of breath, and Liz looked deep into her eyes.

"Do not ever compare yourself to him again," she said tightly. "You are nothing like him, Kris. Nothing."

Kristan nodded, worry still dancing in her eyes.

"You haven't known me long, Liz."

"I've known you long enough."

Liz shook her head.

"I really can't believe the things that go through your head," she exclaimed. "Kris, you are kind. Gentle; compassionate and thoughtful," she added, finally managing to bring a faint smile to Kristan's lips. "And so brave. I feel safe when I'm with you."

"You do?"

Liz nodded.

"I do. It's a wonderful feeling."

"Is it because I am big and butch?" Kristan asked, and this time she was laughing.

Liz rolled her eyes.

"Of course," she grinned.

Kristan kissed her, and then Liz felt her shiver.

She noticed the change in her, the way that Kristan started to slur her words a little, the way she seemed to be having trouble keeping her eyes open. Obviously talking about her past and her addiction had taken its toll.

Liz was so fiercely proud of her.

"You're exhausted. Time for bed now darling," she said gently.

She pushed her down onto the bed, and covered her with the quilt. Kristan did not resist. All of a sudden she felt more tired than she had in years. Liz kissed her, and brushed the hair from her face. She moved extra pillows out of the way. Kristan felt herself start to sink.

"Don't... I don't want to sleep," she murmured.

"Why not?"

"I want to stay with you."

"I'll be right here next to you," Liz murmured against her ear. "Just sleep, honey. I won't leave."

"Promise?" Kristan mumbled.

"Yeah. I'll be right here when you wake up. Then I'll teach you how to cook me breakfast. How's that?"

Kristan chuckled. She looked like she was going to say something else, and then she just smiled. She closed her eyes, and she snuggled deeper against Liz, and within seconds she was asleep.

Chapter 8

The weather was changing. Autumn was clearly on the way, and Kristan wanted an opportunity to take Liz out on the lake before it got too cold and windy. So she was up at five the next morning, and straight into the office for a few hours. She spoke to the police, to her staff, went through the books, sorted out replacement parts for one of her helicopters, and purposely avoided looking at a bunch of resumes from local pilots who had obviously heard the news about Mike.

By eight o'clock she was done and back at the cottage, and for the next two hours Liz did not give her a chance to think about anything at all. And it was not teaching her how to cook breakfast.

Now Kristan was feeling incredibly relaxed, and she could not stop smiling.

"Do you want a single or a double?" she asked.

Liz stood at the door to the kayak shed, dressed in shorts and one of Kristan's t-shirts, looking like a kid in a toy shop.

"I don't know," she said, her eyes jumping over all the boats, of different sizes, types and colours. "What's best?"

"Well, in a double you get to sit at the front, and I'll be sat behind you. In a single you're just on your own."

"I don't want to spend all morning not being able to see you," Liz protested.

"Okay. Single it is then," Kristan said, happy with her choice.

On the beach she helped Liz to get in, adjusted her foot rests and spray deck for her, and handed her the paddle.

She kissed her.

"All set, doc?"

"Yeah."

"I'll push you in."

As soon as the water was deep enough she stood back, and she watched as Liz started to paddle, almost as if she had been born to it.

"Hey! Looking good," she called out to her.

Liz had good balance already. This was going to be easy.

Quickly, Kristan jumped into her own boat, and caught up with her.

"Is it supposed to be this wobbly?" Liz enquired, looking tense.

"You'll get used to it in a bit. The key is to keep your paddle straight, and use your centre of gravity for balance."

"My bum, you mean?"

"Yes," Kristan smiled. "You got a nice one, so use it."

Liz started to laugh.

"Glad you like it," she said. "You got any other piece of advice? Of the helpful kind?" she added, glancing at Kristan and grinning.

"That was helpful. Relax, and feel the water. You'll be fine."

Kristan slipped her sunglasses on. It was only ten o'clock in the morning, and slightly overcast but still quite warm, and it looked as if the weather would hold for a few more hours. Thunderstorms were forecast for later on, as well as high winds and possibly hail, but by then they would be safely back onto dry land. Kristan adjusted her dry bag onto the deck, and once again her eyes drifted to Liz, who looked back toward her and smiled.

She looked happy now, and relaxed.

"This is kind of nice," she said. "I like it."

"Great. You're looking good, doc. Obviously a natural."

Liz looked pleased at the comment.

"You think so?" she said proudly.

"I do. Now, what do you do if you capsize?"

"I don't want to capsize," Liz exclaimed, looking worried all of a sudden.

Kristan drifted a little closer.

"I know," she said with a smile, "but if it happens I want you to know what to do. There is nothing in the boat that can hold you in," she explained, stopping just ahead of Liz. "So if you go over, just let go of your paddle; grab your spray deck at the front, pull on that loop, and pop if off. Then push with your hands off the side of the boat, and you will just slide out."

Liz nodded.

"Okay, I got it."

"If something happens that prevents you from getting out, stay in, and just bang on the bottom of the boat with your hands."

"And then what?" Liz enquired, puzzled. "What will that do?"

"It's the signal for me to come and get you," Kristan said with a grin.

"Ah. I like that option."

"Really? You wouldn't be flirting with your instructor by any chance, would you Miss Jackson?"

Liz paddled over to Kristan, and rested her incredibly intense gaze on her. She raised an amused eyebrow.

"What if I am?" she said. "Would you mind?"

Kristan leaned over to kiss her.

"I don't mind, and I am happy that you're doing it."

"Good. Now show me the way, coach."

The two women paddled slowly along the coast, chatting and laughing. For once in her life Kristan was happy to go slow. They went up along a small stream, deeper into untouched rainforest, and Liz was astounded by the beauty of it.

"I can see why you like kayaking so much," she observed.

Kristan nodded. She was a little quiet and she was smiling a lot.

"Sometimes it's nice to come up here and just drift," she said.

She reached for a rubber loop on the side of Liz's boat, and clipped a karabiner with a sling to it. She clipped that to her own boat, and relaxed back into her seat.

"Like this," she demonstrated.

"If we're quiet do you think we might even spot a kiwi?"

"Unfortunately not. These guys are only out and about at night."

Liz took her lover's hand and held it tight in both of hers, and they drifted together side by side, just listening to the birds and enjoying the peace.

"Kelly said you're lovely," Kristan said eventually, smiling at Liz.

"Did she? That's nice."

"She really appreciated your spending time with her yesterday."

"Good. I had a good time. She cares about you a lot, you know?"

"I know. So do I. And she loved Mike too."

Kristan scooped a little bit of water in her hand.

"Liz, can I ask you something?"

"Of course. Anything."

Kristan rested her clear blue eyes on her, looking a little uncertain all of a sudden.

"What is it, baby?" Liz asked, suddenly little worried.

"Two things."

"Okay."

"First, I'm flying up to the glacier with a few of my people to scatter Mike's ashes on top. I'd like you to be with me when we do it."

Liz nodded immediately.

"Of course. I will come with you, Kris. And I feel very touched that you would want me there also."

Emotion rose up in Kristan's face, and her eyes filled with tears.

She blinked them away quickly.

"Liz, that job in Wellington you told me about," she said. "When does it start?"

The question took Liz by surprise. She had not thought about Wellington at all since her first night with Kristan, and all of a sudden she was brought back to reality with a bang.

"Well..." she hesitated. "The job's supposed to start in July."

"Okay," Kristan said, and she unhooked the karabiner and grabbed her paddle again.

It was such a sudden move that Liz was taken aback.

"Kris, wait," she exclaimed.

She leaned forward quickly, grabbing on to the side of Kristan's boat and losing her paddle in the process. She paid absolutely no attention to it, her only intention to address the very serious question hidden behind Kristan's apparently innocent one. She had answered it without thinking, and immediately regretted it. Her lover's expression had gone from hopeful and open, to shut-down and completely unreadable, and Liz had spotted the flash of hurt in her eyes before she turned away.

She kicked herself for not reading her better.

"You dropped your paddle," Kristan said flatly.

"Yeah, and I am talking to you right now."

Liz was clearly upset, and Kristan grabbed the abandoned paddle and just hooked them up together again.

"Go ahead."

Liz stared at her silently for a few seconds, and then she simply burst out laughing. Kristan did not immediately follow suit, but when Liz started to laugh so hard she nearly fell out of her boat Kristan started to smile. She grabbed the back of Liz's buoyancy aid to keep her in her kayak, and she shook her head a little.

"Liz, you're scaring the birds," she remarked, only managing to make Liz laugh harder.

"Geez, Kristan!" she exclaimed, and she had tears running down her face.

"What? What did I do?" Kristan protested, and she could not keep a straight face now no matter how hard she tried.

Liz grabbed her face in both her hands, and she kissed her, hard, and slow, only stopping when they both ended up entangled in low branches from a bunch of trees on the side. Kristan got them out of it, and back into the middle of the river, maneuvering both kayaks whilst Liz just sat back watching her, shaking her head with a huge smile on her face.

"I really don't know what's so funny," Kristan pointed out.

"Oh, you don't?"

"No."

"Boy, Kristan, you really are going to have to do something about that temper," Liz exclaimed, and she was serious this time. "Why don't you go ahead and tell me what's really on your mind?"

Kristan met her eyes, and she felt like bursting into tears.

"What, like, I love you and I don't want you to go to Wellington?" she said sharply.

"Yes! Exactly!"

"There you go, I said it."

"You are so bloody gorgeous when you're angry," Liz teased her, grinning again. "Hey, you asked me when the job started and I just told you. Sorry, I didn't catch what you really meant. Don't take me to such a beautiful place when you're looking so beautiful yourself, and ask me to concentrate, okay?"

"Can't you multi-task?" Kristan enquired jokingly.

The light was back in her eyes, and she was holding on to Liz now.

"Not when you're so close, apparently," Liz shot back. "Listen," she added quickly, "I will not be going to Wellington."

"But..."

"But nothing. I am in love with you, Kris. I am not going to leave."

Kristan's eyes had filled with tears again, but this time she looked hesitantly happy. Liz rested her hand on the back of her neck, and softly caressed her hair.

"I am in love with you," she said again, leaning close to Kristan and looking straight at her. "Okay? Wellington will have to find somebody else."

Kristan was about to say something when she was interrupted

by a roll of thunder in the distance. She took her eyes off Liz long enough to glance at the thick row of clouds advancing quickly over the lake, and she straightened up immediately. This one was coming straight for them, and their conversation would have to wait a little.

"Okay, how fast can you paddle?" she asked.

"Faster than you."

Kristan burst out laughing.

They got absolutely drenched, which only made the outing more enjoyable as far as Liz was concerned. She enjoyed kissing Kristan in the rain, she enjoyed looking at her when she was wet and her t-shirt was clinging to her chest, she enjoyed watching her as she lifted her kayak over her head on the beach, admiring a body that was lean, and hard, and so beautiful, and remembering exactly how she could touch her and make that body come alive.

She made spicy sweet potato soup for lunch in Kristan's kitchen, and afterward they both collapsed on the couch, watching heavy curtains of rain blow across the lake.

"I love the rain," Liz remarked.

"Do you?"

"Yes. Especially when it keeps you inside with me."

"Do you miss England?" Kristan asked.

"Not so far," Liz replied softly. "Do you miss America?"

"Absolutely not."

Liz chuckled.

"Not even a little bit?"

Kristan kissed the side of her head, and sighed contentedly.

"I was never really happy there," she said. "So no."

"And here?"

"Yeah. I'm happy here. I love what I do. I love where I live. I have good friends."

Liz closed her eyes as she said that, aware that Kristan was thinking about Mike, and she slid her hand under her shirt and rested it against her stomach lightly.

"I love it when you do that," Kristan murmured against her hair.

"Touch you?"

"Yeah."

"And when I kiss you?"

"Even more," Kristan said, and she grinned when Liz touched her lips to hers. "But come on, your turn."

"What do you mean?"

"I want to know what makes you happy."

"Being with you. Like this."

"And what else?"

"Good food. And painting."

"What else?"

Liz thought about it for a moment.

"Well, let's see. I like the mountains, and going out on long walks. I like hot towels when you get out of the shower in the winter. I like dogs. And I love going up in your helicopter with you."

Kristan smiled.

"We can do that again soon, just you and me."

She was silent for a few seconds.

"What about being a surgeon?" she asked then. "Does that make you happy?"

Liz grew wistful when Kristan said that, and she thought about it carefully before she answered.

"What I like is making people well. Helping them, and making a difference. Being a surgeon was one way of doing it."

Kristan nodded, and she sank a little lower against her lover until they were eye to eye.

"You say 'was' as if that were all behind you now," she remarked. "It doesn't have to be, you know."

"I am not going to change my mind about Wellington, Kris," Liz said gently.

"I know. But there is a hospital here too, so if you wanted to work you could apply. They would be crazy to turn you down."

She needed to ask because they had not discussed the future yet. And she wanted to. Liz was apparently willing to give up a good job in the North island in order to stay close to her, and Kristan was not taking that commitment lightly.

Liz smiled a little as she looked into her eyes, and caught the concern in them.

"I just want you to be happy, that's all," Kristan said before she could even ask. "I have a great life here, but I would not simply expect you to drop everything just for me. If you wanted to do something else, or be somewhere else, that would be okay with me."

Liz nodded.

"Thank you. And I would never ask you to give up a place and a business that obviously mean so much to you, Kris," she added. "The truth is, I am not even sure I want to be a surgeon again."

Kristan was silent, simply allowing her lover to explore her thoughts.

"Being able to save someone's life is such a gift. But the job itself can be hard, intense. Very long hours, difficult shifts. Sometimes people die. After what I went through with Robert... What I want now in my life is for things to be quiet and simple."

"Like what?"

Liz shrugged a little.

"I just want to enjoy living. I want to be happy, and safe."

"Anything else?" Kristan asked a little huskily.

Liz looked deep into her eyes, and she smiled.

"Yes. I want to be with you."

Kristan tightened her hold on her.

"I want to be with you too," she murmured.

Liz nodded, looking happy and excited.

"So if we're talking about the future now Kris, our future, this is what I want. I can cook. I could work in the cafe with Kelly. I could help you in the office. We could do this together."

Kristan nodded seriously.

"You could learn how to fly. Then you could have your own helicopter. I wasn't joking about giving you lessons, you know."

Liz gave a delighted laugh.

"As long as this is what you want," she added quickly. "No lies, no secrets. We make it work, and if it doesn't, if either one of us isn't happy for some reason, then..."

"Then we'll simply work it out," Kristan finished for her. "Together. Come here."

She pulled Liz roughly over her and kissed her. The kiss was deep, slow, proprietary, and when she stopped it took a second for Liz to come back to her senses.

Then she became aware of the pounding on the door, and that Kristan was already getting up off the couch.

"Who is it?" she yelled, turning back to look at Liz, and shake her head in disbelief.

She yanked the door open, and her expression changed from annoyance to concern as soon as she saw Kelly standing there, wet from the rain, a little out of breath and in floods of tears.

"Kel," she exclaimed. "What's wrong?"

"Oh, Kristan, I tried to call but I kept getting your machine..."

"My phone's switched off. What's going on?"

Liz jumped off the sofa as soon as she recognised Kelly's voice, and both she and Kristan helped her to walk inside.

"She's in shock," Liz declared, when Kristan asked Kelly another question and again got no answer. "Darling, can you get me a cover please, and something to drink?"

"Sure."

Kristan was back almost immediately, and she draped a light quilt tight over Kelly's shoulders, and put a glass of water in front of her. She sat by her side and kept her hand on her back, watching in silence as Liz talked to Kelly gently, helped her to get her breathing back, checked her pulse and made sure that she was okay.

"Better now?" Liz asked quietly after a couple more minutes.

Kelly nodded. Her colour was back, and she glanced around, looking for Kristan. She grabbed her hand when Kristan smiled at her, and again she burst into tears.

"Tell me what's wrong, Kel," Kristan repeated impatiently.

"Oh, Kris, how could anyone do this?" the woman cried. "My poor Charlie..."

"Who's Charlie?" Liz asked immediately, feeling her stomach tighten.

"Charlie's my cat, dear," Kelly answered her, her eyes red and full of pain. "They tortured the poor animal..."

She took her face in her hands, and sobbed quietly.

"Who's 'they'?" Kristan asked tightly.

Her face was like thunder and her eyes were flashing.

"Where?"

"In the cafe... And I don't know... I just found him..."

Kelly was breathing hard again, and Kristan stood up. She looked angry and just about ready for a fight, and Liz reached for her immediately.

"Please don't," she said urgently. "Not on your own."

"Someone needs to stay with Kelly."

"Then we'll all go," Liz said firmly. "Okay?"

Kristan relented. It made sense.

"Okay," she agreed. "We'll go together."

To be quicker, and because Liz was still a little bit concerned about Kelly, they drove the little distance to the cafe. Kristan parked right in front of it, and before Liz could stop her she jumped out of the big 4x4, ran up the stairs, and disappeared inside.

She did not have to go far.

Right in the middle of the dining room, Kelly's beautiful little cat Charlie had been nailed to a table. Kristan stopped dead in her tracks, feeling anger course through her as she stared at the poor animal, and realised that not only did he have a knife through the stomach, but also that his eyes appeared to have been scratched out.

Would that have been done before or after his death?

Kristan's stomach lurched as she started to imagine the scene in her head, and what terror and pain the poor animal must have felt. Because she had a feeling that whoever was sick enough to do something like this would have enjoyed making it hurt. She spun around, only to collide with Liz.

"What happened to..." Liz started, and the words died on her lips.

She reached for Kristan, and covered her mouth with her hand at the same time.

"Oh my God," she murmured.

Kristan stood in her line of sight, blocking the view of the table and the rest of the room.

"Don't look at it," she murmured.

Liz had grown rigid. She was pale as they walked back out of the café, and onto the stairs where Kelly was waiting.

"Who would do such a thing, Kris?" she murmured. "Oh my God..."

Kristan was already on the phone to the police. When she hung up she went to sit down next to Kelly. She wrapped her arms around her and held her tight.

"How're you doing, Kel?" she asked quietly.

"A bit shaken up, Kris," the woman replied, and she looked it. "A bit shaken up."

"I know. I am very sorry about Charlie," Kristan said gently.

"That poor little thing, Kris…"

"When is the last time that you saw him?"

"Just after lunchtime when I closed up. You know I had my dentist appointment today, right?" Kelly said, and Kristan nodded and listened patiently. "When I got back I found him…"

"What time was that?"

"Oh, I'm not sure... I think probably just after two o'clock..."

Kelly looked at Kristan, the look in her eyes heartbreaking.

"It's my fault, you know," she sobbed.

"Of course not," Kristan exclaimed. "Why would you think that?"

"I forgot to close the back door. That's probably how that person managed to get in, and..."

Kristan was adamant.

"It is not your fault, Kel," she said softly. "Look, the police will be here in a minute, and I can talk to them on your behalf. Would you like to go home now?"

Kelly simply nodded.

"No problem. Just give me a couple of seconds, okay?"

"Okay, Kris, I'll just wait for you right here."

Kristan stood up, and she went to find Liz, who was standing over to the side looking tense.

"Are you all right?"

Liz nodded, looking worried and white as a sheet.

"This is not right, Kris," she murmured. "Who would do something like this?"

"Someone very angry," Kristan mused, wondering where her partner's brother had been around lunchtime.

"Someone very sick," Liz said in response, and she looked troubled.

Kristan met her eyes.

"Look, I need a favour."

"Of course, what can I do?"

"Could you take Kelly's car and drive her home?"

This did nothing to reassure Liz.

She was beginning to see that when most people were feeling scared, Kristan became angry instead. And when she was angry she had this tendency to do stupid things, like the other morning when she had almost ended up fighting in the middle of the road with

James. Her temper could get her in trouble, and Liz hated the thought of her getting hurt.

"What about you?" she asked suspiciously. "What are you going to do?"

"Nothing much. I'll just wait for the police. I want to talk to them about what's going on, and I'm sure they'll have questions."

"Don't stay here on your own after they've gone, okay?" Liz insisted.

"I won't. I'll drive over to pick you up as soon as we're done here."

Liz took a deep breath and sighed.

"Okay."

"That is if you are all right to drive," Kristan added, frowning a little as she looked at her partner. "You've gone very pale."

"I'm fine. I'll take Kelly home now. Be careful, okay?"

She pulled Kristan into her arms and hugged her hard.

"Don't worry," Kristan promised. "I'll be as quick as I can. I love you."

Chapter 9

It took a little while for the police to get there, and Kristan realised it was a good thing that Liz would not know exactly how long, or what she had done with the time. She was on her own for a good forty-five minutes, and she put it to good use.

She walked through the empty shower blocks, the cafe, the shop and reception, looking for any other nasty surprises, looking for signs that someone had been around where they did not belong. Basically, she went prowling around the Park hoping to bump into the guy who had killed Charlie, and she was disappointed when she did not.

Jen was manning reception, and Kristan quietly filled her in on what had just happened. When given a choice to stay or go home, Jen firmly declared that she would stay.

"I'm on my cell if you need me, okay?" Kristan told her.

The small redhead nodded.

"No worries, boss. If I see anyone around I don't recognise I will call you straight away."

Kristan gave her a thumbs up and a smile, and she walked back to the cafe to wait for the cops.

When she picked Liz up a few hours later at Kelly's she was in a somber mood. She declined an invitation to stay for dinner, and she drove them straight into town, parked on the high street, and killed the engine. She leaned over the wheel with a frown on her face, and it took Liz's gentle touch on the back of her neck to bring her back to the present.

"Sometimes I really wish I could down a bottle of Scotch and forget about the world for a while," she declared, and her jaw flicked.

Liz immediately scooted closer to her, and she wrapped an arm around her shoulders, pulling her close.

"Something bad is going on, isn't it?" she said tensely.

Kristan sighed.

"Maybe. Looks like it," she admitted.

She reached into her pocket for her cell phone and scrolled through the screens.

"The cops found a piece of paper stuck under Charlie. It had a written message on it," she said as she found the picture she was looking for. "Look."

Liz took the phone from her and stared at the photo. The paper was bloody, but on it you could clearly see that somebody had scribbled a few words.

It simply said, *'I will hurt you'*.

Liz shivered so violently that she dropped the phone. She grabbed Kristan, and pulled her against her once more. She held her as hard as she could, whilst the old panic twisted her stomach and squeezed her heart.

"Liz," Kristan murmured against her ear. "What's going on? Are you okay?"

Liz pulled back, and her eyes were huge and full of tears. She was so upset she could only shake her head no, and then she started to hyperventilate and the colour drained from her face.

Kristan was out of the car like a shot. She ran around it, pulled the passenger door open, and slid the seat as far back as it would go with Liz still on it. Then she supported her as Liz leaned forward, looking white as a sheet, and almost ready to collapse.

"Keep your head down," Kristan instructed. "That's it. All the way. Breathe."

She held Liz's left hand in hers, and with her right she softly kneaded the back of her neck with her fingers. She flinched when Liz started to cry, and she wanted to help her so much it hurt.

"It's okay," she whispered. "It's okay, baby, I'm here..."

It was several long minutes before Liz was able to breathe properly again, and another five before she could speak.

"You think it's him, don't you?" she said then, almost choking on the words.

Kristan shook her head.

"Who, James?" she said. "No, I don't. I did think of him at first, but I think if James had a problem with me he'd probably just come over and yell at me. This is different. This is sick, and seriously vindictive."

Liz shivered again.

"I didn't mean James," she murmured.

Kristan stared at her, biting her lower lip. She hated seeing that look of fear in Liz's eyes. She hated to see her cry; she hated to see her in such obvious distress.

She sighed.

"Okay, yes. When I saw the note, because it kind of fits what you told me about him, the next person I thought about after I discounted James was your ex," she admitted, and she felt Liz start to tremble again.

On impulse, she leaned over and she kissed her.

"I love you so much," she whispered. "I will not let anything happen to you."

Liz reached out and touched her face.

"You don't know him, Kris... You don't know him like I do."

"Stop, Liz. It's okay."

"What if he's responsible for Mike too?" Liz murmured.

This did hit home.

Liz watched as Kristan's incredibly clear blue eyes shifted to almost black, and Kristan pulled back. She stood there for a couple of seconds, watching Liz with an intense look on her face.

Then she extended her hand and waited until her lover took it.

"It will not change how I feel about you," she said fiercely. "Never. Now come on. We need to go talk to the cops."

They were at the station for two long hours. The police were very interested to hear the details of Liz's relationship with Robert, and Kristan sat silently by her side as Liz went through it. She left nothing out, and by the time they finished both women were emotionally spent. Liz because she hated talking about Robert, and Kristan because it simply made her feel sick to hear the woman she loved calmly describe the abuse she had suffered at the hands of that thug.

When they left the police station they simply walked for a while, holding on to each other.

"How're you doing Kris?" Liz murmured after a while.

She was beginning to understand her lover's patterns. It was not good when Kristan was so silent, and still.

"I had no idea," her partner said roughly. "I had no idea it had been that bad. You should have told me."

"Why? It was not ever going to change anything."

He had broken her arm in three places, and threatened to kill her. She had not wanted to tell Kristan because she was so ashamed of it.

"Ashamed of what?" Kristan exclaimed, turning her head to look at her.

"I should have been stronger. I should have left before it got to that point."

Kristan exhaled sharply.

"Liz; please don't do this. It is not your fault, okay? And if he is responsible for Mike, I will…"

She almost choked on her words.

She did not finish her sentence, but she did not need to.

Liz understood exactly how she felt.

"Nothing good ever comes out of violence, Kris," she pointed out.

Kristan stopped walking when her lover said that. She turned to her slowly, and Liz did not think anyone had ever looked at her with so much love in their eyes before.

"What?" she smiled.

Kristan just returned her smile, shaking her head a little in wonder.

"You are such an amazing woman," she observed. "It would be so easy for you to be bitter and angry about everything. And yet you're just kind, and gentle, and just... amazing."

"Yeah, well... Bitterness, anger, all that stuff you know, it would only be another way to hurt myself."

Liz took Kristan's hand in both of hers and she kissed the bruises on her knuckles.

"I choose to be happy. I want you to do the same."

In Kristan's idea, happiness always started with a good meal. Sandwiched in between a surf shop and a garage was a non-descript wooden door with a sign painted on it that simply said 'Paradise'. She pushed the door open with a smile, and stepped aside to let her lover go in first.

"After you, babe."

Liz walked in and immediately felt like she had entered another world.

"Oh, wow..." she whispered.

Right behind the unassuming wooden door was a large patio with a beautiful fountain tucked away in one corner. Tropical plants and lush flowers were hanging from the balcony above. The floor was beautifully tiled, the space was warm and lit with candles, and

Kristan was pleased when she saw the delighted look on Liz's face.

"I was hoping you would enjoy spending some time in Paradise with me," she murmured, and she wrapped her arms around Liz from behind, and kissed her neck softly.

Liz giggled, smiling at the soft calming sound of the water and the wonderful smell of lilies in the air.

"Oh, Kris, this is great. I love it," she said, beaming.

A waiter appeared almost immediately at their side and greeted Kristan by name, and he led them to a table in the corner. Liz sat on the comfortable cushioned bench with her back to the wall, and Kristan slid in right next to her. They sat with their thighs and shoulders touching, and Liz relaxed against her girlfriend.

"Feeling better now?" Kristan murmured.

"Yes. This place is so peaceful… I needed that."

"I know."

"So this is a restaurant?"

"Indeed."

"You would never guess it from the outside. And you have been here before, obviously."

Kristan nodded.

"Yes, Mike took me here last year for my birthday."

Liz opened her eyes wide.

"Do you realise that we have slept together, and decided on a future together, and I don't even know when your birthday is?"

Liz sounded genuinely astounded, and Kristan burst out laughing.

"July 19. I'll be thirty-five. You?"

"March 12. I turned forty-one."

Kristan's eyes sparkled, and she laughed.

"You're kidding, I missed your birthday this year? Well, we'll have to do a post official birthday celebration type thing for you then," she declared, smiling. "Do you like surprises?"

Liz raised a dubious eyebrow.

"Depends."

"On what?"

"On whether I think I can trust you or not," Liz replied, looking suspicious.

"Well I guess you'll just have to wait and see, won't you?" Kristan declared with a grin.

They shared quinoa salad and spicy spring rolls, and drank lemonade because Liz was sticking with her decision to remain sober. Not that she needed alcohol to keep her going anyway. Just sitting so close to Kristan, being able to feel the heat of her body through her jeans and her t-shirt, listening to her speak, and watching her smile was intoxicating enough.

They played the Questions game, finding out about each other. They were not shy or delicate with it either. The questions were deep, targeted, loaded. And every single time Liz answered one of hers, Kristan found herself falling more and more in love with her.

"You know, it's weird," she remarked after a while.

"What is?" Liz enquired.

Kristan leaned forward with her elbows on the table.

"How can it be," she mused, "that the most wonderful thing in the world, and the most awful thing, can happen to me pretty much right on top of each other?"

Liz's eyes grew soft.

"You really are beautiful," Kristan murmured.

"And so are you," Liz said thoughtfully. "Although big and butch might not be the best way to describe yourself, darling," she added, amused.

"What do you mean?"

"I mean I think you are very capable, and independent. And strong, too; physically and mentally..."

"Except for when I am crying like a baby, right?" Kristan pointed out.

"I think that was probably a one-off. You know what I mean,

don't you?"

"Yeah," Kristan said slowly. "I think I do. I'm not weak, that's just who I am. You, uh… you don't like it?"

"Oh yes. I sure do," Liz said with an amused little smile.

"Really? The way you said that, it didn't sound like you like it at all."

Liz nodded, touched at the way that Kristan seemed to need the reassurance.

"I love it that you are strong and self-reliant," she said. "I like it that I feel so safe when I'm with you. But that is not my favourite thing about you."

"Should I quit now while I'm ahead?" Kristan asked, smiling a little.

"What makes you think you're ahead, stud?"

Kristan burst out laughing.

"And keep me real, too," she said, grinning. "Am I ahead? You tell me, Liz."

Liz smiled, her eyes sparkling with happiness.

"The thing I really love about you is that you let me see inside," she said.

She rested her hand on Kristan's heart, inside her shirt, on naked skin. She watched as Kristan's eyes darkened immediately, and she almost gasped.

"There," she whispered. "This is it, right there."

"I don't get it," Kristan mumbled.

"I mean this." Liz pushed harder. "This is what I love about you. Inside, you feel."

Kristan's eyes suddenly grew a little bit hot.

"I do feel," she said huskily. "Sometimes wish I didn't."

"Hence the alcohol and the drugs?"

Kristan shrugged.

"We can work on that," Liz said quietly.

She was feeling exhausted by the time they got back to the Park, and Kristan drove right up to the cottage and parked under a tree. Liz reached for the door, pulled the handle, and she was about to step out when Kristan stopped her with a firm hand on her shoulder.

"Wait a minute, Liz," she said softly.

She peered straight ahead into the darkness, and all of a sudden she hit the central door lock and reached for her cell phone. She kept the lights on and the engine running.

"Son of a bitch," she murmured under her breath.

Her cheeks were flushed and her eyes were flashing, and Liz recognised anger in the set of her jaw.

"What? What's wrong?" she asked, fully awake once more, her adrenaline running.

"I locked the cottage door when we left with Kelly this afternoon, didn't I?" Kristan said. "Can you remember?"

Liz thought back on it, and yes, she remembered that Kristan had taken the time to lock the door to the cottage before they had driven with Kelly back to the cafe. Now as her eyes adjusted to the darkness on the outside, she clearly saw that the front door was ajar.

Fear shot through her and she gasped.

"Police please," Kristan said into her phone, and at the same time she reached for Liz's hand, and squeezed gently. "Breathe," she murmured.

This time the police were back in less than ten minutes. Two cruisers showed up, their lights flashing, and Liz recognised Omaru, the lead investigator in Mike's murder enquiry as he climbed out of one of the cars.

"I'll come round," Kristan said.

She jumped out from behind the wheel and made her way to the other side to pull the car door open for Liz. She took her hand immediately, checked that she was okay, and they both went to speak to the officer in charge. Meanwhile, two men in uniform entered the cottage and did a thorough search of the premises.

It was empty.

Liz and Kristan went in next, and had a look around. Kristan walked through every single room of the place she had lived in for the past three years. The one place she had ever called home, and actually meant it. In the kitchen she found a plate had been left out on the table, and a half-smoked cigarette was abandoned on it.

"We don't smoke," she said darkly.

She spotted that look of absolute distress in Liz's eyes again, and she wanted to punch something. Kevin Omaru, the man who had insisted on pursuing the 'thief' line of enquiry in Mike's murder to the exclusion of anything else, was standing in the middle of the room looking grim.

Kristan settled her gaze on him, feeling her temper rise.

"Now you believe me that my partner would not just let some idiot thief creep up on him?" she said. "Mike just wouldn't. He was way better than that. Okay?"

She wanted to remain strong for Liz, and so she kept on breathing, and she kept her temper in check. If Liz had not been standing right next to her she would probably have lost it completely.

She was furious.

"I think it might be best if you did not spend the night here tonight," Omaru stated, looking at her.

"No kidding, genius," Kristan snapped.

Liz stepped forward.

"We need you and your men to hang around a bit longer please," she said softly. "We just need to grab a few clothes and things."

"They will," Kristan said sharply.

"Of course," Omaru nodded. "Take your time. We'll wait outside."

Kristan went into her bedroom, grabbed a suitcase from under the bed and started throwing clothes into it. Liz watched her from the doorway, not knowing what to say.

"Kris..."

"He's been here, Liz," Kristan said quietly. "We can't stay."

"I am so sorry..."

Kristan walked over to her and simply held her face in her hand. She kissed her gently.

"It is not your fault," she whispered. "And we'll be back. He's just trying to scare us."

"Are you scared?"

Kristan's eyes sparkled.

"No," she said sharply. "I'm pissed off."

Her hands shook as she said that. She turned away and walked into the bathroom. She threw a bag of toiletries into the suitcase, and turned to Liz.

"I am pissed off because this is my home!" she exclaimed. "And we slept together in this bed, and I wanted it to be our space. Ours, no one else! Now some idiot has ruined it. He has no idea what he's taken on."

"We'll be back, my love," Liz reminded her gently.

Kristan stopped what she was doing suddenly.

She looked back toward her lover and she grinned.

"Yes, we will. Sorry I'm such a moaner. Feel free to tell me to stop anytime."

"Okay. Shut up moaning."

Kristan chuckled.

"Anything else?" she asked.

"Yes. I love you so much."

"Me too," Kristan replied, finally slowing down.

"This sucks, and you know what, I feel awful about it..."

"I told you..."

"Shh..."

Liz simply rested a finger against Kristan's lips.

"You know what?" she repeated

Kristan shook her head no, smiling faintly.

"We're alive, we're in love. No one can take that from us. Please stay calm. It's shit right now, but it won't last."

"You still want to be with me?" Kristan asked.

"Of course. Why wouldn't I?"

"Because I wanted to protect you from stuff like this, and now it looks like I can't."

"Oh, Kristan," Liz exclaimed, smiling softly. "You love me, and that is all I care about."

Kristan finally relaxed.

"Okay," she said. "We'll go to your camper and get your stuff."

It was no surprise to either of them that Liz's van had been broken into as well. Someone had done a thorough job on her clothes. Every single item had been slashed, every single shirt shredded, her bathroom was thrashed, and her paintings had been cut to pieces.

To her credit, Liz did not get overly emotional about it.

"I expected nothing less," she murmured as Kristan stood by surveying the damage, feeling helpless and trying hard not to let it show.

"I will take you shopping tomorrow."

Liz nodded quietly.

"Okay. Can we just go now, please?" she asked.

Chapter 10

They spent the night at a local motel, and Liz woke up just after two a.m. to find the side of the bed next to her was empty. Worried, she sat up and scanned the room, and then relaxed immediately as soon as she spotted her partner.

Kristan was there. She had not left.

She was sitting in front of the window, wearing a t-shirt and a pair of sweats. She looked lost in thoughts. Her profile was beautiful in the half moon light, her dark hair just a little messed up from the pillow.

"Hey gorgeous," Liz said softly from the bed.

Kristan turned to smile at her.

"Right back at you," she said. "Did I wake you?"

"No. Can't sleep?"

Kristan shook her head and crossed the room back to the bed. She undressed quickly, slid under the covers, and pulled Liz tightly against her.

"You smell nice," she murmured, resting her cheek against her hair.

"What were you thinking about?" Liz asked.

"About Mike," Kristan murmured. "I miss him."

"Oh, honey, I know..."

Liz pulled Kristan against her until her lover was lying close, with her head on her shoulder, and her arm wrapped securely against her waist.

"I wish I had got to know him better," she said.

"He was an amazing guy. He was the only one at the Park I told about my past. You'd have loved him. And he would have loved you."

Liz was silent, simply stroking her lover's shoulder gently.

"I will arrange for a cleaning team for home as soon as they're open," Kristan said tiredly, her thoughts as always drifting to what needed to be done.

"Okay, my love."

"Does you ex smoke?"

Kristan drew the line at saying his name. She did not want him in the room with them. She hated the thought that he even existed.

"Does he?" she repeated.

Liz frowned a little.

"No," she said. "He doesn't. At least he never used to when we were together."

Kristan was silent again.

"I can't think who else would want to hurt me like this," she reflected eventually. "I know almost everyone in town, and I have no problems with anybody. Neither did Mike."

"Let it go," Liz whispered gently. "Just let it go for a few hours, Kristan."

She kissed her roughly, slid her leg in between hers, loving the instant flash of heat in Kristan's face.

"Don't move," she ordered, and she slowly blazed a trail of hot kisses down the centre of her chest and across her stomach.

"I can't think when you do this," Kristan panted.

"That's the idea," Liz pointed out with a smile, and then she drifted down a little lower.

Kristan could not remember falling asleep, and she slept like a rock for a couple of hours. Then she was up at first light raring to go. Running away was not in her blood. The police had suggested closing down for the winter and going somewhere else for a while, but Kristan was adamant. She would not run. She would not hide. She would protect what was hers, and she made it clear to Omaru that she expected him to do his job, and find the person responsible asap.

Robert's name had not shown up on any Customs records at any of a number of potential airports he could have arrived at, but it did not do much to alleviate Liz's fears. She knew he had contacts in the military still, and if he had wanted to travel under a fake identity she believed it would have been fairly easy for him to do so.

Kristan still had some doubts, but whoever it was she now had a healthy dose of respect for that person, and their level of obsession.

At least the police had now completely veered away from the thief theory in Mike's murder. Whether that had been an accident or premeditated Kristan was not sure, but when Omaru decided to offer her and Liz protection at the Park Kristan accepted immediately.

She was brave but not crazy.

Now she stood in front of her staff, and calmly explained what was going on. Most of her crew were seasonal anyway, and had already left. A few of them were more or less permanent.

That meant Jen, who worked at reception, maintained the website and generally handled phone calls, email queries and bookings. Kelly, who looked after the cafe and the shop. Julie and Braxton, who worked in the kitchen. And Pam, the kayak instructor and mountain guide, who along with Mike was probably Kristan's longest friend at the Park.

They all listened intently as Kristan went through what had been going on, and filled them in on the latest police theories. She explained that she would not close down for the winter, but that she would not hold it against any of them if they decided that they would rather take some time off.

Then Liz stepped forward a little, and Kristan smiled.

"The good news is," she said, her eyes sparkling as they settled on her girlfriend, "that we have a new member of staff. Liz?"

Liz went to join her.

She gave a friendly wave to the group, feeling strangely nervous all of a sudden now that she was standing in front of them all.

"For those of you who don't know her yet, this is Liz," Kristan said, smiling and reaching for her hand. "She's from England, so if she starts to speak funny don't worry, just please teach her the appropriate Kiwi word, okay?"

People started to laugh, and Liz did so as well.

"She's a surgeon, so Jen," Kristan carried on, "next time you get a paper cut just talk to her, right?"

"Yeah boss," Jen replied, looking serious as always. "You got it."

"Liz and I, we, uh…"

Kristan glanced toward Liz, and immediately got caught in her eyes.

She grinned.

"Get on with it, Kristan," Kelly hollered from the back. "We're all waiting for the good part."

Both Liz and Kristan started to laugh.

"Okay," Kristan said, smiling. "So, simply put, Liz is not a member of staff. I am in love with her, and I feel incredibly happy that she is here, and has decided to stay. Permanently."

Her face turned red when everybody started clapping and cheering.

She raised her hand.

"Thanks, guys," she nodded. "So, just to confirm, there will be a police presence at the Park for a little while. If you need to talk to me privately, then please feel free to come and do so. Other than that, thank you for being here, you know I appreciate all the hard work that you do around here; and let's just get on with our jobs."

Everybody wanted to welcome Liz to the family, and Kelly was the first one to do so, hugging her fiercely, almost crying.

"I am so happy for you," she said a few times. "So happy."

Jen, Julie and Braxton all came forward to hug Liz as well, and Kristan was delighted that they all wanted to meet her and make her feel welcome. Only one person did not come forward, and Kristan noticed Pam slipping away quietly. She would have thought Pam would be the first to want to congratulate them, so it was strange that she was the first to go.

Leaving the rest of the team to chat, Kristan jogged after her.

"Hey Pam," she called. "Wait up, mate."

The tall, slender blonde woman turned around, and waited for Kristan to catch up with her. She looked serious, and her green eyes were unusually cold.

"What's up?" Kristan asked her quietly. "Are you okay?"

Pam simply shrugged, looking annoyed.

"I don't know, Kristan. You tell me."

"What do you mean?"

"Isn't it obvious?" Pam snapped, and Kristan was taken aback by her attitude.

She had always been very close to Pam. The woman was a talented kayak instructor, an excellent mountain guide, and an even better communicator. Her passion and enthusiasm for her job, her knowledge of the local flora and fauna, and the way that she enjoyed sharing all that with her clients so much made her extremely popular. Kristan appreciated her skills, and she also liked the woman as a person. Pam had a cracking sense of humour, a great can-do attitude, and along with Mike she was one of the people Kristan considered a true friend.

Now all of a sudden it was as if a wall had suddenly come up between them.

"Sorry, Pam. I'm not sure..."

"Oh, come on! Think about Mike, Kristan."

Pam's eyes were flashing, and Kristan suddenly realised how angry she was.

"I think about Mike all the time," she said, not liking the

accusation in the woman's voice.

"Oh, really? Doesn't seem like it to me. He would still be around if not for her," Pam spat, just before she turned on her heels and stormed off.

Kristan was stunned.

She went after her.

"Hey, hang on a minute," she exclaimed, "how can you say something like that?"

Pam spun around to face her once more.

"Because it's the bloody truth! It's her fault. And there you are, treating her like she's something special."

"She is very special," Kristan countered immediately. "I love her, Pam."

The woman shrugged angrily.

"Oh yeah, I'm sure she makes you feel good. I'll give you my take on it though: she deserves all the shit that happens to her. Don't ask me to stick around and pretend like I am happy to have her with us."

Kristan's blood turned to ice in her veins.

"I am not asking you to be happy about it," she said sharply.

She worked to control her temper. After all, she had told her staff that they could speak to her freely if they needed to. Pam was doing just that.

Kristan tried again.

"I know that you loved him, Pam," she said calmly. "And believe me, there isn't a single second that I don't miss him or think about him. But Liz is not to blame for what happened."

Pam snorted.

"Jesus, Kristan. What the hell do you…"

Kristan raised a hand, interrupting her.

"I love her, and she is here to stay," she said, careful to keep her tone even. "I'm sorry if that is going to be a problem for you."

"Yeah. So what if it is, uh? What if I've got a huge problem with it all?" Pam said angrily. "I can get lost, is that it?"

"No. That is not what I was going to say. I have lost one friend already, I do not want to lose you too."

"But?"

It was as if Pam were taking pleasure in forcing Kristan to choose. Maybe she was enjoying it, but Kristan had no time for games, and her patience was wearing thin.

"Look, I'm sorry you feel that way," she said. "But I can't bring Mike back, and Liz is my partner now. That is just the way it's going to be."

Pam stared at her with tears in her eyes. She looked like she was going to say something else, but then she seemed to change her mind. Without another look at Kristan she walked over to her car, got in, slammed the door shut and drove off.

Kristan stood alone in the middle of the driveway.

"Shit..." she murmured under her breath.

She hated to think she may have come across as insensitive. She hated to think she had hurt a good friend. Maybe introducing Liz to everyone, and sharing their happiness with the rest of them had not been the right thing to do after all. But what was she supposed to do, hide? She felt close to her staff, they were her friends, and she was damned if she was going to lie to any of them.

She shared her thoughts with Liz and Kelly later on as they were having lunch in the cafe together.

"That is absolute nonsense," Kelly said immediately. "We all need all the good news we can get, what with everything that's been going on."

"Well. Yeah, that's what I was thinking," Kristan nodded, frowning a little.

"And everybody else was happy for you," Kelly insisted.

"That's not the point. Pam really did not take it well. Maybe I was wrong."

Liz could see that her lover was upset.

She took her hand and rubbed her thumb lightly over her still bruised knuckles.

"Give her some time, darling," she said quietly. "I'm sure she'll come round."

Kristan gave her a gentle smile.

"Yeah… I really hope so."

"And after all, she is right in a way. I am responsible for…"

"You are not," both Kristan and Kelly exclaimed in unison.

Liz smiled weakly.

"Pam might not see it this way," she said hesitantly. "I can see why; she does have a point."

She caught the intense look in Kristan's eyes.

"Look, Kris," she said, looking distraught. "Maybe I should go away for a while…"

Kelly wisely stood up and walked away, and Kristan took Liz's hands in both of hers, and leaned forward.

"Mike really liked you," she said softly. "Did you know that?"

Liz was taken aback.

"Did he? I barely knew him…"

"I know. But he knew me, and he could see how much I wanted you. And this, between us," Kristan said with feeling, "that is exactly what he would have wanted for me. For us."

"Kristan…"

"Don't, Liz. Okay? I love you, and nothing that happened is your fault."

"I love you too."

Kristan nodded, looking a little pale.

The thought of Liz leaving was almost too much for her.

"I'll speak to Pam," she declared. "You belong here with me."

Chapter 11

Incredibly, things started to settle. Things got quiet. For a full week the weather was horrendous, matching Kristan's mood and spirits. Heavy winds and big rains drove almost everyone away from the Park, and little by little it started to empty. Kristan was working less and less, 'going into hibernation', as she called it. Normally she would have been enjoying her downtime season, but this year was different. There was a police car parked in front of her cottage, and she was getting daily updates on absolutely no progress from Omaru. Mainly she was exhausted, and on the fourth day of rain, at last, she slept.

Liz woke up just after eight in the morning to the sound of heavy drops beating the roof, and she smiled when she realised that her lover was still in bed next to her, lying on her stomach, sound asleep. She very carefully got up, walked over to her side of the bed, and collected her cell phone from the table. She knew Kristan wanted it on at all times, and so she would be looking after it whilst her partner got some proper rest.

She drew the blinds lower on the window, grabbed her clothes, and tiptoed out of the room, closing the door quietly behind her. She showered, got dressed, and wrote Kristan a quick note to tell her she had gone into town. Then she grabbed her car keys and slipped out of the cottage.

In town she bought fresh vegetables, groceries, her partner's favourite mango juice and bread, and on impulse she also popped into the local art shop.

She bought more painting supplies, and got interested in a display of locally crafted white gold rings. She did not buy one, but she had a long conversation with the artist, and she walked out of the shop grinning, and feeling on top of the world. She quickly walked back to where she had left the car, and when she got there she was surprised to find Pam leaning against it.

When the woman looked up and spotted Liz it was obvious to her that Pam had been expecting Kristan, and not her. She immediately broke eye contact, and started to walk away.

"Pam, please, wait," Liz said, hoping against all hopes that they could have a conversation. "Pam!"

But the woman simply sank her hands in the pockets of her trousers and carried on walking. Liz sighed as she watched her go. She hated the thought of Kristan losing a friend because of her, but then again, Pam's persistent bad mood and resentful attitude was starting to annoy her a little. Why couldn't she just come and talk?

Shrugging, Liz pushed the thought out of her mind and got back on the road.

It was just after lunchtime by the time she got home, and Kristan was in the shower. Liz dropped her purchases on the counter and went to push the bathroom door open. It was hot in there, and all the mirrors had steamed up.

"Kris?" she called, smiling.

The shower door slid back a little, and Kristan stuck her head out.

"Hello," she grinned. "Fancy joining me?"

Liz had already started to take her clothes off. She nodded, kicked her shoes off and stepped in, sliding the door shut behind her.

Kristan had done well with the bathroom, she reflected approvingly. The shower was big, bright and modern. Plenty of room for what she had in mind, and she smiled.

Kristan was standing under the nozzle, her head tilted up to it, her eyes closed. Liz's eyes slowly drifted over her body. Kristan was lean and slender, and also hard and strong, soft in all the right places. Her hair had grown recently. She was the sexiest thing Liz had ever seen, and she quickly went to stand behind her, molding herself to her body. Her hands rose up to her lover's breasts, eliciting a gasp and a giggle from Kristan.

"You go straight to the point, don't you?"

"I'm not at the point yet."

Kristan laughed and turned around.

Every time she looked at Liz naked something inside her heart went a little quiet and calm. Liz was shapely, yet trim; she was feminine where Kristan was athletic; her body was soft and welcoming, and Kristan could have watched her for hours. And touched her for even longer. She started to do so now as Liz stood in front of her, smiling a little.

"Hey, sleepy head," she murmured, as Kristan caressed her shoulders, let her hands roam down her back, over her bottom, back up to caress her breasts.

"Hey, doc."

If there was one thing Liz liked about Kristan it was that look on her face when she was touching her. That intense look of concentration and delight, like Liz was the most precious thing in the world, and she had been entrusted with a very important possession. She reached for her and caressed her cheek softly. She kissed her gently, then harder, loving that Kristan always responded so quickly to her. Her eyes had turned a hazy blue, and her nipples were hard.

"I keep wanting to go slow," she said, "but you make it so hard for me..."

"Me?" Kristan protested. "I'm just standing here, babe, what are you talking about?"

Liz laughed, and she wrapped her arms around her neck. She

kissed her thoroughly, loving the gentle trembling that kiss started in her lover.

Then Kristan's hand slowly drifted down and between her legs.

"Oh, Kris," Liz gasped.

Kristan started to stroke her, softly, almost teasing.

Liz moaned and raised her leg a little.

"Hold on to me," Kristan instructed.

"Yes. Oh, yes..."

Kristan could feel that she was close, and she wanted to make it last. She took her hand off, twisted her fingers into Liz's hair, and looked deep into her eyes.

"You make me feel a little crazy, you know that?" she murmured.

"Good. I want to."

Kristan touched her again, and Liz's knees buckled.

"Hold on to me," Kristan repeated. "Just keep looking at me, babe. I want to watch you."

She kept on touching her until Liz's eyes lost their focus, until she felt like she was going to fall.

"Close?" she whispered against her cheek.

Liz nodded wordlessly, and she pulled Kristan down onto the floor with her.

"You?" she mumbled.

"Yeah," Kristan replied tightly.

Just touching Liz and feeling her ride her hand had almost been enough to send her over the edge. She wanted to finish, but she had no real urge to stop Liz when the woman rolled on top of her, and her mouth closed around one of her nipples. Liz's hand drifted low, and her fingers found her, and Kristan reacted and hit her head on the hard floor.

"Careful," Liz panted. "I can't stop."

"No, don't. I don't want you to..."

Liz swallowed the rest of her sentence with a scorching kiss. She pressed harder against Kristan, riding her leg, stroking her at the same time. Kristan had thought she would be able to take her time. She was surprised at the force of the orgasm that took her, and as she climaxed it was made even more intense by the sound of Liz, crying out her name as she came.

"So, what did you get when you were in town?" Kristan asked later, much later when they finally emerged from the bedroom.

The session in the bathroom had only been a warm up. By the time they decided to take a break it was night again, and Kristan was starving.

"Well, I was hoping to start on your cooking lessons," Liz replied, surveying the abandoned groceries on the table.

Kristan had a quick look through the bags, looking interested.

"Cool. What did you have in mind?"

"Vegan pizza."

"Just my kind of thing. Okay, so what do I do?"

Liz smiled at the expression on her face.

"Don't look so intense, baby," she laughed. "If you can fly a helicopter I'm sure you'll be able to handle pizza."

"Don't be so sure. I can mess things up pretty bad in the kitchen."

"You won't mess this one up," Liz assured her. "And I got a ready-made base just to help with that," she added, grinning.

Kristan looked happy and relaxed as she spread pizza sauce on the base as instructed, and added vegan pepperoni, red onion, red pepper, mushrooms, olives and vegan cheese.

"That's it?" she asked, surprised at how good the end product looked, and it was not even cooked.

"That's it. Ten to fifteen minutes in the oven now and we'll have chow."

"Awesome. Let's do it."

Fifteen minutes later Liz pulled the pizza out of the oven, and the smell was just amazing.

"I don't think I'll be ordering takeaway anymore," Kristan commented. "Hang on, I'll take a photo."

Liz gave a soft laugh.

"Nice to see you're proud of your work."

Kristan smiled at her.

"That's for your cookbook, dear," she said.

"My cookbook?"

"Yeah. You like cooking, I like taking photos. I say we write a Vegan Cookbook, and sell it in the cafe. We could put the recipes on the menu."

Liz's face broke into a huge smile.

"This is such a great idea," she exclaimed. "I love it!"

"What other things do you think we could put on the menu?"

"Well, I was planning on teaching you to do a roasted veg lasagna, and vegan Shepherd's pie; corn and jalapeno chowder, lentil and quinoa burgers…"

She looked excited as she went through the list, and so happy, and Kristan stepped forward a little. She wrapped her arms around Liz's waist, and kissed her on the mouth gently.

"Never, ever leave me," she whispered.

"I wasn't planning on it, darling," Liz replied seriously. "You have no idea."

"What does that mean?"

Liz grinned, and simply shook her head a little.

"I am not telling you just yet."

Kristan's eyes sparkled.

"That's okay," she said softly. "I will enjoy the wait."

Liz grinned at her, and gestured toward their food.

If she was not careful she would say too much, too soon.

"How about pizza for now?"

"You bet," Kristan smiled. "I swear I am going to faint if I don't eat something soon."

Her phone went off as they were about to start eating.

"Ignore it," Liz advised.

"Yeah…"

But Kristan could not resist glancing at the new email that had come through, and she reached for her phone. Her expression changed slowly as she clicked on the email and started to read it. At first she looked troubled, then happy, and then her eyes filled with tears.

"What's wrong?" Liz asked immediately.

Kristan shook her head.

"Nothing," she reassured her. "It's good news, actually."

"Have they found who we are looking for?" Liz asked expectantly.

"No. Sorry, babe. This is an email from James. I was really hoping he'd get in touch, and now he has, finally."

"What's he saying?" Liz asked, and she slid off her chair to come stand near to Kristan.

"He says he hasn't had a drink since Mike…"

Kristan had to clear her throat.

"Since Mike," she said simply. "He'd like to meet up and have a chat."

"Is he asking you for a job again?"

"No, he's just asking if we can talk."

Kristan took a deep breath, and then she read the email out loud to Liz. She was smiling by the time she finished.

"I have a good feeling about this," she declared. "And if Mike were here he would be over the moon."

Liz nodded.

She had only had one experience of the man so far, and she did not care to repeat it. But she wanted to trust that he would not fail Kristan once more, and so she thought about it as she went back to her seat, and took another bite of pizza.

"Where does he want you to meet?" she asked.

"He just says I pick where and when, and he'll be there. I guess somewhere in town tomorrow will do."

Liz pursed her lips and gave a small shake of the head.

"What?" Kristan smiled.

"Well, I'm just thinking meeting in town would be really too impersonal. Why don't you invite him round for breakfast tomorrow morning? I'll make pancakes."

A huge smile illuminated Kristan's face.

"You're amazing."

Liz just shrugged.

"I just think the guy's probably feeling a little shaky, and you both loved Mike very much. You deserve to be able to talk in a safe and quiet place. I can't think of anywhere better than here."

"You're right," Kristan agreed. "And I'm going to call Omaru and tell him to recall his police car."

Liz visibly tensed at that.

"Hey," Kristan said gently. "It can't be forever."

"I know, but just because it's been quiet doesn't mean he's given up."

Kristan nodded.

"No, you're right," she agreed, looking thoughtful. "But let's assume Mike walked in on him that day, and he struck him and ran. Safe to say that by now he has heard about what happened after that. If I were him I would really want to disappear. You know? I wouldn't stick around here, and push my luck."

Liz took a few seconds to reflect on that.

She knew that when it came to Robert she was not thinking straight. She was too scared of him, and everything about him had been blown way out of proportion. She knew she could trust Kristan's judgment better than her own at this point.

"Maybe," she reflected. "I really hope you're right."

"Anyway, I won't get rid of the police if you're happier with them around, Liz," Kristan decided as she started to type an email in response to James. "I'll just tell him they're there but that he's got nothing to worry about, and I'll make sure the officers know he's coming."

"Thank you," Liz said with feeling.

Kristan simply looked up and smiled.

"That's okay," she said. "This is your home now, babe. I don't get to make all the decisions."

"Yes, but you built it all," Liz pointed out. "Your business, the Park, the cafe, your reputation with your clients…"

"And?" Kristan asked softly. "I like it that I'm not on my own anymore, you know?"

"I think I do, but…"

"I've been single for a long time, but believe you me, I'm a sucker for joint bank accounts, and checking in by text twenty-five times a day."

Liz started to laugh.

"Really?" she challenged. "You want to be domesticated like that?"

Kristan nodded seriously, joy dancing in her eyes.

"Yes, doc, that is exactly what I want," she declared. "With you, that's what I want."

Liz started to melt as she looked into Kristan's eyes, and saw that she meant exactly that, every word.

"What have I done to deserve you?" she murmured, smiling.

"Likewise, baby."

Chapter 12

James was on time and bearing gifts when he slowly walked up the steps to the cottage the next morning just after nine. Kristan had been up for hours already, been for a run and spent some time working. She spotted him as he neared the door, and pulled it open before he could knock.

"Hi."

"Hey, Kristan. I, uh, I'm a bit early, sorry."

"No problem. I'm always early too. Come on in."

He nodded, looking slightly hesitant.

"Sure. This is for you, by the way…"

The man had bought her flowers.

Kristan smiled at him, feeling tears burn the back of her eyes as she watched him standing there, all formal and unsure. She thanked him, and he looked away quickly before meeting her eyes again.

Kristan thought of something else to say to him, but then she just grabbed him and gave him a hard hug. He was stiff at first, but eventually he did hug her back, and he was smiling when she released him.

He was tall, slim, with blond hair, blue eyes, and a quiet look about him which Kristan was struggling to reconcile with the drunken James she had met twice before. He looked a little drawn but his eyes were clear, his hands steady, and when he smiled back at her she saw a little bit of Mike in him.

"How're you doing James?" she grinned, and he matched her

with the same expression.

"Getting there, Kris."

Liz walked out of the kitchen and came to stand next to her lover.

"Hi James," she greeted him, smiling. "My name is Liz."

"Hi, Liz."

"Liz is my partner," Kristan said with a smile directed at her. "She's an absolute genius in the kitchen, like Mike was, and she wanted to invite you over for pancakes. Are you hungry?"

"Yeah. I'm starving actually."

"Good," Liz approved, sounding happy as she took his arm and led him toward the kitchen. "So, where are you staying at the moment, James?"

"I've got a room at a bed and breakfast in town."

"Must be expensive," Kristan remarked as they both settled at the table.

James shrugged a little.

"I can afford it for a little while. It's fine."

"Okay."

Kristan was not good with idle chit chat, and so she jumped straight into it.

"How long have you been sober now?" she asked. "Three weeks?"

"Twenty-three days."

"Great. How are you feeling?"

He gave her a tired smile.

"The first week was awful. The second got better. Now I am getting my appetite back, and I am sleeping again at last."

Kristan gazed at him intently.

"My first three days were the worst," she said. "I had a fever and I kept throwing up."

"Same here," James smiled.

"Shit, uh."

"You bet. But worth it in the end."

"That's for sure," Kristan said gently. "So what happened to make you want to clean up for good this time?"

"You," he said immediately, and he glanced toward Liz as he said that, and tears welled up in his eyes. "You thought I'd killed my brother. Shit, Kristan, that hurt, you know."

"I'm…"

"No, don't say you're sorry," he interrupted. "I deserved it. I'd become that scary guy you thought could have killed Mike. All of a sudden I saw myself through your eyes. I saw what I had become. That guy's not who I am inside, Kristan."

"I know that, James."

"I'm a soldier. I flew Apache helicopters in Iraq, saved lives every single day that I was there. I got injured in the line of duty, even got a medal for bravery. My only regret is that I let my brother down when he wanted to help me, and I am sorry he's not here today to see us all talking at last. The thing is, Kristan, I am never going back. Whatever it takes, whatever happens, I will never, ever drink again. And I am very sorry for all the shit I threw at you on the road the other day. And you, Liz."

All of a sudden James was sitting up straighter, and when he grinned at her Kristan knew for sure that the man was back for good. She smiled, and she watched happily as Liz walked over to him and gave him a huge hug. She kissed him on the cheek and he blushed, and all of them burst out laughing.

"James, please help yourself to some pancakes before Kristan has them all," Liz urged him. "There's maple syrup and blueberry compote, and there's coffee and tea if you like, and juice too."

"That's wonderful, Liz, thank you so much," he said, and everyone looked and sounded a little emotional.

Kristan was very grateful that Liz was there to help them through it.

"Hey, what'd you mean before I have them all?" she protested.

"You know what," Liz shot back at her, laughing.

She went to sit next to her lover and clasped her hand in hers.

"I think we have some empty cottages James could move into, don't we Kris?" she asked as she poured orange juice for Kristan, and helped herself to a glass.

"Yes, we certainly do."

"Look, guys," he said immediately. "Thanks a lot, I appreciate it. But I really only came round to apologise. I am not asking for a job or a place to stay."

He was sincere, Kristan could see that, and she shrugged a little.

"Okay, that's fine," she said, as she reached for a pancake and maple syrup. "You don't have to, but the offer's there if you want it. Also, I need a pilot for next season. So I'm just letting you know there is a job available if you wanted to apply for it."

He smiled, looking happy as he tucked into his breakfast.

"Wow," he exclaimed. "Mate, that is great food."

"Thanks," Liz replied, and she nudged her partner under the table.

Kristan knew exactly what she wanted, and she squeezed her fingers lightly.

"James," she said, "you were crap at answering my questions the other day, but how about we go flying together today, and you show me what you can do?"

He paused, and his eyes twinkled.

"I can fly in dust storms, at night, with zero visibility," he said with passion in his voice. "I can fly with a broken engine, over the mountains with a rotor down and the other one going. I can make sure your clients feel safe, happy and excited all at the same time, and that they have the experience of a lifetime. I can…"

Kristan raised her hand.

"Hey, James, please stop," she laughed. "I'm turned on already."

The man burst out laughing, and Liz shook her head with a smile.

"James," she said, "would you like to be a pilot here?"

"Yes ma'am," he replied, smiling. "Very much so."

"Good. Kris, would you like James to move into one of the cottages?"

"Yes, darling," Kristan said with a firm nod. "Absolutely."

"I think we have a deal then, right?" Liz said, looking pleased. "Now let's eat, and then you two can take me up to the mountains."

James was an incredible pilot. Liz sat in between him and Kristan during the flight, and several times her stomach dropped, she forgot to breathe, and she had to grab on to her partner.

"James, you're scaring the customers," Kristan remarked with a smile, squeezing her lover's hand.

"Sorry, Kris. Liz."

"But I like it," Kristan laughed. "Come on, show me more!"

By the end of the flight James was on the books officially, and in the afternoon Liz took him on a tour of the cottages.

"You can pick any one you like," she said. "It would be great to have you here at the Park, you know."

"Thank you so much. I just need you and Kris to know that even if I had left after breakfast this morning without a job, or a place to live, I still would have been happy."

"We do know that," Liz said gently, "and Kristan would be okay with it too if that's what you really wanted."

She glanced at James as he looked thoughtfully at one of the cottages, which Kristan had said he could move into straight away if he wanted to.

"You know what Kris really wants?" she said.

"Maybe... What does she want?"

"She wants to give you a job you'll enjoy, and also a decent place to live for free. She loved Mike very much, and she loves you because you're connected. And probably also because you're a super talented pilot, and a soldier to boost," Liz added, smiling at him.

He nodded, a soft smile dancing on his lips.

"It would be great to have a place to live, and a job that keeps me very busy for a while," he admitted. "A job that I like, too. I love flying."

"Well, then I guess it's a win-win for all of us."

"Looks like it," James agreed. "Thank you."

He looked happy, and Liz squeezed his arm.

"You do know the police still haven't been able to find the person responsible for Mike, right?" she said.

"Yeah," he replied tensely. "And I heard about the other weird stuff that's been happening around here."

"So you know you need to keep an eye out, and be careful. We have a police presence at the Park, but I don't know how long they'll be here for, and…"

James nodded.

"Don't worry, this won't stop me from moving in. Liz, the guy they're looking for, you think it's your ex?"

Liz nodded, looking pale all of a sudden.

"It might be," she said.

James gave her a warm smile.

"Hey, relax," he told her. "Now that I'm here that bloke's got another huge problem on his hands."

Later on that night Liz got out of the shower and joined her lover in the lounge. Kristan had a fire going. She sat comfortably on the couch with her computer resting on her lap, slender blue-jeaned legs stretched out in front of her.

She smiled when Liz appeared in the room wearing nothing but one of her old sweat shirts, her hair wet from the shower.

She was slowly getting used to having Liz around the place with her. She always smiled whenever she saw something that belonged to her somewhere inside the cottage. Little by little they were turning the place into a home, and Kristan could not have been happier about it.

"Hey, doc. You look lovely," she said when Liz came to sit next to her, snuggling close.

"Thanks. What are you doing? Not working still, are you?"

"No," Kristan said with a chuckle. "Just googling helicopter parts."

"Working then."

"Not really. I'm a nerd, remember?"

Liz laughed softly, and she wrapped her arm around Kristan's shoulders.

"There are so many things I don't know about you," she reflected.

"Ditto, probably," Kristan replied softly. "And you know you can ask me anything you want, right?"

Liz nodded, and Kristan switched her laptop off and turned to look at her.

"Something in particular you'd like to know?"

Liz seemed to hesitate, and then she nodded again.

"Yes," she said softly.

"Go for it babe."

"The other night, when we were in town, you said that sort of stuff would normally drive you to drink."

Kristan just shrugged a little.

"Yeah," she nodded. "It used to. Not anymore though."

"How confident are you that you'll never do it again?"

Kristan let out a sharp breath, and her expression grew a little distant.

"One million percent," she replied, and she was clearly unhappy with the question.

Liz rested her hand on her cheek, and tilted her head a little until she could kiss her.

"I'm only asking because I care about you," she murmured.

"I know. Sorry."

"No need, honey. It's just that you mentioned drinking the other day, so I just want to make sure that you're okay. With what's going on here at the moment you're bound to be feeling a bit stressed."

"Liz, I am about as likely to have another drink or do a line of coke as I am to start wearing high heels and dresses," Kristan declared, smirking.

She chuckled as Liz burst out laughing, and leaned harder against her.

"Ooh, no, don't do that," she grinned. "I like you big and butch."

Kristan laughed at that.

"When I'm stressed I go running babe, so don't worry," she added, and she grabbed her mobile off the table as it started to ring.

"Hi Kel, how are you? Liz? Yeah, she's right here next to me."

She handed the phone over to her partner.

"Call for you, honey," she smiled. "It's Kelly."

She stood up and went to the kitchen, giving her lover a chance to chat in peace. When she walked back in with two steaming mugs of hot chocolate Liz was just finishing the call.

"That is very kind, Kelly, and we would love to come. Okay. See you tomorrow."

Liz's eyes lit up at the sight of the chocolate.

"Oh, that smells wonderful, thanks," she said.

"No problem."

"I need to buy a New Zealand mobile," Liz remarked. "Can't keep using yours, and then we can keep in touch when we're not together."

"And when would that be?" Kristan asked, frowning.

"When you're working. Or when I send you to town for groceries and I realise I forgot something, I can call you and request it," Liz replied with a sparkle in her eye.

"Is that how you figure it's going to be?" Kristan laughed.

"Yep!"

"So what did Kelly want?"

"Her daughter and grand-children are in town, so she wants to invite us for Sunday lunch tomorrow."

"Us as in you and me?"

"Yes. And James as well, if he wants to come. And Pam." Kristan frowned a little at that.

"Pam is going?" she asked. "Does she know we are too?" Liz nodded with an eyebrow raised.

"Apparently so."

She had told her lover about bumping into Pam in town, and about how the other woman had simply walked off, and ignored her.

"I sure hope she'll be in a better mood," Kristan said darkly. "I won't be very patient with her if she starts in on you again."

"If she does, let me handle it, Kris," Liz said quietly.

Kristan glanced at her, and saw the calm yet determined look on her lover's face. She liked that her partner could look after herself.

"Sure thing, doc," she smiled.

Chapter 13

"It's always made my Sunday lunches a bit difficult, you know," Kelly announced, as she set a big pot of lentils and mushroom stew on the table.

"What has?" Liz enquired curiously, catching Kristan as she rolled her eyes and made a face.

"Well, you know, that vegan thing that Kristan does."

"Oh," Liz nodded, grinning. "That thing, yeah. Of course."

"Stop moaning about it, Kel. There is nothing difficult about it, and it will keep you alive longer," Kristan declared from her side of the table, where she sat feeding Kelly's six-months old granddaughter her bottle.

The baby had cried and cried, and been passed from adult to adult until she landed in Kristan's arms, and immediately got quiet. Kristan made faces at her and talked to her, allowed her to touch her face and pull her hair, and pretty soon the baby was smiling and giggling happily.

"That baby's fallen in love with Kristan," James commented.

"Difficult not to," Liz murmured so only he could hear, and he laughed a little.

Kelly's daughter Jennifer nodded gratefully as she stood in the kitchen enjoying a glass of apple juice.

"Thank God for Kris," she said tiredly. "I was up all night with Tim who was having bad dreams, and then Marion started crying as soon as we got into the car, and pretty much hasn't stopped until now. It's like having two full time jobs when Brad is away on business," she added, smiling at Liz.

"Brad is your husband?" Liz enquired.

"Yes. He's just started work for a big Australian firm, and he has been away a lot this year."

"Must be nice having your mum around to help," Liz observed.

Jennifer nodded vigorously.

"You have no idea!"

Kelly deposited a big plate of couscous on the table, some salad, more fruit juice and thick slices of bread, and finally sat down herself.

"Here you go, people," she said brightly. "Please help yourselves."

Pam, who had been very quiet up until then, reached over and grabbed a plate. She started piling stew and couscous on it for Kristan, who was still busy with one very hungry baby.

Once again Liz chose not to comment.

Pam had claimed the seat next to her partner as soon as they had arrived, and Liz had said nothing. After all, if the woman wanted to make amends she had no problem with that.

Pam had been polite with Liz, and she had hugged Kristan hello, and asked if she could talk to her in private. The two women had disappeared in the garden for ten minutes. When Kristan had come back she had walked straight up to Liz, wrapped her arms around her waist, and given her a warm kiss.

"How are you doing babe? Enjoying yourself?"

Liz had been having a good time getting to know Jennifer, and James had helped with the cooking. It was obvious that Kelly really liked him. She had gone out of her way to make him feel welcome, and he was paying her back by being an absolute gentleman. Funny, helpful, and a pleasure to have around.

"This feels like having a family," Liz had observed with a smile.

"That's right."

"How is it going with Pam?"

Kristan had just shrugged.

"Not wonderful, but she has apologised. I think she's finding it a bit hard to be around everyone."

"Why?"

"No idea."

"Maybe she feels bad about the other day still."

"Maybe. I told her to forget it. If she wants to hang on to it that's her problem."

Then Kristan had kissed Liz gently on the cheek, and released her.

"I love you," she had whispered.

Now as Liz watched her girlfriend hand Marion back to Jennifer she smiled at the happy look she could see in her eyes. It was clear that Kristan had enjoyed spending time with the baby, and Liz liked that about her.

She liked it a lot.

"Thanks," Kristan said as Pam handed her a full plate, and she intentionally broke eye contact when the woman tried to linger.

Pam had met Liz, and she knew what the situation was, and so why she was finding it necessary to flirt with her now when she had never done it before Kristan did not really understand. And she wanted absolutely no part in that game whatsoever.

She took a mouthful of stew, and closed her eyes.

"Kel, this is incredible, as usual," she declared.

"Glad you like it," Kelly said, looking pleased. "James, are you doing this vegan thing as well?"

"I haven't been, but this is so delicious I might start," he replied, drawing another delighted smile from Kelly.

Kristan caught his eye and smiled, and when she nodded at him some silent communication passed between them. Liz knew that James' first impulse had been to decline the invitation to lunch. But Kristan had spoken to him, promised that there would be no alcohol on the table, and finally he had agreed to join them. Kristan had explained to him how much everybody had loved his brother, and that they all wanted to welcome him into the family. She was delighted that everyone had embraced him into the group, even Pam.

Pam, who even though she was not drinking now appeared a little bit tipsy. She had regaled them with funny stories of guiding in the mountains, and Liz had to hand it to her; the woman was funny, quick-witted, and she had a gift for telling tales. But she also could not help but notice that she seemed to be touching Kristan a hell of a lot.

Quick touches, leaning against her every so often, pouring her juice, and all that kind of stuff, and Liz's mood was slowly turning dark as she watched the woman flirt with her partner, to the point that even Jennifer wanted to bring it up.

"What's going on with Pam?" she asked as they were getting pudding ready in the kitchen.

Liz forced herself to smile.

"You noticed, eh?"

"Well, I think everyone's noticed."

Kristan was sprawled out on the floor playing with Tim and the baby, happier it seemed with the little kids, and Liz really did not like the look on Pam's face as she watched her partner. The woman looked like she was only one step away from taking her clothes off and jumping on her, and Liz was slowly beginning to get really, really angry.

"Hey, Liz, go get her now," Jennifer said with feeling.

Liz stared at her, eyes wide.

"Get her?" she repeated, astounded. "Who, Pam?"

Jennifer burst out laughing.

"I don't mean get violent with Pam, honey, I mean go get your girl. No one but you is allowed to touch her, right?"

"You've got that right," Liz said fiercely.

She flashed Jen a quick smile.

"Thanks. I will."

But Kristan was quicker.

She had been keeping an eye out for her partner, and looking for an opportunity to be alone with her. She had noticed how Liz had been getting very quiet for a while, and she was concerned. She met her just outside the kitchen, and reached for her hand.

"Babe, come here," she said softly.

"Hey you. I thought you were playing with the kids."

"Yes. Trying to get away from Pam more like."

She saw the tense look in Liz's eyes as she said that, and she held her a little tighter.

"What the hell is wrong with that woman?" Liz exclaimed, and Kristan smiled and shook her head.

"I don't know. I kept thinking I was going to get up and come sit next to you, but I want to make today work. For James and for Kelly, and Jen is exhausted with the kids, and…"

Liz relaxed immediately, and she leaned forward for a quick kiss. When she looked into Kristan's clear blue eyes again all of her anger was gone.

"You are so kind," she said softly.

Kristan smiled.

"You must be rubbing off on me, darling. And something's not right with Pam either, so until I know what it is I don't want to do anything to hurt her."

"Okay."

"But Liz," Kristan added, holding her back as Liz started to walk toward the living room. "You are the only woman in this room I want to go home with tonight."

Liz felt her heart tighten.

"And not just tonight, but every day for the rest of your life?" she asked.

"Oh yeah. That more than anything," Kristan said with feeling.

"Stick with me, okay? You don't have to make yourself scarce for Pam's benefit."

They walked back into the lounge, holding hands, and Jen made space for them on the sofa, purposely leaving no room for anyone else.

Pam was on the other side of the table speaking to James, and she glanced in their direction a couple of times, especially when Liz started feeding Kristan her ice cream and fruit pudding, and made her laugh. It was no surprise to anyone when Pam suddenly announced that she had to leave. She did thank Kelly profusely for inviting her, and promised to pop round again soon. She shook James' hand, waved at everyone else, and her eyes lingered on Kristan, who sat safely inside the circle of Liz's arms.

"Need to talk to you about a climb on Fox," she said brusquely.

"Sure, no problem. I'll be in the office tomorrow if you want to pop round."

"Okay, see you tomorrow," Pam snapped, and she was gone.

Liz took a quiet breath, and Kristan kissed her softly.

"Thanks," she murmured.

James also went not long after because he wanted to move into his new cottage, and Kristan was pleased to see the excited look in his eyes.

"Call me later if you need anything, okay?" she said.

"No problem. Kelly, thank you so much for lunch. I shall see you in the cafe soon, all right?"

"For sure, James, for sure," the older woman promised, and she went over to kiss him on the cheek. "It's good to have you with us, young man."

"Cheers, Kel. Jen, nice to meet you, good luck with the little ones, okay?"

"Yep. And James, if you ever want to babysit you just call me," Jen shot back with a grin.

James chuckled, waved at Liz, and left.

"He's a good guy," Kelly declared, and Kristan smiled and nodded.

"Sure is."

Once she could relax, Liz was more than happy to spend the rest of the afternoon with Kelly and Jen. Kristan sat with Marion on her lap, looking happy, and enjoying having all of her favourite people together.

"James was right," Liz observed with a smile. "Marion really has fallen in love with Kris."

"Do you like babies, Liz?" Kelly asked innocently.

Kristan started to laugh quietly. She was amused by Kelly's pointed and less than subtle question, but her eyes were on Liz, curious and excited as to what her lover would say.

"I do like babies, Kel," Liz replied, smiling. "I don't think I'm quite as good with them as Kristan is, but…"

"Of course you are," Kristan said immediately. "You just need practice. Do you want to hold her?"

"She needs feeding again," Jen stated. "Do you want to do it, Liz?"

"Uh…"

Before Liz had time to say anything else Marion had landed in her arms, and Jen was handing her a bottle.

"I've checked it's not too hot, so you just go ahead," she said.

Marion was already reaching for it, smiling her sweet little smile and making happy noises. Liz got lost in her pretty quickly, and she did not see the loving look in Kristan's eyes as she watched her, but Jennifer did, and she smiled.

"Won't be long before you two have one of your own," she declared.

"I don't think so," Kristan and Liz exclaimed in unison, but there was a definite sparkle in Liz's eyes when she glanced at her lover.

"Well, it's picture time I think, you are all too cute not to," Kelly announced. "Kris, Jen, go sit with Liz and the baby."

"Can we have one with just us?" Liz asked when she was done, blushing furiously when Kristan glanced at her. "What?" she grinned. "I just want a photo."

"No problem. Hey, Jen, make sure you send it on to me as well, okay?"

She laughed when Liz stared at her with an eyebrow raised.

"What? I just want a photo."

On the way back to the Park Kristan drove, and Liz scooted over across the front seats until she was pressed tightly against her.

"You really got pissed off with Pam, didn't you?" Kristan asked, smiling a little.

"You can say that again. She's lucky we were at Kelly's, and I didn't want to make a scene."

"What would you have done otherwise?"

Liz did not even have to think about that one.

"I would have told her to keep her hands off what belongs to me, and I would have made you sit next to me."

Kristan shot her a quick glance.

"Wow. Really?"

"Yes."

"That's sexy, doc. Remind me to make you jealous more often…"

"Don't even think about it!" Liz exclaimed, and Kristan laughed harder.

"I mean it," Liz said, running her fingers over the back of Kristan's neck, and kissing her temple, then her neck, and then sneaking her hand under her shirt.

"Hey, I'm driving," Kristan protested half-heartedly.

"What, can't you multi-task?" Liz murmured.

"I could, but…"

Kristan hit the brakes when Liz started to kiss her harder, and she pulled over onto a layby, way off the road into the trees where it would be safe.

"Liz…"

"Shut up, darling."

Kristan started to laugh as Liz straddled her and wrapped her arms around her neck, kissing her like her life depended on it. Liz's fingers went up into her hair, twisting her head until she could kiss her better, harder and deeper.

"What'd you say before?" Liz asked, wrenching her mouth away for just a moment.

It took a second for Kristan to be able to see straight again.

"I don't know… What?" she said, and she was breathing hard.

"You said I was the only one you wanted."

"Yeah, you are."

"Please say it again," Liz demanded.

Kristan looked up into her eyes, and she saw the heat in them. She could have lost herself in Liz's gaze and never come up for air ever again. She pulled her closer against her, and never broke eye contact.

"I love you, and you are the only woman I want," she said softly, gently. "The only woman I want to touch, kiss, make love to and be with, for the rest of my life."

Liz was silent for what seemed like a long time.

"What?" Kristan asked, smiling.

"I think you should drive me home so I can show you how much I love you too."

"Done deal."

Liz slid back to her seat, and Kristan launched the heavy 4x4 onto the road again. They got a red light just on the outskirts of town, and Kristan stopped at the junction with an impatient sigh.

"I don't know why they put a traffic light on the least travelled road in the country," she remarked impatiently.

The light turned to green, and she pulled forward.

"Hey, can I have your phone?" Liz said suddenly. "I want to see if Jen sent us that picture, and…"

She never got to finish her sentence. She never saw it coming, never knew what hit them. There was a flash of lights and a massive shock. The car seemed to fly off into the air, and all of a sudden there was just silence, and everything went black.

Chapter 14

Liz woke up because she was feeling so cold. Everything was pitch black around her, and she struggled to remember where she was. Lunch, she thought after a while. And Pam being a jerk.

Kristan.

She had been kissing her, holding her… Where was she?

"Kris?" she mumbled.

Gosh, it was hard to talk. She swallowed, wondering why she was so cold, and why everything hurt. She could smell gasoline. Why could she smell gasoline? She managed to sit up, and things slowly started to come back to her.

Something hit us, she thought.

Something came at us.

"Kristan?" she called.

She glanced to her right and realised that she was still inside the car, and her heart nearly stopped beating when she caught sight of her partner, collapsed on the other side of the truck.

"Kris! Kristan, hey! Are you okay?"

Kristan was slumped against the wheel, unconscious. There was blood in her hair, on her face and on her shirt. The car window had exploded under the impact, and the door was twisted and folded inwards. Kristan had been too close to it to avoid being hit full on, Liz understood that, and she rested her fingers against the side of her lover's neck, closing her eyes and breathing hard until she found a pulse. It was racing, but it was strong.

"I'll get help," she said loudly. "Okay, Kris? Damn it, wake up, Kristan!"

There was no response from her partner, and Liz got on her knees and searched for her phone.

"Shit!" she exclaimed when she could not find it.

She pushed hard against the passenger door and found that it would not open. At the same time she became aware of a dull, throbbing pain in her left thigh. When she touched her leg her hand came back all bloody.

"Shit," she muttered again.

She knew she had to find the phone, and be quick about it too. She carried on looking despite the pain, and eventually she did manage to locate it, stuck in between Kristan's leg and the door. She grabbed it with both hands and dialed 111.

"Yes, ambulance," she said urgently, and she was looking at Kristan the whole time. "We're just outside of town. I… I don't know the name of the road… My partner is unconscious, and she has a head wound. We need help."

It felt like an hour but it took less than five minutes for the emergency services to get there, during which time Liz tried in vain to get Kristan to wake up. She could not risk moving her because she did not know what injuries she might have. So far it looked like a dislocated shoulder at least, plus a deep cut on the side of the head, and God only knew what else internally.

The side passenger door would not open no matter how much Liz pressed against it, so she had to climb onto the back seat, and kick that door open with her good leg. She limped around to Kristan's side, and bit her lip when she realised the extent of the damage.

Something had hit them all right.

She did not know what, but when it happened she had not been wearing her seat belt. The force of the impact had thrown her across the car, and her left leg hurt a hell of a lot but fortunately nothing was broken. Kristan on the other hand had still had her seat belt on, and so it had kept her in place, holding her in when something hit them so hard it was enough to almost bend the car in two.

The 4x4 stunk of gas, and Liz's stomach was in knots.

The Fire Service got there first on blues and twos, they made the car safe immediately, and then it was a simple decision for them. They cut inside it from the back, removed the seats, then got to Kristan. They got far enough in that they could pull her seat back, and out from under the weight of the crushed door.

"Take it easy, take it easy," Liz cautioned as they worked. "We need a rigid board and a cervical collar. Okay? You got that?"

A medic crawled inside the car as she was giving instructions.

"Can I help?" he enquired.

Liz glanced back at him.

"My partner is unconscious. Possible neck injuries. She has a bad shoulder too, and it is dislocated. And a head wound. She got hit really hard…"

He nodded calmly.

"Got that. You're bleeding too, are you aware of that?"

Liz glanced at her leg, and as she shifted position inside the wrecked car she suddenly felt excruciating pain inside her knee.

She gritted her teeth.

"We need to get my partner out first."

"Why don't you let me handle it."

"No."

He gave her a friendly smile. He understood stubborn.

"Okay, that's no problem. What's your name?"

"Liz. I'm a surgeon. I know what I'm doing here, okay?"

"My name's Paul. I know what I'm doing too. As soon as your friend is out of the car you need to let me look at your leg."

Liz ignored him, and she returned her attention to the front seat as one of the firefighters leaned over Kristan with a cervical collar in his hand.

"Wait. I'll do it," she said loudly. "Let me do it, please. Paul?"

"Right here," the man said.

"Can you help me?"

"Sure."

Between them they had Kristan onto the board and secured pretty quickly. Two guys carried her toward the ambulance, and Liz jumped out of the car only to find that she could not use her left leg at all now. The pain was excruciating, and when she stumbled Paul was there immediately to support her.

"Can I help you now?" he asked, looking at her.

He was tall, with black hair, black eyes, fit-looking, and he was watching her intently.

"I need to go with Kris," Liz said tensely.

"You need to get off that leg."

She shook her head.

"Later."

It turned out she had a large piece of glass stuck in her thigh. The wound was deep and painful, and it required several stitches. She had also pulled a couple of ligaments in her knee, but fortunately it was nothing that a lot of rest and regular icing would not fix.

Other than that she was fine.

Later on, too much later on for her liking, she managed to find some crutches and she hobbled over to Kristan's room. Liz had been right about her shoulder. It was dislocated. Her left wrist was badly sprained. The cut in her head was deep, and it had taken a while to pull all the bits of glass from the car embedded in it. Fortunately the scans revealed no serious internal injuries, just a concussion, bruising to the brain that would leave no lasting damage. Liz found it difficult to breathe when she thought about how much worse it could have been for the both of them.

Kristan could have been killed.

Just as she was about to enter her room someone called her

name, and she looked up to see James walking quickly toward her.

"Hey, James..."

To her surprise her voice caught in her throat, and she could not say much more. He grabbed her and hugged her tightly, as she dropped her crutches and started to cry.

"It's okay. It's okay," he murmured.

"How did you know we were here?" Liz asked, trying her best to stop crying and regain her composure.

"I know Paul," James said softly. "The paramedic who was at the scene. He called me."

"Oh, yeah," Liz remembered. "Paul was very good. You know him?"

James nodded.

"Yeah. He's a very good friend. How are you, Liz?"

"Worried about Kris," Liz said with difficulty. "She got hit full on."

His expression darkened.

"Is she going to be okay?"

"Yes. She will be. But she has a concussion, and her shoulder was weak to begin with, and I hate it that she's hurt..."

He rested his arm on her shoulders and pulled her close.

"I know. But from what I know about Kristan that won't keep her down for very long, right?"

Liz chuckled a little.

"Yeah, I think you're probably right," she agreed, smiling through her tears. "She's tough."

"What hit you? Can you remember? Did you see it?"

"Had to be a big truck," Liz ventured, shaking her head as she tried to remember, and drew a complete blank.

"Had to be. Look, the police are here and they want to talk to you."

Liz took an immediate step back.

"Not now. James, I need to go and see Kris first. Okay?"

He nodded, and gave her a warm smile.

"Of course. Of course, no problem. I'll go tell them that. I've brought you both some clothes, by the way."

Liz hugged him again.

"Thank you," she said. "And thank you so much for being here."

She opened the door to her lover's room, looked toward the bed and found it empty.

Her heart sank.

"Kristan," she called anxiously. "Kris? Oh, God…"

"Liz."

Liz spun around at the sound of Kristan's voice, and found her leaning against the bathroom door. Apparently she had been in the process of putting her bloody clothes back on when Liz had walked in on her. She had managed to get as far as her jeans, and she was still wearing her hospital gown on top of them.

"What are you doing out of bed?" Liz exclaimed, frowning.

"I was… coming to find you," Kristan said slowly, and with difficulty. "Are you okay?"

Her hair was dirty and stiff, and sticking out of the large bandage that covered her forehead. Her eyes were limpid blue, her face chalk white. The cervical collar she was supposed to be wearing was abandoned on the floor.

"Baby, what are you talking about?" Liz enquired, moving toward her. "You need to lie down, my love, come on."

"Are you okay?" Kristan repeated loudly.

"I'm fine," Liz assured her gently. "Just pulled a muscle. I'm okay."

Kristan nodded and attempted a smile, but then she swayed as if she were going to fall. Liz wrapped her arms around her waist to steady her.

"You need to lie down," she repeated.

"No, I don't," Kristan murmured even as she leaned against Liz more heavily. "Not safe here."

"We are at the hospital, we are safe. You have a concussion. Kris, please listen to me."

Liz had her on the bed again before Kristan even realised what she was doing. She winced when she tried to move her right arm, and found that she could not.

"What's wrong with my shoulder?" she mumbled.

"You dislocated it. It will be fine, darling, but you need to lie down now."

Carefully but firmly, she pushed Kristan back against the pillows. Her lover was fading fast but still fighting.

"I don't want any drugs," she said thickly. "Okay? Will you tell them?"

Liz climbed in next to her and rested her arms around her.

"No problem."

Kristan sighed deeply when she felt Liz settling on the bed next to her. She closed her eyes at last.

"No drugs..." she murmured.

"Don't worry. You haven't had any yet, and I will make sure they do not give you anything."

She had had the presence of mind to tell the doctors that Kristan would not want any pain killers, even when they set her shoulder back in and put the stitches in her head. It had helped that her lover had been unconscious then. She was relieved to find that she had made the right decision.

Kristan tried to sit up again, and Liz tightened her hold on her.

"Shh. Relax," she murmured. "Stay still, my love."

"I've got a headache," Kristan mumbled.

"I know. You should try to sleep."

"What happened?"

"Something hit us."

"On the road?"

"Yes."

Kristan was feeling dizzy, and she relaxed back against Liz, thinking about that. She was silent for a few minutes, her breathing slowed, and Liz was hoping that she had fallen asleep at last. She closed her eyes, eager to join her, when Kristan spoke again.

"I pulled off the road. It can't be… We were way off the road, Liz."

"We got hit at the lights, darling. Remember?"

Kristan sighed.

"Not really…" she said. "Everything's fuzzy…"

"I know. You will feel better in the morning. Just sleep."

"Liz, can Mike come over?"

Liz breathed out slowly. She did not reply immediately, and instead just rested her hand against her lover's cheek.

"You're burning up, Kristan," she remarked, concerned. "Please stop thinking, and try to get some sleep."

Kristan struggled against her and started to get agitated again.

"We need to speak to the police," she protested. "Where's Mike? I need to talk to him."

Liz bit her lip and hesitated for a second. She knew it would do no good to try to reason with Kristan right now, so she simply cradled her in her arms, and tried to offer whatever comfort she could.

"We'll tell him in the morning, okay?" she murmured. "You'll be fine in the morning, I promise. Close your eyes, baby."

Kristan winced in pain as she tried to turn over.

Suddenly it felt like a million nails being fired at her brain.

"Don't move," Liz ordered immediately. "For God's sake, Kris."

"There' something I need to do…"

"No," Liz said firmly. "You're injured. You need to be still, and give your body time to recover. And baby, I need to get some sleep as well."

Kristan went still immediately.

"Why? You said you were okay," she said, her voice trembling.

"Yes. I am. Just pulled some ligaments in my leg. It's fine. I just need to rest a little."

Dislocated shoulder or not, concussion or not, Kristan was very clear when it came to Liz, and she wanted to be able to look her lover in the eye. She twisted until she was lying flat on her back, and she pulled Liz against her with her good arm.

"You're very pale," she remarked, frowning.

"You're one to talk," Liz replied with a tired smile.

Kristan narrowed her eyes at her.

"Are you okay, really? You're not just saying that?"

"I'm fine. Don't worry."

"You had some pain killers for your leg?"

"Yeah, I'm pumped full of them. I feel great."

But she was not lying about the drugs, and she knew she was about to crash.

"Kristan, please promise me you'll stay in this bed with me until I wake up," she murmured. "Okay, darling?"

"I promise," Kristan said immediately. "I'll stay with you."

Liz gave a sigh of relief.

"Okay. You are a handful, you know."

"No, I don't know... Sorry. I love you."

Liz smiled a little. She could barely think now, and she just wanted to close her eyes and forget about everything. Kristan would be there, she believed her, and so she simply allowed herself to drift.

Within seconds she was fast asleep.

Kristan felt her sink lower against her, and she was quiet as she listened to her breathing. She knew she was too wired to sleep, and her shoulder was way too painful to allow her to relax. Her brain felt foggy, she had a splitting headache, and there was something she knew she ought to be able to remember.

She could remember kissing Liz in the car, stopping at the lights, and then nothing. She took a deep breath and shifted a little. Her shoulder was throbbing, and it made her want to throw up again. She knew all she had to do was ask the nurse for some pain killers, and she would dose her up with morphine. For a second the need was so fierce she forgot to breathe. If Liz had not been asleep right next to her she might even have tried. Broken her commitment, just like that.

That's how bad the pain was.

Kristan clenched her teeth and stared at the ceiling, trying to imagine she was somewhere else, maybe on a nice run through the forest or out on the lake in her kayak. But her brain simply would not stop, and she could not help trying to reconstruct in her mind what had happened to them out on the road.

"Something hit us," she murmured.

Liz mumbled something in her sleep but she did not wake up, and Kristan kissed the top of her head.

"It's okay," she said softly.

Liz just sighed, and her fingers tightened briefly around Kristan's wrist before they relaxed again. Kristan tried to remain calm. Her mind kept flashing images at her of Mike, non-stop like a mad projector.

Something about Mike.

For several hours she just held on to her lover, and thought about Mike, and that was it. When she finally fell asleep there were no dreams, no thoughts. Just peace at last.

Chapter 15

When Liz woke up the following morning a nurse was in the room with them, making notes on an iPad. She smiled at Liz when she saw that she was awake.

"Good morning," she said quietly. "I'm Judith."

Liz returned the smile, feeling a little disconcerted and disoriented, wondering how long the woman had been there. She did not like it that people could just walk in on them whenever they felt like it, but then again this was a hospital after all, and these people were here to help. She glanced at her partner as the nurse returned to her notes, and she was happy to see that Kristan was still fast asleep.

"How are you doing?" Judith murmured as Liz slid off the bed.

Liz took a quick inventory of her injuries.

Everything hurt, but at least she could move.

"Sore, but okay," she replied.

She rested a soft hand on her lover's forehead.

"That fever has not gone down yet," she murmured, dismayed.

"I hear your friend did not have anything for the pain last night, is that right?"

"That's right. And she's not my friend, she's my partner."

The tall brunette shook her head, smiling a little.

"No worries. And that's brave," she observed.

Liz's eyes filled with tears at the heartfelt comment.

"She is brave," she whispered, looking at Kristan.

Judith rested a soft hand on her arm.

"She will be fine," she said gently. "Try not to worry too much."

Liz nodded as the woman left the room, and she returned her attention to her partner. Kristan was clutching her phone in her good hand, and when Liz saw the number she had tried to call four times during the night she started to cry.

It was Mike's number.

Taking the phone, careful not to wake her, she stepped out of the room to call Omaru.

"You ladies okay?" he asked immediately.

"Yeah, getting there," Liz said tiredly. "Kristan had a bad night."

She could walk without her crutches now, barely, but she could, even though she knew she should keep the weight off her leg. Surgeons always made bad patients, and she was no exception.

"Bad how?" Omaru enquired.

"She was asking for Mike. She called his number a few times while I was asleep."

He was silent for a few seconds.

"I guess you'd expect this sort of thing after a hard blow to the head, right?" he said eventually.

Liz nodded.

"Unfortunately, yes. It won't last."

"Good. Listen, we found the truck that plowed into you," Omaru carried on. "Abandoned in a field thirty minutes from town. We also found an unlit cigarette under one of the seats, and we are dusting for prints."

Liz's heart jumped in her chest.

"Why? You don't think it was an accident?" she exclaimed.

"We would be doing the forensics regardless, but I doubt very much it was an accident."

"Does the cigarette match the one we found in the cottage?"

"Indeed."

Liz closed her eyes and tried in vain to stop the tears.

"I hate this so much," she murmured. "You think it's my ex

still?"

"I don't know. We've been going round with pictures of him, in town and out of town. Nobody seems to have seen him. Not to mention the fact that Customs did not pick him up. I am beginning to think it might be somebody else."

"I don't really know how to take this," Liz reflected.

The relief when she allowed herself to think it was not Robert was immense. The fear was even greater. This was not about scaring them anymore, it was much more serious. Someone had tried to hurt them badly, maybe even kill them.

"Listen, I know Kristan doesn't want to abandon the Park," Omaru said again, "but it would be great if you guys could go away for a while."

"Where?"

"As far as you possibly can."

"For how long?"

"A few days. Just until she gets better, that sort of thing."

He was not telling her that he had a feeling the situation was escalating. He wanted them gone and out of harm's way until he could get a grip on it.

"Take a few days off, Liz. Wouldn't hurt, you know."

"I know," Liz sighed. "I'll talk to Kristan."

"Okay, thanks. We'll keep on working here. You take care, and keep me posted, okay?"

"Sure."

Liz hung up, and she looked up to see Pam striding down the hallway. The woman was dressed in jeans and a heavy fleece, mountain boots, and she also sported a very angry look on her face. She was probably the last person on the planet that Liz wanted to see at that precise moment.

"Liz, what's going on?" Pam said in lieu of a greeting. "Did you crash?"

The emphasis was on it being her fault, obviously, and Liz

visibly bristled at the woman's cheek.

"Something hit us," she advised her.

Pam looked her up and down, and she did not bother even asking how she was.

"Where's Kris?" she snapped. "She okay?"

Now Liz was getting really fed up with the woman's attitude.

"She's sleeping," she said sharply.

"I need to talk to her."

"Not now," Liz said quietly.

She stepped in front of the door, and at the same time gestured to the nurse in charge.

"Who the hell are you to decide?" Pam said loudly.

The woman was incredibly confrontational, Liz reflected, and she was wondering why. She stood her ground in front of her lover's room, and refused to engage in any further conversation.

"I will tell you the exact same thing," Judith intervened. "Please be quiet."

This made Pam quite furious. Liz saw it and she tensed, but fortunately the woman had enough sense to back down.

"When can I see her?" she wanted to know.

"How did you know we were here?" Liz enquired.

"Small town. Everyone's heard about the crash by now," Pam snapped as if Liz were somehow stupid.

"I'm afraid it will be a while before Miss Holt can have visitors," Judith informed her coolly.

Pam looked outraged.

"But she gets to go in?" she said, gesturing toward Liz.

Liz stepped forward in a very uncharacteristic loss of temper.

"I get to go in because I am Kristan's partner. Okay? I love her, and she loves me, and nothing will ever change that. Get used to it, and stop acting like such a fucking idiot, Pam!"

The look in Pam's eyes was so full of rage that Liz wondered suddenly whether the woman would try to hit her. Instead, she took a step back.

Good move, Pam, Liz thought, and she was boiling inside.

"Tell Kris I came by," Pam barked one last time.

Then she turned around and walked back out the same way that she had come. Exhausted, Liz swayed a little, and leaned against the wall for support.

"Hey, are you okay?" Judith asked as she caught her arm.

"Yes, just tired," Liz replied with a grateful smile.

"Could have done without her, right?" the nurse nodded.

"That's for sure."

"You should go home for a bit, and get some proper rest."

"No, I don't want to leave Kristan," Liz replied immediately.

Judith smiled a little.

"I knew you'd say that. How about I put another bed in the room for you then? You need to be able to recover properly too."

Liz gave her a tired smile.

"That would be great. Thank you so much."

"No problem. And please use your crutches if you're going to be walking around."

Kristan drifted in and out of consciousness for just over a day, and the next time that she woke up for good she was in a terrible mood, and wanted to leave immediately.

"I'll never get better in this place, Liz," she declared. "The food is horrible."

"You mean not vegan. And you haven't even had any yet, so how can you tell?"

"I just know. It's awful. Not going in our cookbook any time soon."

Liz smiled a little.

"Headache?" she asked, daring her lover to lie.

Kristan looked her straight in the eye.

"Yes. Full on. But it won't kill me."

Liz shook her head, wondering how on earth she managed to look so sexy, with a bandage around her head, a badly damaged shoulder, and dark shadows under her eyes.

Probably something to do with spirit, she thought.

Kristan had endured a concussion and a dislocated shoulder with no drugs whatsoever, and Liz did not know exactly how she would be feeling right now, but good certainly was not an option.

"I'll go have a word with your doctor."

"No need. Just tell her we're leaving," Kristan advised. "My choice."

Liz smiled a little, amused at her commanding tone.

"Okay. I will tell her just that, and I will get the paperwork sorted out."

"Thank you."

Liz hesitated on her way to the door.

"By the way, Kris," she said, "Omaru says we should disappear somewhere for a while…"

Kristan's smile immediately died on her lips.

"He does have a point, you know," Liz added softly.

Kristan rested her head back against the pillows, and she closed her eyes for a few seconds.

"No. I don't want to leave. I don't want to give up," she said after a while, and as she straightened up and looked at Liz again her eyes slowly filled with tears.

Liz hated seeing that look in her eyes.

"I know darling," she said gently. "But that's not quitting, we would just be going away for a few days to recover. Just you and me. Nothing wrong with that, right?"

"Of course not. It's the only thing I want," Kristan murmured. "To be with you. Just us. But…"

Liz simply threw her arms around her and pulled her close, mindful of her shoulder.

"If I were your doctor you would not be leaving this room any time soon, you know that?" she murmured.

"Guess I'm lucky you're my lover then, right? And that you want me. I'm signing myself out right now."

"I am serious, Kris."

Kristan gave an impatient shake of the head.

"So am I. I've had enough of all this. And you're one to talk anyway. How is your leg?"

"It's fine."

"Why don't I believe that?"

"I don't know, but you should. It's nothing that some stretching and a knee brace won't be able to fix. And I've been able to take pain killers for it so I don't feel any pain."

"And you think we should take Omaru's advice?" Kristan asked with a sigh.

"Yes, I really do."

Kristan had a sudden vision of her office, with the phone ringing and people queuing to book flights. In three years she had never closed down once, not even for a day, and the thought of doing so now made her feel a little sick.

"It would only be for a few days, darling," Liz insisted.

"What is Omaru hoping to achieve during that time?"

"I don't know. Perhaps he just wants us out of the way for a little while."

Kristan took a deep breath.

She was feeling sore, tired, and very, very pissed off.

"Okay," she agreed reluctantly. "A few days away would be great, Liz."

"Really?"

"Really," Kristan said weakly, trying to convince herself that she really meant it.

"That's great, Kris. I'll let Omaru know."

"I don't suppose he has any idea about location?"

"His words were 'as far away from here as you can get'," Liz admitted.

Kristan rolled her eyes.

"Okay. Well, Crystal Springs comes to mind."

"Where is that?"

"Crystal Springs is a small town about six hours away from here. Not that far, but I have a house there. No one knows. I only ever told Mike."

"How come?" Liz enquired.

Kristan tried to shrug, and could not quite manage it.

She winced a little.

"When I first got here I loved the idea of being able to disappear, if and when I ever needed to. Crystal Springs is an old mining town, and the best place in the country for whitewater sports. It's great for walks and mountain biking too. I bought a house there, and just never told anybody. I could fly us over."

"Maybe we could make a road trip of it?" Liz suggested, smiling and getting excited at the prospect.

Kristan rested her eyes on her, and nodded slowly. Her lover looked pale, tired and worried, but when she smiled like that her eyes sparkled, her entire face lit up, and she was still the most beautiful woman Kristan had ever known.

"I love you," she murmured. "And I love road trips too. We can do that. I can drive."

"Kris, give it a rest. I'll drive."

"Not if your knee's hurting…"

"I'll drive," Liz interrupted firmly. "We'll take it easy. Take lots of breaks, and make it last. What do you say?"

Kristan knew when she was beaten. She liked it that Liz could do that to her. She nodded and smiled a little, and she let her lover enfold her in a tight embrace. What had happened to Mike had come back to her now, and she was feeling tired and weak. She wanted out of that hospital room, and she wanted the world to give them a break. The thought of being with Liz on the road, alone, just the two of them was just incredible, and if she allowed herself to think about that, and not her work, she had to admit that it was exciting.

It was hard to forget about the Park though.

"We'll need to speak to James before we go," she said.

"I already have."

"Really?"

Liz nodded.

"He's been here a lot."

"Really?" Kristan repeated, and her eyes filled with tears again. "I only remember the one time when everything was blurred. Is he okay?"

"More than okay. You remember Paul?"

"Who's Paul?"

"The paramedic who helped me get you out of the car."

"I don't know," Kristan said, frowning. "I can't remember much about that."

"Don't worry about it. Just turns out that Paul and James are very close."

Kristan looked into her lover's eyes, and she smiled when she understood what Liz meant.

"James has a boyfriend?"

"Yes."

"That's great."

All of a sudden her colour was back, and she sat up a little straighter, and rubbed her eyes.

"Okay, let's do this thing," she declared.

"I've got clothes for you," Liz said tentatively. "If you really feel up to it."

"Absolutely."

"Sure you can stand up?"

"Yes," Kristan smiled. "We're leaving, babe. I'll grab a quick shower, and I'll meet you outside."

Liz waited outside the room, feeling a mixture of anxiety and excitement, wondering if she was making the right choice in allowing Kristan to walk out of the hospital so quickly. Then Kristan walked out, wearing clean trainers, a pair of jeans and a simple white t-shirt, her hair wet from the shower and the bandage on her head gone. She was smiling, there was a sparkle in her eyes and Liz felt her heart jump in her chest at the sight of her.

"How're you doing, doc?"

"Great," Liz replied, smiling tenderly. "And you look amazing. How's the headache?"

"Kind of pounding," Kristan admitted. "But I'll get used to it."

She wrapped her arms around her partner, and nodded a little as she looked down the hallway.

"Oh, bummer. The cops are here."

Liz glanced behind her to see Omaru walking toward them, and he looked a little tense.

"You guys are leaving then?" he asked.

"Yes. I hear you got us a car," Kristan replied. "Thanks."

He nodded at her, relaxing just a little when he realised that she was not on the war path.

"You are planning on putting some mileage on it I hope?" he ventured.

"We are. Do you need to know where we are going?"

He could not help but roll his eyes a little.

"I will know where you are going, Kristan, seeing as I'll have a couple of guys on your tail the whole time."

"You're joking," Kristan exclaimed disappointedly. "Isn't it enough that we are leaving? You have to tail us as well?"

He shook his head.

"It is for your own good I'm afraid. But I can promise you one thing."

"What's that?"

"You'll be safe, and you won't even know they're there."

Kristan snorted and immediately regretted it.

"Don't make me laugh, Omaru, my head hurts."

Liz squeezed her hand, a gentle signal to be nice.

"Safety first," she said firmly. "We're going to Crystal Springs."

"Crystal Springs," Omaru smiled. "Nice place. A good distance away. Good choice."

Kristan sighed a little. Deep down she knew that Liz was right, but she hated having to share her plans with the police.

"We might stop in Motuhano along the way," she volunteered reluctantly. "Just so you know."

He nodded.

"Thank you, Kristan. I appreciate your letting me know."

"Any news on what's going on?" she enquired.

"The cigarette we found in your cottage was a Marlborough light, same as the one we found in that abandoned 4x4 several miles from here. The front is busted, and it's got your Ranger's paint all over it. We'll find him, Kristan. I promise you that."

Kristan nodded, and she shook the hand he offered.

"Thank you. And for the escort too. Will you be keeping an eye on the Park for me?"

"Sure thing. You guys have a good time, and don't you worry."

He caught Kristan's dubious look, and simply shrugged.

"I know it's easier said than done. But I am working on it."

"Sooner rather than later, Omaru," Kristan reminded him.

He smiled at her.

"No worries. Keep your mobiles switched on; watch your six; and I'll be in touch."

Chapter 16

Kristan did smile when she saw the replacement car the police had arranged for them, and it did a lot to restore her spirits. It was enough to make her forget about her headache, for a little while at least.

"Doc, I don't care what you say, I am driving this thing," she exclaimed.

Liz laughed a little, and opened the passenger door to the brand new black Porsche Cayenne.

"I promise you will, but not just yet."

"When?" Kristan protested.

"Once you have some proper food in you. For now you get to ride shotgun."

Kristan relented, albeit reluctantly. She was feeling wound up, and the sight of the powerful car had triggered a desire to take it out on the road, and break every single rule in the book at least twice and more.

"Where are we going?" she asked.

"I was thinking about a quick pit stop in Paradise for lunch, and then we can swing by the Park to get some clothes and things. Then we can go. Is that okay?"

Kristan nodded, making a conscious effort to relax.

"All right. I might need to spend an hour or so in the office, to close down officially and let everybody know."

Liz glanced at her, catching the impatience in her voice.

"Of course. Are you going to tell James where we're headed?"

Kristan hesitated.

"No, I don't think so..."

"You don't trust him?" Liz asked, surprised.

"I do trust him, I just think the less people know about what we are doing the less they have to lie."

"Makes sense," Liz agreed.

She started the engine, and laughed at the way that Kristan immediately smiled and leaned forward a little.

"What is it with you and big machines?" she asked, laughing.

"I don't know. But I'm a nerd, remember?"

"You don't look like one. You miss your Porsche?"

"Stop talking dirty to me," Kristan muttered, and when she smiled Liz knew that she would be okay.

In Paradise Kristan ordered sweet potato and spinach soup, and soothing fruit tea, one of her favourites, but despite her initial enthusiasm she had to force herself to eat. Liz glanced at her over her quinoa and mango salad, and smiled in sympathy.

"It will get better," she promised. "You are very fit. You probably just need a good night's sleep."

"Hope so." Kristan said morosely. "I hate being injured. And I don't often struggle with food, as you know."

"Oh, do I?" Liz said mockingly.

Kristan chuckled, and gave her a knowing look.

"It's already noon," she stated.

She was feeling nervous at the thought of leaving, and she did not want to delay things unnecessarily.

"We need to get a move on if we want to pack and get on the road."

"Sure. Just one thing before we go, darling."

"Sure, what is it?"

Liz leaned close to her lover and lowered her voice.

"I don't believe Robert is behind all this anymore," she

whispered.

Kristan did not look all that surprised.

"I was never a hundred percent sure that it was him," she reflected.

"I know. I think you were right."

"So what made you change your mind?"

"Well, Omaru says they've been busy looking for him, and yet there is no sign of him. And I was very careful, you know. When I stop being scared of him long enough to think clearly, I start to realise there is no way he could have found me."

Kristan nodded seriously.

"That's good. I wasn't looking forward to hurting him."

"But who else could it be?" Liz insisted. "Who could hate us so much?"

"I don't know. Maybe I pissed somebody off and I don't even know it."

"And how do you feel about that?"

Kristan shrugged.

"I don't feel any particular way about it. I don't think I'm to blame for any of it. Or you," she added, and there was a dangerous sparkle in her eyes as she spoke. "Somebody's got a problem with us, and that is their issue, not ours. I want them found, arrested, and I want to go home and feel safe."

James was not at the Park when they arrived back at the cottage, and so Kristan simply left a note for him telling him they were going on a short holiday in order to recover from the crash. She left him her mobile number with a request to call her as soon as he found it.

She went to her office, tidied up, switched her computers off and locked the doors. She called every single person on her staff and had a long conversation with them, explaining what was going on and answering any question they had, but not telling them where she was headed. She found it harder and harder to talk with every single call, and when she got to Kelly tears were running down her cheeks.

"I don't want to go away, Kel," she said, her voice trembling.

"I know that, Kris, but the police think it's better, don't they?"

"Yeah..."

"Then do what they say, please, Kristan. Trust them, okay? And if they want to give you protection, then for God's sake, please go with that."

Kristan sighed loudly.

"Omaru says he'll have someone with us the whole time. And with you too."

"Good."

"And he said they'll keep an eye on this place too."

"Even better," Kelly said firmly. "How is your lovely girlfriend doing?"

"She says she's fine," Kristan replied. "But I know she's hurting."

"What does she think about going away for a while?"

"She thinks it makes sense. She says we should make a road trip of it, take our time and enjoy it."

"Hallelujah!" Kelly exclaimed. "The woman has a good head on her shoulders."

"I love her, you know," Kristan simply said, and she could not for the life of her stop crying.

"I know you do. And Kristan, from the way she looks at you, I know that she feels exactly the same way. Listen to me, honey. Nothing matters but you both. Not the Park, not the helicopters, not that sicko, whoever the hell he is. Believe me Kristan, when you find love like the one you have with Liz, you protect it."

"I know. I do want her to be safe, and..."

"Then do what the police tell you, Kris," Kelly interrupted. "I love you, baby, and I can't wait to see you again. For now I just want you and your darling to put some miles in between you and the Park.

Don't tell me where you are going," she added quickly, and Kristan smiled. "Actually, do not tell anyone where you are going. I'll check in on James. I will text you. Okay?"

"Okay," Kristan agreed.

At last she managed to stop crying.

"I love you Kel. Be safe and I'll see you soon, all right?"

"Absolutely. I'll get Jen over, and I'll cook you and Liz some vegan delight when this is all over."

Kristan put the phone down with a smile, and she turned around to find Liz standing in the doorway, watching her with a gentle look in her eyes.

"Hey," she said. "Are you all set?"

"Almost," Liz replied, walking toward her.

She realised that Kristan had been crying, and she wrapped her arms around her neck and pulled her close.

"I know this is hard for you," she whispered.

Kristan nodded a little.

"Yeah. Just hard to say good bye, that's all."

Liz pulled back to look at her.

"We'll be back soon, Kris," she assured her.

"Yeah, I know. I'm just worried. It feels like permanent..."

Liz understood how difficult this all was for her lover. She had lost her best friend in extremely distressing circumstances ,and then had to deal with a couple of seriously weird events. Now she was fresh from a car crash and a concussion, and Liz understood how much Kristan probably just wanted to be home right now.

"I wish we could stay," she said gently.

"Me too."

"But at this point," Liz added, "frankly I would rather do whatever Omaru suggests. I could have lost you in that crash, Kris. I don't ever want to lose you."

"I'm not going anywhere," Kristan said firmly. "I'm right here, Liz."

She saw the fear in Liz's beautiful dark eyes, and it made her shiver. Kelly was right, she realised. Nothing else mattered but Liz. All of a sudden the office felt cold and empty, and Kristan just wanted out.

"I'm ready to go," she said firmly. "Did you pack?"

"Yes."

Liz smiled at her, and Kristan held her hard against her as they made their way out of the office. She locked up, and they walked quickly back to the cottage, holding on to one another.

Kristan threw some clothes and toiletries together, they loaded their bags into the back of the car, and Kristan took one last look around her home. Everything was in order, just the way that it should be.

Only home now was with Liz, wherever she wanted to go.

She locked the door and climbed in next to her, and her partner gunned the engine.

"Ready?"

"Yes," Kristan smiled, and this time she really meant it.

It was a three hour drive to Motuhano, and despite her best intentions Kristan fell asleep pretty much as soon as they left the Holiday Park.

She was exhausted.

She woke up a couple of hours later when Liz pulled off at a petrol station, with a sore neck and a bad shoulder, but amazed and very pleased to discover that her headache was completely gone.

"Sorry doc," she said as she straightened up. "Lousy company."

"Of course not, I'm glad you got some rest."

"Did you notice anyone following us?" Kristan enquired as Liz stopped at the pumps.

"Not a thing."

"I wonder if the cops are with us."

"I think they're probably picking us up at specific points along the way," Liz observed. "I'm sure Omaru must have a unit waiting for us in Motuhano, since he knows that's where we are headed."

"Probably," Kristan said wryly. "I'll go and pay. Do you want anything to eat or drink from the shop?"

"Orange juice would be nice."

"Sure."

Kristan smiled and leaned over for a quick kiss, and she walked over to pay for their gas and a couple of bottles of juice. They were the only ones there. Her head was clear once more, and as she watched she clearly saw Liz stumble and hold on to her leg when she put the petrol hose back in place. If anything, she was limping harder now than when they had left the hospital, and Kristan hurried back.

"How about you let me drive for a while?" she suggested, and she was not prepared to take no for an answer.

Fortunately, Liz was in no mood to argue.

"I could do with taking a break," she admitted.

"I know. I feel good now, so you can rest."

"Okay, darling," Liz agreed immediately, and Kristan knew her leg must be hurting quite a lot then, but she did not comment on it.

She got behind the wheel with a smile on her face.

"I used to own one of those, you know," she said as she started the engine again. "The Turbo model. This isn't as good, but you know what, if Omaru thinks he is getting his loan car back he should think again."

They put Tracy Chapman on the CD, Liz got comfortable on the passenger seat, and Kristan drove slowly for once. As the beautiful West Coast highway unfolded in front of them she realised that regardless of their circumstances, going away with Liz was going to be an amazing experience. Leaving the stress behind would do them both a world of good, and Kristan was happy that they would get to be completely alone for a few days. It was the first time in three years that she was putting herself first ahead of her work, and that was a little bit scary to her. But when Liz rested her hand on her leg gently she knew that she had made the right decision.

"All right, darling?"

"Perfect," Kristan smiled. "How is your knee?"

"A bit sore. But not too bad."

Kristan nodded, and her smile widened.

"What?" Liz grinned.

"You tell me off for being a bad patient, but you really are even worse," Kristan replied with a laugh.

"I am a surgeon," Liz teased a little. "We're tough like that."

"Well, I think we should definitely stop in Motuhano anyway, and spend the night. We should be there in about forty minutes or so. Then we can both get some rest."

"Okay. Sounds good."

"And we don't even have to start driving again first thing tomorrow," Kristan added. "We could have a slow walk on the beach if your knee is okay."

"It will be," Liz said firmly.

"If not, you can always lean on me."

Liz smiled a little.

"I know that, baby. I love you."

Kristan smiled, her hands light on the leather steering wheel, the feeling bringing back memories of a life she had purposely left behind. Her head was clear and she could not feel her shoulder now.

"I do miss my Porsche," she said lightly.

Liz turned to her as Kristan downshifted and accelerated, enjoying the feel of the powerful car in her hands. Memories of driving hard and fast in LA came back to her all of a sudden.

"It was exciting working for that firm, you know," she reflected.

"Yeah? How come?"

"Creating new technology was exciting. Knowing that I was doing stuff no one else had done before."

"And the perks?" Liz enquired.

"Yeah, the perks," Kristan said tightly.

"What about them, Kris?"

"Well, it's been three years…"

"Time is all relative," Liz said softly, using Kristan's words from their first night together.

She saw her lover smile a little.

"Yeah," she nodded.

Liz grasped her free hand and held it tight in both of hers. Kristan drove on, slow enough that her partner would feel safe, not fast enough that she got any real satisfaction out of it.

"What about the perks?" Liz asked again gently.

"Well," Kristan said eventually. "Nothing comes close. Or at least it didn't, until I met you."

She glanced at Liz, and noticed the expectant look in her eyes.

"Making love to you, and being with you is better than all the cocaine and fast cars in the world, doc."

"I hope you know I feel the same way about you, Kris," Liz replied, staring at her lover's profile, not sure she could ever express exactly how much she loved her.

She was so in love with her it hurt. Every single time Kristan smiled at her, every time they connected, with a glance, a touch, a simple smile, it was always almost more than Liz could bear.

"I know," Kristan said softly, and she glanced at her lover and smiled. "I can feel it."

"You know, when I first landed in New Zealand, for a couple of days I wondered if I'd made the right choice," Liz reflected.

"Really?"

"Yes. And now I know I have. The closer I was getting to the Park the better I started to feel… I didn't know why at the time. Now I know that's because you were there, and I was coming to be with you."

Kristan tucked Liz's hand against her chest, and she kissed her fingers.

"I know a little hotel on the beach that's bound to have a room for us at this time of year," she said.

"Okay, great."

"They have a good Italian restaurant on site too, so once we're there we won't have to drive anywhere else."

"I don't care about the food," Liz tightly.

Kristan laughed a little.

"I was hoping you'd say that."

"Then step on it, darling."

There was a call from James when they arrived at the hotel, and Kristan stayed in the car to take it whilst Liz went to check in.

"Hey, how is your secret boyfriend?" Kristan enquired straight away, smiling.

James was laughing.

"He's fine, Kris, he's fine," he said happily.

"Why didn't you say anything, man?"

"Well, things have been busy, and I was planning to introduce you soon, but…"

Kristan sighed.

"But I did a runner," she finished for him.

"That's not what I was going to say."

"Well, that's pretty much how I felt going away like this. But the truth is now I am enjoying it. I don't really care where I am, so long as I am with Liz."

"And so you should. Speaking of safety, we have us a nice police car here keeping an eye on things," James informed her as he glanced out the window of his cottage.

"Good."

"To be honest with you Kris, I don't think it's your girlfriend that guy is after."

"The thought has crossed my mind," Kristan agreed, watching

the ocean in the distance. "It might not be a guy either."

"Really? Any idea who it might be?"

"Nope. Everybody loved your brother. The Holiday Park creates business for the town, I know pretty much everybody there, and I never got into trouble with anybody."

"What about any jealous ex-girlfriends?" James asked.

Kristan shook her head.

"No," she said.

"You sure?"

"I'm sure. Why, what's on your mind?"

"Well, Pam was acting pretty weird with you at Kelly's the other day. I wondered if maybe there was a link there."

Kristan winced a little at the thought of Pam. She had not been able to reach her to tell her she was going away. After four unsuccessful attempts she had simply left her a message, and asked her to get in touch. Liz had told her about her coming to the hospital and her angry behaviour with her, and it was strange all right but Kristan did not want to believe it.

"Something's definitely not right with Pam, and I am going to need to have a good talk with her about it," she said. "But I know her. She wouldn't go crazy on us like that."

"Okay. Well listen, don't worry about anything regarding the Park. You've got an ex-soldier in the cottage, and the police is outside. Everything will be okay."

"Thanks buddy. I really appreciate it, and I am very happy to hear about Paul."

"I'll introduce you soon, Kristan."

"Cool. Take care and we'll see you soon."

Chapter 17

The room was a delight, and Kristan had not lied about the view. They snuggled together in bed under the heavy quilt, and Kristan ran her fingers carefully over Liz's injured thigh and the bandage that covered it.

"How many stitches again?" she whispered.

"Eight."

Kristan winced a little.

"How many did I get?"

"Five."

"You win this one, doc."

Liz burst out laughing, and she tilted her lover's head back gently so she could take a closer look at her injury. The cut just above her hairline looked clean, and the stitches were holding up well. In a week or so she would probably be able to pull them off.

"Is everything a competition to you?" she asked.

"Not everything. I do know how to take my time, when it is worth it," Kristan said with a smile.

As she spoke she gently carried on with her exploration of Liz's body, caressing her leg, then the inside of it, and running her fingers over her hip and drifting lazily up to her breasts.

"That's nice," Liz murmured, smiling warmly.

"Turn over, darling," Kristan whispered against her ear. "I think I owe you a massage."

Liz obeyed without another word, stretching out over the large comfortable bed, smiling a little when she saw Kristan's expression.

"I love it when you look at me like this," she said softly.

Kristan reached for the bottle of essential oils on the bed stand next to her, and she poured some into her hands, warming it up carefully before she lay her hands on her lover. Then a simple few strokes, shoulders, neck and back, drifting down lower for just a second, then back up. And starting again, only going lower every single time. And again. And again.

Kristan stroked and caressed her for a long time, and when she paused eventually Liz was feeling almost liquid with pleasure.

"I need you," she whispered, turning over and reaching for Kristan.

Her partner grinned.

"Yeah? Then ask me nicely."

Liz burst out laughing, and she pulled Kristan against her, wrapping both arms around her neck and then rolling over on top of her. She clasped her hands around her right wrist, pinning her arm back, not touching the other one for fear of hurting her. She rested her leg in between hers and pressed herself harder against her, loving the way that Kristan immediately gasped and arched her back.

Liz smiled.

"How about you ask me nicely?"

"Anything you want, Liz," Kristan murmured.

She looked up at her lover straddling her, thinking how it blew her mind every single time she looked at her like this, and meaning every single word.

Liz simply nodded, and she lay down over her body, kissing her like Kristan belonged to her, like she wanted to belong to Kristan. She went on until Kristan's heart was beating faster than on any hard run she had ever done, and then she took her, gentle and hard, tender and rough all at the same time.

When the two women finally made it to the dining room that night it was almost nine o'clock, and Kristan was feeling a little bit faint, whether from hunger or from their lovemaking session she was not really sure. She held on to Liz's hand as they were led to a table in the back, next to a small window and a roaring fire.

"I think we should do this more often, doc," she remarked.

"What? Make love?"

"That, and going away," Kristan replied with a laugh.

"You will never have to ask me twice. On both counts."

They ordered tagliatelle cooked with tomatoes, spinach and black olives, with thyme and a hint of chili, and Kristan chose a non-alcoholic root beer than reminded Liz of drinking Guinness. Just as they were about to start eating Kristan's phone went off, and she glared at the screen.

"Oh come on! Get lost," she exclaimed, looking annoyed.

"Who is it?"

"Omaru."

"I'll take it," Liz said immediately.

"He could wait until we're done, Liz."

"I'll take it."

"Okay."

Kristan handed the phone to her partner, and she returned her attention to the plate in front of her.

"I might have to order another one of these," she declared, scanning the room for their waiter. "I'm starving."

Liz shook her head a little, looking amused.

She was smiling, listening to Omaru, and then she frowned.

"How do you know we're eating pasta?" she asked.

"Because he knows this place has an Italian restaurant," Kristan said as she tore a big bite off a piece of garlic bread. "Not 'cos he's a genius."

Liz rolled her eyes at her, but she could not help herself from smiling.

"Yes, everything is fine," she informed him.

"You didn't spot any unwanted on your tail?" Omaru asked.

"Nope. Not even you guys."

"That's how good we are. Listen, Liz, did Kristan ever mention Mike had a girlfriend?"

Liz repeated the question, and Kristan shook her head.

"No," she said immediately. "Mike did not have a girlfriend."

"Because we found some pretty explicit love letters in his apartment," Omaru carried on.

"Explicit how?" Liz asked.

Kristan looked up at that very moment, and she frowned at her girlfriend.

"What?" she mouthed.

"Look, I'll put you on to Kris, okay?" Liz told the detective.

"What's going on?" Kristan asked as Liz handed her the cell phone.

"You need to speak to him I think."

"Kristan, hey," Omaru said cheerfully when he heard her voice on the phone. "How're you doing? How's the Porsche going?"

"Going great; thanks for buying me one."

He chuckled.

"And how are you enjoying that olive sauce?"

"Quit playing with me Omaru, and tell me what's going on," Kristan snapped.

"Okay. I just told Liz we found some pretty disturbing letters in Mike's apartment."

"Disturbing? Tell me more."

"The letters start off rather tender and erotic, and then little by little they get threatening. Lines like 'I'll make you pay for not wanting me', 'you will live to regret this', and 'I am not playing anymore, I will hurt you if you hurt me'."

Kristan rested her fork on the table. All of a sudden her appetite was gone, and her stomach tightened.

"Explicit all right," she murmured.

"I thought so."

In her mind Kristan was rapidly sifting through the last few weeks with Mike. The conversations, the casual comments. She could remember nothing, nothing at all that would have indicated he was worried about anything. And he would have told her if something had been going on, she knew that.

"So how come you only just found those letters, Omaru?" she asked, sounding frustrated.

"Well, we used to think everything was connected to your girlfriend's ex, remember?"

"No, we didn't. You thought it was a thief, even when I told you otherwise."

"Look, Kristan, I am not calling you to argue about it, okay? Did Mike have a relationship?"

"No. He never mentioned anyone to me, and he would have done," Kristan said again. "He never mentioned he had a psycho on his hands either."

"Well, I'm just telling you what it looks like."

"And how do you know it's a woman by the way?"

"Was Mike gay?"

"No. Doesn't mean anything though, does it?"

Omaru had to agree with that.

"But at least we're making progress," he said.

"Are we?" Kristan argued. "How? If Mike had a stalker, and she ended up killing him, why is she now stalking us? Doesn't make sense."

Omaru took a deep breath, and he tried to calm things down.

"How are you two doing, seriously?" he asked.

Kristan exhaled loudly.

"We're fine, doing great," she said, and as she looked at Liz sitting across from her she relaxed a fraction. "You give us a great car and you send us away on holiday, what do you expect?"

"That's good, that's good. Listen Kristan, I don't know what's going on, but we're getting close, I can feel it. And these letters, when

I was reading them, they made me feel kind of bad. So I need you to take it seriously too."

Kristan paled.

"Believe me Omaru, I am taking it seriously. Ever since my partner got killed by some low-life piece of shit in fact; every fucking second. Now what about you?"

If Kristan had been alone she would have slung the phone across the room, but because Liz was with her she did not. And she kept her voice down so the other diners could not hear her; but she was shaking.

Liz grew still when she heard her partner's words, and she froze on the other side of the table.

"I am taking it seriously too, Kristan," Omaru said calmly. "I'm glad you are. Stay away for a few more days, okay?"

"Mike's brother is at the Park. Can you guarantee his safety?" Kristan said sharply. "Because if you can't even…"

"James is okay, we have him and Paul under surveillance. We have Kelly under protection as well. This thing is about to unravel."

"So you keep telling me."

"Because you need to be careful."

"I am always careful," Kristan snapped.

"That's good to know. I'll call you again soon."

Omaru disconnected, and Kristan leaned back against her seat. She closed her eyes for a second, and she took a deep breath.

"I swear this guy needs a good shaking," she said tensely.

She glanced at her food and pushed the plate away.

"No. Come on, Kris, you need to eat," Liz protested, dismayed.

"It's okay, I'll have it in a doggy bag. I just can't right now. Or maybe in a few minutes."

Liz reached across the table for her lover's hand.

"Whatever was going on, and if anything was going on," Kristan said fiercely, "I'm sure that Mike had no idea how serious it was. Otherwise he would have told me."

"Did he usually talk to you about his love life?"

"He talked to me about the serious things. He talked to me about James. You know."

Liz nodded a little, and she left her seat and went to sit next to Kristan.

"Funny how I can't seem to keep my hands off you, eh?" she whispered as she wrapped her arms around her shoulders.

"You won't get any complaints from me," Kristan said softly, and she turned her head to rest her forehead against Liz. "Gosh, I hate this…"

"If you want your food in a doggy bag I'll let them know, and we can go back to our room. You've gone very pale all of a sudden."

Kristan shook her head.

"No, it's okay. No reason we can't linger a little, and I don't want to ruin your dinner either."

"Only if you're sure."

"I'm sure. This root beer is excellent, and I want some more."

Kristan held Liz back against against her as she started to move away.

"I want to sit with you and talk."

"I'd love to sit and talk. About what?" Liz asked with a gentle smile.

"Not sure," Kristan replied, and Liz nodded a little when she caught the exhausted look in her eyes.

She understood Kristan wanting to stay put, because she as well wanted this night to never end. But she also knew that her lover was about to cave in, and to be fair she was surprised it had not happened earlier.

"How about we take some root beer back to our room, and drink it in bed?" she suggested.

Kristan's eyes sparkled, and she started to laugh.

"What?" Liz asked with a grin.

"You're rampant, darling."

"But you like it, right?"

"Maybe," Kristan said, laughing harder.

She took the hand her lover offered, and she let her pull her up from her chair.

"Unsteady?" Liz asked as she caught her in her arms.

"Maybe a little."

"Tired?"

"Kind of," Kristan replied, and she could not stop herself from yawning.

"I asked them at reception what's the latest that we can check out tomorrow, and they said five o'clock in the evening." Kristan smiled.

"Yeah," she said. "Off season and all that."

"That means we can take our time tomorrow."

"And it means we can stay up as long as we like tonight," Kristan remarked.

"Absolutely."

Liz got food to go for both of them, and a few bottles of beer as well, and she walked with her partner back to their room. By that time Kristan was flagging big time. She brushed her teeth, slipped under the covers, and she watched as Liz busied herself around the room.

"Hey doc," she said softly. "Your food is getting cold."

"Don't worry, I'll get to it in a bit. Are you feeling okay?"

"Tired," Kristan admitted. "My shoulder hurts."

She noticed that Liz was extra careful about checking that the door was locked properly, and then she did the same with the window. She was about to draw the curtains shut when Kristan stopped her.

"It's a full moon," she pointed out. "If you just switch the lights off no one will be able to see in, but we'll be able to see the ocean."

Liz hit the switch, and she smiled at the soft light that suddenly inundated the room.

"Gosh, Kris, this is beautiful," she said.

"Told you."

Liz slid under the covers, and she snuggled close to her lover, wrapping her arms around her from behind, and pulling her tightly against her.

"Relax," she murmured.

"Can you see the waves?" Kristan murmured.

"Yes."

"Nice, uh?"

"Very."

"So what are you going to do about Robert?"

"What do you mean?" Liz asked, surprised at the question.

"Sorry. I should have said what are you going to do about being married to him," Kristan corrected.

Liz held her a little harder against her.

"I don't want to be," she said with feeling. "You know I don't, right?"

"I know. And lately I like it less and less that you are married to somebody else."

"Do you think I can initiate a divorce from here, and keep where I am a secret?"

"Can't see why not. We'll just need to find a good lawyer."

Liz relaxed against the pillows and wrapped herself more comfortably around Kristan. It was windy outside, and she could see white froth on the waves crashing on the beach a little way away. Kristan was silent as she closed her eyes, and let herself rest against her partner. Her headache was back, but not as bad as before. The need to sleep was overwhelming though.

"Liz," she murmured.

"Yes, baby."

"Go eat."

Liz smiled.

"No worries darling. You just sleep, okay? I'll be right here..."

She went silent when she realised that Kristan was asleep already, and she smiled and held her for a little while longer.

Then she slid off the bed as quietly as she could, even though she had a feeling her lover would probably sleep through a nuclear blast. She settled at the table and reached for her food, glad that it was still warm and absolutely delicious.

As she ate she went through her newly acquired New Zealand iPhone, checking emails.

She had a couple from Jennifer, and she smiled when she realised that Kelly's daughter had sent her the photos of their day together. There was that one they took of her, Kristan and the baby, and also a couple more. In one of them Kristan was sitting right next to her, looking at her and smiling at something Liz had been saying. The look in her eyes brought tears to Liz's eyes. This was normally how Kristan looked at her. It was love, affection, lust and protection all rolled into one, and captured perfectly on camera. Jen had a good eye. Liz stood up and went to the bed to pull the covers a little tighter around Kristan.

"I love you," she whispered.

Next there was an email from Kelly, saying she had adopted a new kitten, and again there was a picture and it made Liz smile.

James had sent one of his newly decorated cottage, and also one of Paul, and Liz clearly remembered the respectful medic from the night of the crash. She sent a heartfelt email back saying they looked beautiful together, and that she was happy for them and could not wait to meet again in person under happier circumstances.

She clicked on the next email without thinking, and immediately recoiled in horror. She dropped her phone and swore under her breath, and she looked toward the bed immediately, hoping that Kristan had not heard her. Fortunately her lover was still fast asleep, and Liz slowly picked up the phone and went to the window to lower the blinds.

The photo was one of Charlie, Kelly's cat, pinned to the cafe table with a knife through his stomach. The email simply said, 'your turn soon', and Liz's blood turned to ice in her veins. She hit the forward button and immediately sent it to Omaru, and the officer was back on the phone within seconds.

"Where are you now?" he asked.

"Still at the hotel. Kris is asleep. Should I wake her up? Do we need to leave?"

"She hasn't seen the email yet?"

"No."

"Okay. No need to wake her up, Liz."

Liz stepped into the bathroom and pulled the door shut behind her.

"Are we safe here, Omaru?" she said sharply.

"Listen, Liz, my officers have been trailing you all day," he replied, and he sounded serious and calm. "We recced the hotel when you checked in, and ran checks on personnel; I've been there before, and it's the same staff. Nothing to worry about as far as they're concerned. Right now I have a unit parked outside keeping an eye on things, and everything's quiet. You guys are safe."

Liz sighed a little, and she glanced at Kristan through the half open door.

"Thank you," she said a little more warmly. "I'm sorry we are giving you such a hard time."

"Hey, don't worry about it. I understand. I'm doing my job, and this will be over soon."

"Should we carry on to Crystal Springs?"

"Sure. No one knows where you two are going so that's still fine. Tell me, how many people did you give your email address to?"

"Just Kris, Kelly, Jen and James."

"Fine. You go to bed now and relax. We'll trace that email and see where it came from."

"Okay."

"I'll call you in the morning.

"Okay," Liz repeated. "Thank you."

"Don't mention it. Hang in there, Liz. Won't be long now."

Liz disconnected but she kept the phone on loud just in case Omaru needed to get back in touch with them. She slid into bed next to Kristan and wrapped her arms around her.

"Shh, it's okay, I've got you," she whispered when Kristan mumbled something in her sleep, and struggled against the covers. "I love you baby."

Kristan reached out for her, pulled her close against her, wrapped her arms around her neck and sighed.

"Love you," she whispered. "Sleep. I love you."

Chapter 18

Jason Omaru was not fazed by Kristan Holt's attitude, and he was hoping she could end up keeping that Porsche if it made her happy. But he was annoyed that someone had managed to murder Mike Anderson, a man he had not known personally but had a good feeling about. Now whoever had done it was trying to turn the lives of two very nice women into a living nightmare.

This simply would not do.

Omaru was the only cop left in the huge open plan office he shared with another ten or so senior officers. He poured himself a cup of coffee, dropped several big spoons of sugar into it, and returned to his desk where the disgusting email that had been sent to Liz was open on his PC.

He reclined in his chair, rested his legs on his desk, and got to thinking.

Kristan awoke just after seven o'clock the next morning feeling fantastic. She ordered scrambled olive tofu for breakfast, beans, tomatoes, fried bread, toast and marmalade, and Liz was pleased to see that she seemed back to her normal self.

"Do you ever miss meat?" she asked her as Kristan reached for the orange juice.

"Nope. Never. There are enough good foods out there that I get all the flavours and textures I need to be happy."

She smiled at her lover.

"When I lived in the US I was a cheeseburger addict. Now I choose to be kind."

Liz raised her glass, smiling.

"I'll drink to that."

Kristan ate quickly, and then she relaxed against her seat.

"That should do me until lunch," she declared with a grin. "How about we go for a small walk on the beach before we leave? How's your knee doing this morning?"

"It's fine."

Liz was loathe to bring the mood down but she needed to tell Kristan about the email from the previous night, and so she did. She passed her phone over to her, and she watched as Kristan stared at it for a few seconds, her normally clear blue eyes darkening noticeably.

"So now he's sending emails," she mused. "Or she, whoever the hell that might be. Omaru is right, this thing is about to start unravelling."

She looked across at her lover.

"You got this last night?"

"Yes."

Kristan sighed. She knew why Liz had not woken her, but she wished she could have been there to comfort her.

"Did you sleep okay?" she asked.

"It took me a long time to fall asleep," Liz admitted.

"I'm sorry babe. We can take it easy today."

"I'm not tired. I'm just worried it's someone very close to us doing this, and that's scary. Has Pam been in touch?"

Kristan was not surprised at the question because she had been thinking the same thing. Someone close, someone pissed off, someone out for revenge. Liz had only ever experienced Pam at her worst, and Kristan thought about the woman she knew, who was smart, funny, kind, and a good friend.

"Not yet," she said. "I'm worried about her."

She went silent, and Liz glanced out the window, at the

amazingly clear blue sky, and the white beach that led to a glittering ocean.

"It's such a beautiful morning," she said. "Let's not waste it. Let's go for a walk."

Omaru and his amazing sense of timing never failed, and he phoned just as they were crossing the road. This time Kristan did not suggest they make him wait.

He informed them that the email Liz had received had been sent from an Internet cafe in Queenstown. Again, he reiterated that the two women would be safe if they kept on moving, and that Crystal Springs still sounded like a reasonable destination.

"I'm fed up being on the run," Liz pointed out.

"Think of it as a holiday. And Liz, I have good news for you. I have contacts in London, and I called in a favour from one of them. Your ex has been spotted going to and from work in the City all week last week, so there is no way he can be behind what has been going on here. You guys take care, okay? I'll speak to you soon."

Liz put the phone down, beamed at Kristan, and almost burst into tears.

"I think we were due some good news at last, right?" Kristan smiled as her lover hugged her tightly.

"You have no idea how happy this makes me," Liz exclaimed excitedly. "He has given up on me, he's let me go. I am so, so happy!"

She laughed, and Kristan laughed with her. They carried on walking on the beach, holding on tight to one another, and the smile never left Liz's lips.

"You were great with Marion the other day," she reflected after a while.

"Well. When she stops crying she's a great baby."

"And you really do like kids, right?" Liz enquired, wanting to be sure.

She was on a roll now. She felt lighter than she had in months, and the woman next to her was so beautiful it made her feel invincible. She wanted to love her, be with her, create a life with her that no one else could touch. Now she really felt that she could, regardless of what else was going on.

"I do like kids," Kristan replied after a quick glance at Liz, smiling when she noted the colour in her face, and the sparkle in her eyes.

Liz nodded.

She grinned at her.

"Okay. So would you like to have a baby with me?"

Kristan stopped walking immediately.

"Do you?" she asked.

"I asked you first."

"Depends," Kristan replied seriously.

"On what?"

"On what you are talking about. Adoption, surrogacy..."

Liz wrapped her arms around Kristan's neck, and she kissed her gently.

"Pregnancy," she said softly. "For me."

Kristan held her against her, her head spinning a little. Her crystal clear blue eyes turned thoughtful as she considered the idea, and Liz ran a gentle hand through her hair.

"What are you thinking?"

Kristan breathed deeply.

"You've never mentioned kids before," she said. "So I'm just a bit surprised, that's all. This is fast, Liz."

"But it feels right."

"And I want to make sure this is really what you want. Because I wouldn't be the one doing all the hard work."

"Like being fat and emotional for nine months?" Liz ventured.

"Yes," Kristan chuckled. "That, exactly."

Liz shook her head a little.

"There would be plenty of hard work besides that," she remarked.

"I know."

"Kris, I never thought kids would be an option for me," Liz reflected thoughtfully. "But now things are different."

"Because we are together?"

"Yes. And the other day when we were at Kelly's, when I was holding Marion and feeding her, and looking at her like that, I was thinking what an amazing adventure it would be to bring another life into this world."

"Bit scary, too."

"I'm not scared. I know enough about what is important in life to understand the huge responsibility that it would be."

"Huge is the right word. It would be about caring for another human being when they are small and young, and learning…"

"And making sure that we equip them with all the resources they will need to be happy and successful in this world," Liz finished.

Kristan smiled.

"My thoughts exactly."

"Looks like we're on the same page then. And I am ready for it," Liz said, her eyes shining. "I am ready for it, with you."

Kristan smiled again, her heart beating so fast she thought she might faint.

"Then yes," she said simply. "Yes, I want to have kids with you."

Just before lunchtime they packed up their gear, threw the bags into the back of the car, and got on the road again. Kristan felt better and happier than she had in years. Her shoulder had stopped hurting as if by magic, her headache was gone again, and her mind was clear. She got behind the wheel, smiled when Liz put Melissa Etheridge on the CD, and she hit the gas.

"I could get used to this travelling thing," she said happily.

"Is that what you did when you first got here?"

"Yep. Spent a couple of weeks in my campervan driving all over the place. Of course I was sick the first few days, but it got better eventually. I'm ready to settle down now," Kristan added with a smile.

"Glad to hear it, my love."

They turned off Highway 6 after a while, and Kristan switched her lights on as they left the ocean behind and headed inland toward the mountains. It had gotten cloudy, and as they started to climb the temperature dropped noticeably. Liz switched the heating on and zipped up her fleece. After a few minutes it started to spit a little.

"I love this kind of weather," Kristan remarked with an excited smile. "In the mountains especially."

"Weather in the mountains," Liz nodded. "Only one word for it."

"What's that?" Kristan asked.

"Temperamental, darling. You should know."

Kristan shot her lover a quick glance, taken aback by the unexpected comment.

"What?" she said. "You think I'm temperamental?"

"I think you have a temper," Liz said gently.

"I get passionate about things. What's wrong with that?"

"Nothing," Liz assured her. "Nothing at all. And I like it. Passionate is good."

"I sense a big 'but' in there somewhere," Kristan said, glancing toward her again, and looking slightly worried.

Liz leaned over and kissed her on the cheek tenderly.

"But sometimes," she said slowly, "I think it's scary. Like the other day when you were all ready to go charging into the cafe on your own, regardless of what danger might be there waiting for you. Or when you almost ended up in a fight with James. When you get angry, you forget to be careful."

Kristan gripped the wheel tighter, and she breathed deeply. It was not the first time someone had taken issue with her rather explosive and fiery character. Mike used to tell her her off for it.

Kristan smiled a little when she thought of him.

"I know," she said eventually. "I just… sometimes I just react to things, and…

"And it might get you hurt one day," Liz interrupted. "The thought of that happening, it makes me feel sick, Kristan. It makes me…"

Liz hesitated, shaking her head and looking pale.

"I just can't bear to think about it, simple as that."

For a while Kristan was quiet, focused on her driving, taking each bend with absolute commitment. Her reading of the road was sharp and precise, her use of speed just perfect, and it was enough to make Liz excited but not enough to make her scared.

"I understand," Kristan said after a while. "I promise I will do something about it."

"Thank you," Liz whispered.

"But I will lose control from time to time, Liz," Kristan added fiercely. "And there is nothing that I can, or want to do about that."

She glanced to her left, smiling a little at the worried look in her partner's eyes.

"I mean when I make love to you, darling. Only when I make love to you."

Liz gave a soft laugh and sat up a little straighter.

"That," she said, "is a deal."

"Yeah? For sure?"

"For sure."

Kristan smiled, and she reached for Liz's hand and wrapped her fingers through hers.

"Thank you for being honest with me," she said quietly. "That's one of the things I really love about you."

"Good. I wouldn't know how not to be."

They carried on climbing, and Kristan leaned forward and

narrowed her eyes at the leaden skies above.

"Wow, it looks like snow," she remarked, frowning.

"I love snow," Liz replied excitedly.

"Well, Crystal Springs is quite high up, so it's not unusual to get some at this time of year."

"Great."

"I just hope we don't get snowed in."

"I hope we do," Liz shot back immediately. She laughed. "I'd love to get stuck in Crystal Springs, alone with you for a few days."

"After, we load up on groceries, right?" Kristan pointed out with a grin.

"Oh yeah, of course."

The road became narrower, and the skies grew darker, and Kristan grabbed her phone when it bleeped inside the pocket of her jeans.

"We have just lost phone cover," she announced, frowning at the screen. "Under normal circumstances I would be delighted."

"Then again, we haven't seen a single other car since we got on this road," Liz pointed out. "I think that's a good sign. I'm not worried."

Kristan nodded.

"Good. We're not far from town now."

"Okay, so what's the plan when we get there?"

"Load up on some food and head straight to the house before this weather gets worse, if that's okay with you."

"Perfect. How far is your house from the centre of town?"

Kristan smiled a little.

"About three miles," she said, almost sheepishly. "In some bit of forest. You know me, I like privacy."

She drove them straight up to a shopping outlet on the outskirts of town, and parked in front of a Whole Foods.

"Great," Liz commented, looking at the shop through her window. "I intend to carry on with your instruction whilst we're here."

"Cooking lessons, yes?"

"Absolutely."

"How about lasagna for tonight? I'm starving again, Liz."

It was a good sign, Liz thought happily, and they walked hand in hand to the shop and spent some time stocking up on vegetables, fruit juice, rice and pasta. When they walked back out again it had started to snow.

"Unbelievable," Kristan exclaimed. "This is so early in the season for snow…"

"It's our welcoming present," Liz declared, grinning, her face turned toward the skies.

Kristan looked at her and smiled. She dropped the bags she was carrying, walked up to her lover, and wrapped her arms around her waist.

"You are so beautiful," she murmured.

She kissed her, right in front of all the shops.

"Kristan," Liz protested, blushing and smiling.

"What?"

"People are watching…"

"I don't care," Kristan replied.

She kissed her again and this time Liz responded, wrapping her arms around her neck and pulling her harder against her. When Kristan pulled back she was beaming.

"Thank you," she said softly, and she rested her head against Liz for a moment.

Liz had to shake her after a while.

"We need to go," she laughed.

She was right, and it was snowing hard now.

They got back into the car and Kristan drove off quickly.

"You got phone cover now?" Liz enquired.

"Nope. You?"

"Nothing."

Kristan just shrugged. She was feeling too happy to worry about it, and when they turned left off the main road onto the country lane that led to her house she spotted the police unit parked under a bunch of trees, and came to a stop right next to them. She rolled her window down, and smiled at the two officers who were sat in it.

"Omaru's team, right?" she asked.

"Kristan and Liz?" one of them replied.

"You got that right."

"The coast is clear. Welcome home, ladies."

Kristan smiled at them and carried on driving. She would have hated to admit it, but she was glad that Omaru had come through for them. She was not so worried about herself but she wanted Liz to feel safe, and now she knew that she could relax. They turned a corner and came within view of her house, and she stole a quick glance at her lover. Liz was leaning forward in her seat, staring at the house with a big smile on her face.

"Home sweet home, darling," Kristan announced. "You like it?"

The house was small, made of wood and large expanses of glass, and it looked just like a jewel in the snow.

"I love it," Liz exclaimed.

She jumped out of the car and hurried up toward the front door, limping still but ignoring it. Kristan threw her the keys, and she got busy with the bags of groceries in the back. When she joined her lover inside, and pushed the door shut behind her, Liz was already busy getting a fire started.

"Kristan, don't worry about the bags," she instructed loudly from the lounge.

"It's okay, I got it."

"No, really, the shopping can wait."

Liz was beaming as she almost ran into the kitchen and flew into her arms, making Kristan drop a loaf of bread and several bags of spinach onto the light grey flagstone floor.

"Liz, what are you…"

Kristan stopped talking when her lover started to kiss her, not at all gently but roughly, hard, passionately, pushing her against the wall and pressing herself against her.

"Liz," she gasped, feeling out of breath, and sounding like it.

"Kristan," Liz replied, staring her in the eye, thinking how beautiful Kristan was when she was aroused and a little confused.

"What?" she asked.

Kristan just shrugged, smiling, her eyes a little hazy.

"I forgot," she murmured, and she pulled Liz against her and kissed her back.

The bedroom was freezing cold, and so they made love in the lounge, on the couch, in front of the big open fire. The groceries waited, the mobile phones waited, the world was put on hold. And when they finally came up for air Liz looked into Kristan's limpid blue eyes, and she was alarmed when she saw tears in them.

"Kris," she murmured. "What is it babe?"

Kristan shook her head and smiled a little.

"Nothing," she said. "Just tired. A bit emotional I guess."

"Then it's not nothing," Liz replied immediately. "Tell me."

Kristan simply sighed.

"I've just realised something."

"What?"

"I hate it that I cannot make you pregnant right now," Kristan said quietly. "There is nothing in this world that I would like more than that, and there is nothing I will ever be able to do about it."

Liz immediately wrapped her arms tightly around her, and she rested her head against her naked breast.

"You will," she said gently. "You will. All we need to do is plan a little more than most people. Okay?"

But Kristan believed otherwise.

"Not really," she said darkly. "It is not going to be that easy."

"But it can be," Liz insisted. "There are ways, Kris. Ways we can have a baby together. Don't worry."

"I just don't want it to be all clinical and cold when it happens, you know? I do not want it to be just a medical procedure."

"It won't be. I promise you darling, it won't be, and you will be as much a part of it as me. Okay, my love?"

Kristan nodded a little, a small smile dancing on her lips. She could not look at her lover and not smile, she realised, and that was a good thing.

"Are you hungry?" Liz enquired, smiling back at her.

"Yes. Please don't make me cook…"

Liz burst out laughing, and she gathered her clothes from where she had thrown them on the floor. The house had warmed up by now, and she was looking forward to a nice meal with her lover, and a good night's sleep. She looked around the room thoughtfully, admiring the plush cream carpeting throughout, pale blue and yellow furniture, and the Maori art pieces on a shelf on the far side that stood out beautifully against the darker red wall. Wooden French doors led to an outside patio, and heavy wooden beams on the ceiling gave the room tremendous warmth. Throughout the house it was the same theme, soft colours, warm wood, modern shapes and ancient Maori art.

Kristan definitely had a gift for design.

"Still no phone cover?" Liz enquired.

Kristan shook her head no, laughing when she spotted the delighted look in her lover's eyes.

"Great," Liz declared. "I'm going to grab a quick shower, and then I'll get that lasagna under way."

"Okay. I'll go get some more wood in."

Even though she did not share that information with Liz, this was an opportunity for Kristan to go around her property and check that everything was in order.

In the small shed at the back she smiled at the sight of her mountain bike and kayak waiting patiently for her to return, and her heart jumped in her chest when she spotted the CD case abandoned on the side. Shane Nicholson, Mike's favourite, she recalled, and she picked up the case and gently ran her fingers over it.

Then she looked up toward the sky.

"I'm going to have a baby, mate," she said softly, "what do you think of that, uh?"

Her eyes filled with tears at the thought that Mike would never know, and before she could get emotional all over again she walked back out into the cold. It had stopped snowing but it was getting windy, and it was absolutely freezing. Kristan walked around the house, doing what Liz would not have wanted her to do. She was not sure what she was looking for exactly, but she was pleased when she found nothing of interest, no sign that anyone had been there, no footprints in the snow. She went to the wood shed, happy to find it well-stocked still, and she gathered several big logs in her arms before walking back to the house and the enticing smell of roasting vegetables.

Chapter 19

Despite what Kristan Holt thought about him, Jason Omaru was a good cop, and he had a flair for people. If given the opportunity to spend a little bit of time with them he could pretty much read them like a book, and he was looking for such an opportunity when he arrived at the Holiday Park that morning. He came to a stop in front of James's cottage, not surprised when the man walked out to greet him pretty much immediately.

"James. How's it going?" Omaru enquired, and he shook the man's hand, and was pleased to see that he was stone cold sober.

"Pretty good, chief," James replied, smiling, "pretty good. What can I do for you?"

"I got your email, and I was wondering if we could have a chat."

James looked very comfortable as he glanced back toward his home.

"Sure. My partner was just about to put the kettle on."

"Coffee?"

"Yep."

Omaru smiled a little.

"That would be great," he said.

Kristan was running hard on the side of the road. The tarmac was covered with a thin layer of snow, and it was grippy and soft underfoot, just the right kind of surface for speed. It was only a mile into town, and so she had started slow going the opposite way for a few more; now she was going pretty much flat out, trying to stay ahead of Liz, who was riding her mountain bike and acting as her pace maker.

"Looking good, darling, keep it up," Liz shouted, and she was enjoying watching her partner run.

Kristan was wearing black tights, a brand new pair of Nikes, a red Helly Hansen top and a pair of Oakley's. She looked loose and strong as she powered up the road leading into Crystal Springs, almost taking over, concentrating on her stride.

"Faster," she laughed, as her lover glanced over her shoulder and forgot to pedal for a second.

Liz got out of the saddle and accelerated, getting ahead of her once more.

"How's that?" she yelled back, and this time Kristan grinned and gave her a thumbs up.

"Good," she panted. "All the way now, babe."

Liz's knee was holding up, and Kristan had declared at breakfast that if she did not get a run in pretty soon, no amount of love making would be able to keep her sane. It was a beautiful morning, crisp and light, and they had decided to run into town so that Liz could get a good look at Crystal Springs. As they neared the edge of it Kristan struggled to keep up with her, as she was finally following instructions and maintaining a very healthy seven and a half mile per minute.

"Keep going," she shouted at her lover, and Kristan dug deep for the last five hundred yards.

She slowed down when they reached the main street, to a jog and then a fast walk, smiling at Liz who was now free-wheeling by her side, looking happy.

"How was that?"

"Tremendous," Kristan replied, finally coming to a complete stop in front of the police station and leaning forward, hands on her thighs, catching her breath.

"Did you enjoy running after me?" Liz enquired in a mischievous tone.

Kristan was laughing.

"Oh yeah," she grinned, "best run I've ever had."

Liz dismounted and walked back toward her.

"Thought so," she declared with satisfaction, and she leaned over for a quick kiss, and then stood next to her lover as she started to stretch.

"How's your leg doing?" Kristan enquired. "Feeling okay?"

"Yep, feeling good. It's nice to get it moving a bit."

"Great."

Liz got a warm jacket and a hat out of the rucksack she was carrying, and handed them over to Kristan.

"Make sure you don't get cold now," she said firmly.

Kristan pulled the jacket over her running top and the hat over her head, and she nodded.

"Thanks honey. You'd make a good coach, you know."

"Not so sure about that, Kris. I was checking you out the whole time instead of checking the pace."

Kristan laughed a little.

"Really? I didn't notice. But thanks. So was I."

She took the rucksack from her partner and put it on, and she locked the mountain bike to a nearby lamp post.

"I think we should have mobile cover if we stick close enough to the police station for a second," she said.

"I've got a couple of missed calls from Omaru," Liz announced when she checked her iPhone.

Kristan frowned at her own cell and met Liz's eyes.

"I've got five," she said.

"From Omaru?"

"Nope. From Pam."

Liz sighed loudly and simply waved her phone in the air.

"Might as well call her back now," she declared, and she did not sound too happy about it.

Kristan hid a smile.

"I'll do it now," she said.

She sat on the steps leading to the police building, and dialed Pam's number, annoyed when she got her answerphone. She tried again and got the machine once more, so she left her a message.

"Pam, it's me," she said, and she sounded impatient. "I'm out of range most of the time but I got your missed calls. I should have cover for the next two hours, so call me back when you get this, okay?" She nearly hung up and hesitated. "I hope you're okay," she added a little more softly. "We need to talk, all right?"

Liz was standing not far from her, deep in conversation with Omaru.

"We're fine," Kristan heard her say. "Yep, that's no problem. Speak to you soon."

"Any news?" Kristan enquired as she ended the call.

"No."

"You look worried, what's going on?"

"I'm not sure," Liz replied with a slight shake of the head. "But he sounded in a hurry. Intense. I don't know. Could be nothing."

Kristan nodded, far from convinced. In her opinion Omaru was getting close to something, and he was keeping his cards close to his chest. She considered calling him back and shaking the facts out of him, but then she forgot all about it as soon as she saw the happy smile on her partner's lips. Liz was staring intently across the street, looking excited.

Kristan followed her gaze.

"What? What are you looking at?" she asked.

"Art shop. Just right over there," Liz replied, pointing at a tiny window next to the bakery.

"Oh yeah. Want to have a look?"

"You don't mind?"

"Of course not," Kristan said softly.

Liz stood close to her and clasped her fingers around her wrists, looking deep into her eyes.

"You're not cold? Or sore or anything?" she enquired.

Kristan shook her head, touched by her lover's concern.

"I feel great," she assured her.

"Okay, then," Liz decided. "Let's check out the art shop."

They crossed the busy street, and Kristan was happy to follow Liz as she led the way, first to the tiny shop she had spotted, and then on to the local museum, an art gallery, and finally, when she decided that they should get warm and take a break, inside the local cafe. Before she had met her, Kristan had always been the one who called the shots, the one who was in charge, who made the decisions. Right now she was more than happy to take a back seat, and it was a wonderful feeling to finally be able to relax, knowing that she was no longer alone in the world.

Liz had bought some new painting materials, and as she sat at a table in the window, looking at her partner, she started to smile.

"What's up?" Kristan enquired, leaning forward, her blue eyes sparkling.

"Nothing. I'm just having a great time."

"Me too."

"Are you looking forward to going home?"

"Not at all," Kristan reflected, surprising even herself. "I'm really enjoying being with you, away from everything else."

"You realise we won't have much of that sort of time when the baby comes, right?" Liz said with a smile.

Kristan laughed a little, looking delighted.

"I look forward to it."

Her expression grew tender when Liz left her seat across the table to come and sit right next to her, and she rested her arm around her shoulder gently.

"How're you doing babe?" she murmured.

Liz hooked both her arms around her waist and rested her cheek against her shoulder.

"Wonderful," she replied.

Kristan nodded, and she gazed out the window, enjoying the reassuring feel of her partner against her, her thoughts turning to the future and the life that they would build together. When she spotted a familiar figure across the street she sat up a little straighter, and she looked again.

"What is it?" Liz enquired, still holding on to her, caught in the moment.

Kristan blinked, and she narrowed her eyes at the people walking outside, trying hard to spot the figure again.

"Kris?"

It was gone. No one there. She must have imagined it.

"Nothing," she said, turning to smile at her lover. "Listen, I fancy a hot chocolate and a piece of carrot cake. How about you?"

Liz chuckled.

"I think we deserve it, seeing as we ran in. Well, you ran in."

"Yes, and you biked in despite your busted knee, so you deserve it too," Kristan said firmly, raising her hand to get the waitress' attention.

"I think you need to order at the counter," Liz stated. "I'll get it."

She turned to stand up, started to do so, put weight on her injured knee and without thinking, leaned on it. She felt something twist inside, heard a little crack, and all of a sudden she lost her balance and landed on the floor.

"Liz," Kristan exclaimed.

She jumped to her feet and helped her lover to stand up, but as soon as Liz tried to use her leg she felt a very intense, sharp pain inside her knee.

"Damn," she murmured. "I think I did it again."

"Have a seat," Kristan ordered.

"I'm okay, Kris, it's nothing…"

"Then why do you look like you are about to throw up?" Kristan muttered, glancing at her lover and shaking her head.

In the space of a single second the colour had completely drained from Liz's face, and she definitely looked shaky. The waitress joined them at the table, looking concerned.

"Are you okay, honey?" she asked, and she rested a friendly hand on Liz's shoulder. "Did you slip on something?"

"No, I just have a bad knee, that's all," Liz replied, and she forced herself to smile at the little woman who appeared genuinely sorry for her. "Don't worry."

"Okay, well, I can get you some ice for that if you'd like…"

Liz accepted gratefully.

"Ice would be perfect. Thank you."

"I'll go get the car," Kristan said immediately.

"No, no, there is no need," Liz protested. "I'll be fine, it's nothing."

Kristan looked at her and said nothing, but she gently lifted the leg of her trousers until she could see the extent of the damage.

"It's not nothing, Liz."

She shook her head, staring at her partner's swollen knee, and noticing that a bruise was already forming.

"I'll go get the car," she repeated.

Liz sighed, thinking she should probably count herself lucky that Kristan had not thought about calling an ambulance yet. But she really did not want her to go, and she clasped her hand in hers.

"Wait."

The waitress came back with a big ice pack, and Liz immediately applied it against her leg, wincing a little.

"Does it hurt?" the woman asked. "Can I get you anything else? It's on the house, honey."

Liz smiled at her.

"Thank you. We were just about to order, but my partner here is going to cycle back to the house and get the car. I'll just wait for her to get back…"

"Have that hot chocolate while you wait for me," Kristan suggested gently. "I won't be long."

"How long?" Liz wanted to know.

"Thirty minutes, max," Kristan replied.

"You've got your phone?"

"Yes. And you too?"

Liz nodded as Kristan bent over her and kissed her softly.

"I could probably just ride back one-legged, you know," Liz tried again. "You could push me along…"

"Why would you want to do that when we have a brand new Porsche waiting at home?" Kristan enquired.

She knew what her lover was afraid of, and she understood. But Liz would be safe waiting for her in the cafe, and she could take care of herself if anything happened on the very short ride back to the house.

"You won't even know I'm gone," she promised.

Liz clasped a handful of her jacket in her fist, and she held her back for just a second.

"Be quick. And be careful."

"I will. See you in a few minutes."

Kristan smiled at her, and Liz watched her walk out of the cafe, and start jogging back toward the police station.

She sighed.

"Here you go, honey, this should help make you feel better."

Liz smiled at the friendly waitress and thanked her for the free chocolate.

"I've got another one on stand-bye for your friend when she gets back," the woman told her with a wink.

Kristan rode hard back to the house, and once there she simply threw the mountain bike against the railing and ran inside, looking for the car keys. Within seconds she was safely inside the Porsche, and driving fast toward town. She found a parking space right in front of the cafe, and she ran inside, looking for Liz.

The place was empty.

Kristan looked toward the back, wondering if maybe her partner had decided to sit somewhere else, but Liz was nowhere to be seen. Kristan walked toward the counter, feeling her heart tighten in her chest.

"Oh, there you are," the waitress called out from the kitchen when she saw her looking.

"Where is my friend?" Kristan asked.

"She had to go."

Kristan paled.

"What do you mean? Go where?"

"She got a call, and she said she had to go. Practically ran out the door too, and she looked in pain…"

"Did you see where she went?" Kristan interrupted, trying hard to remain calm.

"She got into a car with this woman… I thought it was you from a distance, but now I remember she had blond hair, and you are dark…"

Kristan did not wait for her to finish. She ran outside again, and scanned the main street in both directions. There was no sign of her partner.

Liz was gone.

"Damn it," Kristan exclaimed.

She checked her phone but there was no message from Liz, and for a second or two she felt fear the likes of which she had never felt before.

Then she jumped into her car again, and performed an illegal U-turn in the middle of the street. There was only one way in and out of Crystal Springs, and so she would take the road out, and try to catch up with whoever Liz was with. As she punched the gas pedal she slotted her phone into the hands-free holder, and speed-dialled Omaru's number.

"Liz is gone," she shouted into the receiver as soon as he picked up.

"Whoa, hang on. What happened?"

"I don't know. I need your guys, where are they right now?"

"Kristan, you're breaking up."

Kristan hit the brakes, and she skidded to a stop on the side of the road just as she was about to leave town.

"Can you hear me now?" she said tensely.

"Yes. I've got you. Tell me what happened."

"Apparently Liz got into a car with some woman," Kristan said, scanning the road as she talked, itching to get going again. "She wouldn't leave without me. Something's not right."

"Okay, just calm down..."

"Don't tell me to calm down," Kristan yelled at the phone. "Tell me what you know, Omaru."

"I am on my way to you right now, Kristan. About two miles away. I've got your friend Pam with me."

"How come? What's going on?"

"Do you know a woman by the name of Denise Ketteringham?"

"I don't," Kristan replied immediately, and she was staring out of the car window, watching little snow drops start to dance on the wind again. "Who's she?"

"Denise Ketteringham, twenty-six, from Auckland."

"Never heard that name," Kristan repeated.

"That's right," Omaru said, and it was obvious he was in a car and driving at speed. Kristan could hear it on the call. "You know her as Melissa Cassidy."

"Mel?" Kristan frowned, and an image of the cute blonde kayak instructor flashed in her head immediately.

"Yes indeed. Five years ago Denise, or Mel, as you know her, was arrested in Auckland on charges of aggravated assault and stalking."

Kristan shook her head a little, and she was feeling very cold all of a sudden.

"What did she do?" she asked, dreading the answer.

"Her boyfriend broke up with her, and she beat him up quite badly. Then she broke into his flat, killed his dog, and painted 'liar' all over the walls with the poor animal's blood."

Kristan closed her eyes, and she leaned back against her seat, feeling out of breath all of sudden.

"Kristan, are you still there?" Omaru said loudly over the speakerphone.

"Still here," Kristan said, and she was finding it a little hard to breathe.

"Denise was arrested but spared jail because it turns out she has a personality disorder. She spent some time in a mental hospital in Auckland, and then as soon as she was released headed straight to the South Island."

"How long ago was that?"

"About three years ago."

"I had no idea," Kristan replied, shaking her head and feeling a little like she had been punched in the stomach. "I never suspected she had a problem."

"We found letters in her apartment that look very similar to the ones Mike was getting," Omaru continued, and he sounded very calm and in control. "Denise is a smoker too. Likes Marlborough Lights by the look of it."

"But Mel doesn't smoke," Kristan said, not arguing with him but struggling to get her head around news that were so outrageous it made absolutely no sense.

"We don't really know if she might still be suffering from a personality disorder, we don't know what triggered all this. My bet is that Mike wanted none of it, and it made her angry. All I can tell you Kristan is that she is behind everything that has been happening to you recently. And we found her prints all over the car that was involved in your crash."

Kristan punched the dashboard so hard it brought tears to her eyes.

"She must have got to Liz somehow," she said, her voice breaking. "Liz was seen leaving with a woman. A blonde woman. Did your officers pick her up?"

"No, they were busy keeping an eye on you," Omaru stated, and this time Kristan felt a little bit sick.

"Where is she going?" she whispered. "Where…"

"I've got an inkling she's aiming for some kind of a confrontation now," Omaru said. "With you. So I figure…"

"My house," Kristan exclaimed. "She's going to my house."

"Okay, don't…"

"If she hurt Liz I will kill her, Omaru," Kristan interrupted, "so you'd better get there fast."

"Kristan, wait…"

But Kristan did not wait for him to finish, and she floored it. The Porsche's hard tyres spinned wildly for a second, then found precious grip, and the car shot forward. Kristan was doing eighty when she passed the city limit sign, and as she flew past Omaru's car coming the other way she was so focused she did not even see it.

"Damn it!" the man exclaimed, and he swung his car around and got on his police radio.

Chapter 20

Liz had been listening out intently for the Porsche and its characteristic sound, and she knew the very second that Kristan arrived back at the house. She tensed when she heard the car door slam shut, and a second later her eyes filled with tears when she heard Kristan calling out for her. Her heart hammered in her chest as the woman who stood in the middle of the room holding the gun grimaced a horrible smile, and looked up expectantly. She even licked her lips.

Liz had no idea who she was, and it did not matter. She understood now that it had not been her ex-husband trying to scare her, and Pam might be jealous of her and struggling to come to terms with their new relationship, and Mike's death, but she was no psycho. On the other hand, this woman, who had tricked her into getting in her car with her, acted and sounded seriously unbalanced. She was chain smoking, and dropping half-smoked cigarettes onto Kristan's beautiful floor.

Liz hated her with every fiber of her being.

It had all started with a phone call out of the blue, and someone saying that Kristan had been knocked off her bike on her way back to the house. The helpful stranger had offered her a ride home, saying that Kristan was waiting for her there, but then as soon as Liz had climbed into her car she had pulled a gun on her.

Now Liz knew that her lover was there. She was close, she was coming for her. And she started to feel sick when she realised that it was exactly what this woman had been planning all along. She heard Kristan as she burst in through the front door, shouting her name again, and mindless of the danger that might be waiting for her. Liz remembered their conversation that day in the car, about Kristan's tendency to react first and think later.

I promise I'll do something about it.

Kristan had promised, and yet there she was now, running straight into the arms of a woman who wanted to hurt her and probably even kill her. And the worst thing about it was that Liz knew it was all her fault. It was because of her that Kristan was going to put herself in harm's way, and Liz hated herself for being so stupid, and believing a total stranger.

"Fucking hurry up!" Melissa yelled as she stared down toward the hallway.

Kristan walked in a second later, breathing hard, her cheeks flushed and her ice blue eyes burning. She spotted Liz immediately, and she headed straight for the couch where Melissa had ordered her to sit, but the woman stepped forward in front of her, and pointed the gun at her head.

"Where do you think you're going?"

"No!" Liz screamed, jumping to her feet.

"It's okay," Kristan said calmly.

She raised her hands up in a peaceful manner, just as she came to a stop as close to her lover as she could.

"It's okay, Mel."

She could barely recognize her.

Mel had always been pretty, and she was always smiling when she worked at the Holiday Park. The woman she was looking at now looked older, harder, her clothes were dirty, and she looked nothing like the cute kayak instructor that Kristan knew. She had dark circles under her eyes, she looked angry, and the gun she was pointing at her head looked suspiciously like a Glock, and not a weapon to be underestimated.

Kristan glanced at her partner, and she was glad to see that apart from a busted lip she appeared to be okay. Pale, terrified, but okay. Kristan tried very hard to ignore the fact that Mel had hit her. She put that thought, and the anger that came with it out of her mind, because she could not afford to lose control.

She focused on Liz instead.

"Are you all right doc?" she asked, using the familiar nickname she knew her partner liked.

She took her eyes off Mel again for a bit longer, long enough to meet Liz's gaze, and send a silent reassuring look her way.

"Yes, I'm fine," Liz replied in a trembling voice.

There was something in Kristan's voice that was so incredibly calming, and her eyes were so tender and full of love that it helped her to forget about their situation, if only for a second. She forced herself to smile, because she loved Kristan so much, and because she was convinced that she was going to lose her.

"Are you okay…" she started.

"Just shut up," Melissa muttered, interrupting her.

And then she shouted.

"Shut the fuck up, both of you!"

Kristan tensed. She shook her head a little, but she remained silent. She waited a couple of minutes, watching as Melissa paced and smoked in front of them. When the woman glanced at her again Kristan held her gaze.

"What are you doing, Mel?" she murmured. "What is going on with you?"

Melissa glared at her, and she stopped pacing. Before Kristan could react she took a step forward, and she punched her in the face.

"It's all your fault!" she screamed.

Kristan doubled over and tasted blood in her mouth, and she glanced quickly toward Liz again, silently signaling for her not to move. Mel had turned her back on them and she was now facing the back window. Unfortunately Kristan did not think that she would be able to take her down that easily. With her partner in the room still she would not try any desperate moves. So instead, very slowly, she walked over to the couch, and sat down next to her. Liz immediately linked her arm through hers and pulled her close. She was careful to remain quiet.

Kristan gave her a gentle smile.

She could feel Liz trembling against her, and she squeezed her hand as she returned her attention to the woman standing at the back of the room. When Melissa spun around to face them again she instinctively extended a protective arm in front of Liz.

Melissa chuckled darkly.

"Oh, how fucking sweet, Holt. You think if I want to put a bullet in her head that's going to stop it?" she snarled.

"Probably not, but it won't stop me trying," Kristan said flatly. "Mel, what's going on? Tell me what's wrong, okay?"

"I am not your mate."

"What about Mike?"

The woman's troubled blue eyes flashed a clear warning.

"That was your fault, too," she exclaimed.

"How do you figure that?"

"I was in love with him but he wanted none of it. I went to see him that evening in the office, after you'd left. I wanted to talk to him but all he did was laugh at me. He didn't understand."

"Understand what?"

"Me!"

"Did you get angry?"

"Damn right I did," Melissa shouted. "I grabbed that spanner, and as soon as he turned his back on me I hit him."

Kristan tried to detach herself from her words, she tried to stay calm, but Melissa carried on.

"I hit him as hard as I could, and it was good! Shouldn't have made me mad. And now he's gone, just like that," she added, and as Liz stared at her in horror she started to laugh.

Kristan made a conscious effort to keep breathing, deep and slow.

"You need help, Mel," she said calmly. "Let us go, okay? Then we can help you."

"No fucking way," the woman snapped, waving the gun toward Kristan, and blinking furiously. "You're staying."

"Then let Liz go at least."

"No."

"Why not?" Kristan insisted. "You're pissed off with me, not her. So let her go."

"If not for you Mike would have wanted me," Melissa carried on as if she had not heard her. "But he loved you."

"Mike was my friend, Mel," Kristan stated quietly. "Not my lover. My friend."

"He loved you," Melissa spat, taking a step closer. "You got in my way, and I had to hurt him because of you."

"Not because of me."

"Yes! You made me hurt him. Now I am going to fucking hurt you too. Get up!"

"Melissa..."

"I said GET UP!"

Slowly Kristan got to her feet, aware that she was losing control of the situation, and not knowing quite how to get it back. When she moved she made sure that she was standing right in front of Liz, protecting her from whatever might be coming their way, hoping that she could buy them some time.

"Let her go, Mel," she repeated. "You wanted me, I'm here. Just please let her go."

At the same time, Kristan was signaling for Liz to stand up too, and Liz did so very carefully.

"Don't you fucking move," Melissa snapped at her. "You," she said, gesturing toward Kristan. "You come closer to me."

"I don't think I want to, Mel," Kristan replied quietly. "But we could talk. Right? We could talk, like we used to? Why don't you put the gun down?"

And she raised a hand behind her back, and waited for Liz to take it. She pulled her against her, and she made sure that her lover would not be able to step in front of her.

Melissa laughed nervously.

"You do what I tell you, Holt," she muttered. "I had to kill him because of you. I fucking hate you."

"Mel, the police are outside," Kristan said softly.

"Liar."

"The police will be coming in now, and Liz and I are going to leave."

Melissa burst out laughing once more, a crazy laugh completely devoid of humour, and she watched as if in a trance as Kristan started to move slowly toward the back of the room, still holding on to her partner, still shielding her with her body.

"You think you're so fucking smart, uh?"

"We're just leaving, that's all. It's okay, Mel. We're just going..."

Melissa rushed forward all of a sudden, and she hit Kristan again, only this time it was with the butt of her gun, catching her on the side of her head where the stitches were still fresh.

"Get lost," Melissa yelled at Liz. "I don't care about you, it's her I want. Just GET LOST!"

Liz did not move an inch, and instead she held on hard to her partner's hand, as blood started to pour from Kristan's head.

"Go," Kristan murmured.

Liz started to panic.

"No," she said. "No. Kris, don't..."

"Liz, just go," Kristan said sharply.

"I don't..."

"Please," Kristan repeated.

She pushed her partner toward the door, squeezing her arm one last time.

"I love you," she murmured, and then she pushed her hard and shut the door behind her, locking it from the inside.

Liz hit back at it with all her strength.

"Kristan!" she yelled.

Then almost immediately she felt hands on her. She spotted a couple of uniformed officers in the hallway, and before she could utter another single word Omaru was ushering her outside toward his car.

"Stay here," he urged. "Do not go back in there."

He turned back toward the house and raised his radio to his mouth.

"All units, you are clear to shoot. I repeat, you are clear to…"

But he was too late.

Suddenly there was a blood-curdling scream from inside the house, and a couple of shots were fired. Liz could not tell where they had been coming from.

She went wild.

"No! Let me go!"

She twisted out of Omaru's grip and ran up the steps leading back inside, limping, almost falling. The police had already kicked the door open, and Liz burst into the room after them and immediately spotted Kristan, half lying, half sitting down against the wall below the window sill. Her eyes were closed and she was breathing hard.

Liz dropped to her knees in front of her.

"Kris, look at me," she said loudly. "Open your eyes, look at me!"

Kristan opened her eyes, and her first impulse was to pull her partner down on top of her, to shield her from harm, to keep her safe. Then she noticed the police in the room, and she met Liz's gaze.

"Are you hurt?" the woman asked frantically.

She turned back toward the cops.

"Guys, where is that ambulance?"

Kristan shook her head as blood dripped into her eye.

"I don't need an ambulance."

She spotted Omaru and his officers on the other side of the room, standing over a body she knew was Melissa's, and she shivered.

She struggled to sit up.

"Stay still," Liz ordered. "Did you get shot?"

"No. I'm okay, doc."

Liz stared at her, then at her chest, and she paled at the sight of the neat round hole in her jacket, still smoking, positioned right over her heart. She felt faint at the look of it, and she could not understand how her partner was still moving, still speaking, let alone smiling now.

"Liz..."

Liz tore at her jacket, clawed at it and wrestled with the zip, finally managing to pull it down so she could see the full extent of the damage. She stopped when she saw the thick vest that her lover was wearing underneath it all.

"What..."

Kristan rested a soft finger under her chin, and she leaned forward to kiss her lips.

"I told you I would be careful," she murmured.

Liz started to shake. Kristan had been wearing body armour under her jacket...

Without it she would be dead by now.

Liz wrapped her arms around her neck, pulling her hard against her, not knowing whether to cry or burst out laughing. She felt Kristan's strong arms around her, felt her fingers caress the back of her neck softly, and she started to sob.

"It's okay," Kristan murmured gently against her ear. "It's okay, babe, it's all over. It's over."

It was a long time before Liz could let her go, and when she finally did Omaru was standing next to them, pretending to look out the window with an interested look on his face.

"Looks like snow again," he remarked.

Liz stood up, and she hugged him hard too.

"Thank you," she murmured. "Thank you."

And then she spotted Pam standing a little way away, looking like she was about to fall.

"Kris," she said. "I think your friend needs you."

Kristan brushed blood off her brow, and she straightened up.

"Be right back, doc."

Pam was crying, staring at Mel's body, and when she got to her Kristan simply put her arms around her, and pulled her close without a single word.

Pam held on to her tightly.

"I am so sorry Kris," she murmured. "I knew she wasn't right."

"It's okay."

"I knew it, and I should have told you earlier, but..."

Kristan hugged her gently for a minute longer, and when she pulled back she just smiled.

"It's okay, buddy," she said softly. "It's over now. How are you? Not hurt or anything?"

Pam shook her head no, and she looked hesitantly toward Liz as the woman walked up to them, and wrapped her arms around Kristan's waist.

"It's good to see you Pam," she said quietly. "Thanks for trying to help."

"I'm sorry I was too late, Liz. I should have…"

"You were not too late," Liz reassured her.

"Let's get out of here, shall we?" Kristan declared. "You want to grab a coffee with us Pam?" she enquired.

Both women stared at her, frowning.

"What?" Kristan asked, obviously completely oblivious to the fact that she was covered in blood.

"You need your stitches looked at, darling," Liz told her gently, and she turned to glance toward Mel's lifeless body, but only for a second. "You and I are going to the hospital."

"Can't you do it?" Kristan protested, and she looked at Mel as well, and again she shivered a little. "You're a surgeon, surely you can do stitches?"

When Mel had pulled the trigger on her she had been standing by the window, and as the woman fired Kristan had been unaware that one of the sharp shooters outside had done the same thing at approximately the same time. Body armour or not, if the man had missed, she would probably be dead by now.

All of a sudden fatigue hit her like a ton of bricks.

"Kristan?" Liz said gently. "Did you hear what I said?"

"Yes. Okay. Pam, will you be all right?"

Pam smiled, and it was probably the first time that Liz had seen her do so, and actually mean it. She stepped forward and hugged her tightly.

"See you soon, okay?" she said. "Don't be a stranger."

"I won't. Thanks."

Kristan smiled at her friend and gave her a thumbs up, and she was glad when she got a happy look from her back in return. She allowed Liz to drag her away, and she did not protest when she had to sit in the back of the ambulance with her to drive the five miles to the hospital.

She was beyond tired.

Liz stayed close to her whilst a young doctor cleaned her head thoroughly, and put fresh stitches in place.

"I don't need that," Kristan argued when he started to wrap a bandage around her head.

"Yes you do," Liz shot back immediately.

She nodded to him.

"Just do it," she ordered.

Next it was her turn, and Kristan waited patiently by her side while a specialist took a good look at her knee. She grinned when Liz declined the crutches that he offered.

"If I have to wear this," she laughed, pointing at her head, "then you use the crutches, doc. Non negotiable."

An hour later they both stood at the entrance to the hospital, alone, staring at the pale blue Ford Focus that Omaru had got for them from the only hire place in town. Liz shot a quick glance at Kristan, and she leaned against her, bumping her shoulder softly.

"He wasn't able to get another Porsche at such short notice, darling," she explained, amused at the slightly offended look on her partner's face. "Thank you for driving so hard to come and get me that you busted the suspension on the Cayenne."

Kristan shook her head at the replacement car.

"I'm sure I could get us better transport," she observed. "And it's late, too. I don't know about you, but I don't fancy another hotel tonight."

"You're right, it is getting late. And I don't think you should drive."

"I could get James to pick us up," Kristan pointed out with a little smile.

Liz opened her eyes wide at the thought.

"You want to fly back home tonight?"

Kristan nodded.

"What would you like to do, babe?" she asked softly.

Liz thought about Kristan's comfortable cottage back at the Park, with views of the lake and the mountains, tucked away on the edge of a soothing rainforest, and not far from the beach. She remembered the heavy rugs and the big fire, and the comfortable bed where they had made love for the first time. She took out her phone and handed it straight to Kristan with a huge smile on her face.

"I would like to go home please," she murmured.

UNBROKEN

Epilogue

James flew them home, and Kristan was delighted to see that he looked so well. Later he would tell them how he had spoken to Omaru about Melissa, after he had smelled cigarette smoke on her one morning when she was at the Park. He had told Omaru immediately, and then Pam had come forward to confirm it, and share her concerns about Mel; if not for those valuable bits of information, things might not have ended up so well for Liz and Kristan.

But there would be time for talking.

For now the two women opted to sit in the back, holding on tight to one another. It was obvious that they were both exhausted, and James took his cue from them. He was quiet most of the way as he flew nice and safe all the way back to the Holiday Park. Thanks to him they got home just before nightfall, and Kristan was delighted to find the cottage exactly as she had left it.

It was chilly inside at first, but not after they had shared a long hot shower, and changed into warm clean clothes. Kristan quickly built a fire, and Liz thought about food but her partner was not hungry, and to be honest neither was she.

They simply curled up together on the couch, and Kristan sighed as Liz rubbed her fingers gently against the back of her neck, and softly up into her hair.

"Hmmm," she murmured. "That's nice."

Liz smiled a little, stifling a yawn and struggling to keep her eyes open.

"I'm so glad it is all over."

"Me too."

"Now we can focus on the important things."

"Like… sleep?" Kristan mumbled.

Liz chuckled, and she grinned but she was too tired to speak. Kristan laughed with her, sinking lower against the pillows.

"Not kidding," she said, "we need to go to bed…"

But Liz was already asleep, and Kristan decided that the couch would do just fine. She rested her cheek against her lover's hair, closed her eyes, and drifted off with a smile on her lips.

James had not told anybody that they were back in town yet, thus buying them a little bit of alone time, and so they spent the next day sleeping, walking on the beach, and simply enjoying each other's company. It was wonderful to be feeling safe again, and Kristan shook her head a little as they ambled slowly past the kayak shed.

"Penny for your thoughts," Liz said gently.

Kristan looked sad.

"I was just thinking about Mel. I still can't believe what she did."

"To Mike?"

"Yes. And kidnapping you," Kristan said fiercely.

"And shooting you in the chest," Liz added softly, tightening her hold on her lover's hand.

"Yeah. That too."

Kristan looked tense all of a sudden, and Liz did not want her to get anchored in the past.

"It's over now," she reminded her gently.

There was nothing she could do to bring Mike back, and she knew that Kristan was thinking about him. Then her partner said something incredibly beautiful.

"I don't believe in death, you know."

"No?"

Kristan smiled a little, looking up at the sky, and the mountains.

"No. I think it's just a transfer of attention. Mike is still out there in some other form. He's still alive, in another form. There is a lot more to this world than we can see. I know he's okay, even if I can't see him."

Liz looked away for a second because she did not want Kristan to see her cry. She took a deep breath of clear mountain air.

"I booked us a table in Paradise tonight," she said softly.

Kristan looked surprised.

"Really? When did you do that?"

"When you were out getting some wood."

"Okay. Sure. You know I love the place."

Liz nodded, her eyes shining.

"I have a surprise for you," she announced.

"What is it?"

Liz laughed at the expectant look on Kristan's face.

"Wouldn't be a surprise if I told you, now, would it?"

Kristan shrugged, grinning.

"Is it something I can keep?"

"Stop asking."

"Did you buy me a new Porsche?" Kristan exclaimed, enjoying the teasing, and loving the soft blush that suddenly coloured her partner's cheeks.

"I will not tell you anything," Liz repeated with a chuckle. "You may as well give it up now."

"Is it something that…"

Liz threw her arms around her neck and silenced her with a kiss. She slipped her hands underneath Kristan's shirt, and she let her fingers dance over her stomach, caressing the hard muscles there, and remembering what she looked like when she was naked.

"Shall we go back inside?" she murmured.

Kristan nodded, her eyes serious as Liz kissed her again.

"Anything you want," she whispered.

Paradise looked different when Kristan and Liz walked in that evening. Kristan looked around for a couple of seconds before she realised what it was. The place was empty. All the candles were lit, music was playing softly on the speakers, and the atmosphere was as pleasant and romantic as ever, but no one else was around.

"What's going on?" she frowned.

"Nothing," Liz replied with a little smile. "I just thought you might like to spend some time alone in Paradise with me."

Kristan looked at her, her eyes turning soft as always at the sight of her partner. Liz was wearing white trousers and a new red silk top. Her hair was up in an elaborate twist, and a few small strands had escaped to just come brush the side of her neck. Her charcoal black eyes looked as though they were burning with a secret fire.

"Come," she smiled, and she took Kristan's hand.

She led her to a table in the middle of the patio.

"Where are the waiters?" Kristan enquired.

"Doesn't matter. This is ours."

The table was set for two, and someone had scattered rose petals over and all around it. Kristan shook her head in wonder. She was smiling, and she looked incredibly handsome in a simple pair of jeans, and a fitted black blazer over a white t-shirt.

"What have you done?" she chuckled.

Liz gestured for her to sit down, and she took the seat across from her.

"Don't worry," she smiled. "The staff are still here… I just asked if we could have a bit of time alone first thing."

"Okay," Kristan nodded. "What's the occasion?"

Liz leaned forward a little, and clasped her hand in both of hers.

"You know how much I love you, don't you?" she started, looking a little nervous.

"I love you just as much, doc," Kristan said softly.

"And I want to have a baby with you."

"Yes."

Liz stood up, and walked round to Kristan's side of the table.

"You are so beautiful," Kristan murmured.

Liz gave her a soft kiss.

"So are you, my love."

She took a step back, and she fished in her pocket for a little black box.

She got down on one knee.

Kristan stared at her, and she almost forgot to breathe. Her heart started to thunder in her chest as Liz opened the little box, and took a beautiful white gold ring out of it. She looked into her lover's sparkling blue eyes, and spotted love so pure there it made her heart ache.

"Kristan, I want to spend the rest of my life with you," she murmured, smiling softly. "Will you marry me?"

She watched as her lover's eyes filled with tears.

Kristan did not even have to think.

She leaned forward, looking intense.

"Every day I spend with you, I love you more," she whispered, her voice husky with emotion. "Yes."

"Yes?" Liz repeated, delighted.

"Yes."

Kristan stood up, and she pulled Liz up with her.

She was trembling a little, and laughing at the same time.

"Liz, nothing would make me happier than to be your wife. And I want you to be mine."

Liz slid the ring on her finger. She knew it would be a perfect fit. She looked up into Kristan's eyes, and she rested her forehead against hers. When they kissed, it felt just like coming home.

UNBROKEN

NATALIE DEBRABANDERE

Printed in Great Britain
by Amazon